COLDHEARTED 2

RISE OF A STREET TYRANT

LOU GARDEN PRICE SR.

URBAN AINT DEAD

URBAN AINT DEAD
P.O Box 448
Maybrook, NY 12543

No part of this book may be reproduced or transmitted in any form by any means, electronic or mechanical, including photocopying, recording, or by any information storage system, without written permission from the publisher.

Copyright © 2024 By Lou Garden Price Sr.

All rights reserved. Published by URBAN AINT DEAD Publications.

Cover Design: Angel Bearfield / Dynasty Cover Me

Edited By: Veronica Rena Miller / Red Diamond Editing by V. Rena, LLC / reddiamondediting5@yahoo.com

URBAN AINT DEAD and coinciding logo(s) are registered properties.

No patent liability is assumed with respect to the use of information contained herein. Although every precaution has been taken in the preparation of this book, the publisher and the author assume no responsibility for errors or omissions. Neither is any liability assumed for damages resulting from the use of the information contained herein. This is a work of fiction. Names, characters, places, and incidents are either the product of the author's imagination or are used fictitiously. Any resemblance to actual events, locales, or persons living or dead is entirely coincidental.

Contact Author at

Email: IGHOSTWRITEBOOKS523@gmail.com

Address:

Lou Garden Price, Sr.

100 BRIAR AVE

ROCHESTER, NH 03867

Contact Publisher at www.urbanaintdead.com

Email: urbanaintdead@gmail.com

Print ISBN: 979-8-9904701-6-3

STAY UP TO DATE

To stay up to date on new releases, plus get information on contests, sneak peaks and more,
Click the link below...
https://mailchi.mp/6d21003686d1/subscribe

CONTENTS

Soundtracks   9
Urban Aint Dead   11
Submissions   13
Acknowledgments   15

Chapter 1   21
Chapter 2   28
Chapter 3   34
Chapter 4   51
Chapter 5   58
Chapter 6   74
Chapter 7   82
Chapter 8   85
Chapter 9   116
Chapter 10   126
Chapter 11   132
Chapter 12   140
Chapter 13   144
Chapter 14   156
Chapter 15   169
Chapter 16   176
Chapter 17   182
Chapter 18   191
Chapter 19   199
Chapter 20   209
Chapter 21   220
Chapter 22   228
Chapter 23   233
Chapter 24   252
Chapter 25   264
Chapter 26   278

Up Next: Coldhearted 3	287
Other Books By	289
Coming Soon From	293
Books By	295
Stay Connected	297

Soundtracks

Scan the QR Code below to listen to the Soundtracks/Singles of some of your favorite U.A.D titles:

Don't have Spotify or Apple Music?
No Sweat!
Visit your choice streaming platform and search URBAN AINT DEAD.

Currently on lock serving a bid?
JPay, iHeartRadio, WHATEVER!
We got you covered.

Simply log into your facility's kiosk or tablet, go to music and search URBAN AINT DEAD.

URBAN AINT DEAD

Like & Follow us on social media:
FB - URBAN AINT DEAD
IG: @urbanaintdead
Tik Tok - @urbanaintdead

Submissions

Submit the first three chapters of your completed manuscript to urbanaintdead@gmail.com, subject line: Your book's title. The manuscript must be in a .doc file and sent as an attachment. The document should be in Times New Roman, double-spaced, and in size 12 font. Also, provide your synopsis and full contact information. If sending multiple submissions, they must each be in a separate email. Have a story but no way to submit it electronically? You can still submit to URBAN AINT DEAD. Send in the first three chapters, written or typed, of your completed manuscript to:

URBAN AINT DEAD
P.O Box 448
Maybrook, NY 12543

DO NOT send original manuscript. Must be a duplicate.
Provide your synopsis and a cover letter containing your full contact information.
Thanks for considering URBAN AINT DEAD.

ACKNOWLEDGMENTS

Praise God for allowing our voice to reach the masses. Haters, this is gonna really hurt, (I fuckin' promise you). *5-star Ratings*/Top Notch *Reviews* on Amazon. Ayo, Elijah R. Freeman, the whole URBANAINTDEAD.com clan- we bombin' the country and the globe with books. Can y'all believe this shit?! Like, a hundred years ago, Blacks were being lynched, beaten, tortured, raped, and burned at the stake for even trying to learn the spelling to our own names! Now look. *"The World's Monumental Storyteller"* – shinin'!!

1. SOSAFROMSCARFACE: The Sage Beings (Amazon)
2. HITTAZ: Get It Back In Blood
3. HITTAZ 2: Real Killaz Don't Miss
4. HITTAZ 3: Contract Killaz
5. HITTAZ 4: As Grimey As It Gets
6. Coldhearted: Blood Stains and Broken Trust
7. SOSA (Book One)
8. SOSA 2: The Reign

9. SOSA (Prequel) Killing Tony Montana

Coming Soon

1. HITTAZ 5: Everybody Suspect
2. HITTAZ 6: Chapter AK Verse 47
3. COLDHEARTED 2 and 3
4. SOSAFROMSCARFACE: Cocaine Presidentz (Book 2)
5. The Black Gambinos: A John Gotti Hood Tale (Book One of 3)
6. Grimey Grandma
7. Wet Dreamz on Lockdown
8. The Ten Crack Commandments (Book 1 thru 5)

I am honored by those of you who care enough to take the time to give books (mine in particular) a review. And I thank you all for inquiring about "ighostwritebooks"

IGWB…lemme break it down. It's real and not complicated.

IGHOSTWRITEBOOKS523@gmail.com

That's my new email FYI. I've gotten so many people asking me to ghostwrite for them – mainly inmates. Like during *Economic Impact Payment,* cats wanted to invest so I charged them 2 cents per word. (50,000 words I delivered untyped manuscripts, neat, clean to customers). Upfront payment because I do not start work if I don't have payment. 50k words is $1,000.00. I am bound by Agreement, not to mention the names of customers, but the books have been advertised inside of KITE and STATE vs. US Magazines, and my advice to self-publish is paying off nicely at $200 or so in royalties each month.

I really appreciate the inquiries on this. And if you're serious about it and you wish to hire me to freestyle your book then send a *short* request to my email: IGHOSTWRITEBOOKS523@gmail.com or you can also send the request plus $500.00 payment (25k word novella) or $1000.00 payment (50k word full novel). Once I begin on your novel, it usually takes 6-8 weeks to complete. Mail to:

Lou Garden Price, Sr.

100 BRIAR DRIVE

Rochester, New Hampshire 03867

Cashapp: *$DELALEGALACES* (Leave your name in "the Memo" section).

To all the "Coldhearted" mufuckaz in the world- whether by an act or a mind-state-- y'all were in my mind and heart as I wrote this. My homie, Deontay "Nice" Willingham. I'm praying for you, bro. Till da next one, Brooklyn! Love you Fort Greene. Love you Bronx. Shout out to Jenny Bui from Jenny's Spa (@Nailson7th), where CARDI B get them bling nails. King Sun: 180 & Valentine Ave. *"Where You At Kid?"*

Lou Garden Price, Sr.
IGHOSTWRITEBOOKS523@gmail.com

P.S.

Jay René-Prison Riot Radio Interviews Link:
https://youtu.be/epbrNdybHD4?_si=v+kYSD_6ZvTY16dy

DEDICATION

For: Tammy "Honey Sweet" Willingham

CHAPTER ONE

"Hurt"

San Diego, CA

Liza nearly had a heart attack and almost dropped hers and Coldhearted's daughter after receiving a text that told her that he was in the hospital. The text had come from his head of security, OG Bobby Tate. Liza packed up suitcases for her mother, Elizabeth, her child, Isabel, whoever was available from Savage Hoodz and Savage Hoodz Girlz, and booked a flight to Los Angeles International Airport.

"Hurt? Ayo, Liza, whatdafuck 'hurt' s'posed to mean?" Ava Applez asked as they disembarked the first-class flight at the AmeriKKKan Airlines disembarkment tunnel they were walking out of.

"I don't fuckin' know, Ava!" Liza whined as she wrestled with hoisting up her daughter as well as two different carry-on bags. "Will *somegoddamnbody* help me?!" she snapped. "Fuck!"

Barbie, the brown skinned honey with the chipmunk-like high voice, suppressed a laugh because she could do without Liza going off on her. It was bad enough that her man was hospitalized. The only thing that Tate said was that C.H. is hurt and it's kinda serious.

On the flight over, Ava and Juicy P were arguing and carrying on because Juicy was caught cheating-again. And it wasn't that they were arguing, they chose to do it in public - front of Nick Cannon and Fifty Cent. Two celebrity cats that saw these SHZ Girlz acting like fools on a cross-country flight.

Altogether, those who'd come from New York to L.A. with Liza to support and see C.H. was Ava Applez, Juicy P, Isabel, Diamond Girl, Bhad Barbie, Elizabeth, and Dojo. They'd arranged for a blue luxury Cadillac Escalade stretch limousine to take them to The Imperial Monterey Hotel in San Diego. As soon as they arrived they were ushered to their rooms and/or shared apartment units by hotel staff.

Elizabeth, baby Isabel, and Liza were in a two-bedroom hotel apartment suite and everyone else had their own rooms paid out of their own accounts. When Liza entered hers she yelped and held her hand to her chest.

"I thoughtchu was in da hospital, Sage!!" she screamed and burst into happy tears. She observed him laid out on his back across the enormous California brass four-poster king-sized bed.

Elizabeth entered and flopped down into the over-stuffed expensive penthouse recliner. "Them, bog-mouths nearly spoiled the surprise at the front desk," she smiled.

"¿Como esta usted, chico?" Elizabeth helped baby Isabel as she nearly broke her neck to get to him.

"You fuckin' *knew* he was aight?!" Liza yelled at her mom.

"Not really, just that he'd be here at the suite," Liz said as she checked out C.H.'s bandages. "He called me to say he left the hospital a few hours back."

Liza looked at the bandages closely. "What happened thatcha couldn't say in a text or phone call, Papi?"

"What's done is done, mama," he told her as he kissed her and his baby, holding them both firmly. "Won't do you or Isabel no good to make you worry."

Liza just stared at him for a minute and then it was emotional waterworks for her. Isabel saw Mommy crying and she did what she was taught to do: she went over to Daddy's chest, causing him to grimace from his cracked ribs – to Mommy and tried to hug her with a reassuring *tap, tap, tap* hand gesture on her back, as if to say: *"It's okay. Please don't cry Mommy."* What an awesome gesture from a toddler who was barely a year old, trying to soothe her mom, giving her some comfort.

"Damn," Coldhearted choked up, looking at his baby. "You killin' me right now, Izz."

"They love you," Elizabeth told him. "At least tell us the injuries."

"Broken cheekbone, right knuckle, rib, and concussion."

"They give you anything for it?" Elizabeth questioned him.

"Percocet. That's the new popular one," he mentioned. "They instructed me to take one. I popped two and I'm higher than heaven…And dat shit make my buttock itch."

"Sage! My frickin' moms right there, man!" Liza admonished while busting out in laughter at the same time. "And she is, too," Liza indicated the baby.

The doorbell rang.

First, it was Juicy P.

"We unpackin', c'mon Mama," Liza stated with an attitude towards Juicy, taking her mother, leaving the baby.

"I thought you was in da hospital, Bro," she state. At 4-foot 11 inch, 100-pound Juicy P. was rocking a powder pink Prada leather skirt and black Manolo boots. Even the diamonds in her all-platinum lower row grill was pink. Including the cute pink Anita Baker hairstyle wig. "Ya, okay, man?" she inquired.

"I will be," he answered as the thought of eating her from

behind became vivid in his mind. "Why Liza give you da evil eye?"

She told him. "Cuz dis boy I gave my number to from that Gucci Mane concert keep callin' me."

"And Ava think y'all smashed?" he queried.

She nodded. "We was arguing – *while* Nick Cannon and Fifty Cent was up in First Class wit us!"

"So, it was even more embarrassing. Did you give that hole up to the boy?"

"Wit Ava all up my ass like a proctologist? Fuck no."

"Did you want to?" he asked, causing her to blush.

She had a glint of mischief in her eyes. "You know you started somethin' once you let me suck your dick and you tasted me. My pussy leaks all day like a faucet. I can't get nobody to fuck me since then."

"We gonna fuck," he assured her. "If you want me to."

She exited the apartment. Not long after she exited, Ava, Juicy, Diamond, Barbie, and Dojo were all seated inside of the hotel suite bedroom.

"As y'all know, a fuckin' war been goin' on," Sage said as his Rollin 60's homiez came down from the rooms in the hotel which they occupied. "Rock left a half a million in drug debt on *Vulkanyck*. To keep that plug alive I gotta holler at them."

Deuce, Tate, Kaz, Cumba, and Ammo stood by awaiting orders. Liza came in with an ice pack and a towel which she urged C.H. to use on his face.

"Y'all girlz should go hit da stores and shit for some 'Cali weather' outfits." C.H. suggested. "Liza, did you and ya mom work on gettin' Lilly and Lupé out here? I ain't movin' 'til this pain go down and da concussion clear. Our house bein' worked on anyway. And I know Lilly tryna hit the beach."

"We using Ubers?" Ava questioned them.

"Me and Mama hitting da stores, too. You okay holding Isabel down?" Liza wanted to find out.

"I'll be straight," he told her. "Y'all should get rentals. That way errbody got a car."

Coldhearted eyed Juicy, while everyone else was itching to leave. Juicy understood. She went to her room and locked herself inside to shower, make herself smell extra nice, and to put on something cute for him.

He gave his men their week's pay. Deuce, Tate, Kaz, Cumba, and Ammo pocketed the cash, and they took off. Coldhearted dumped the Dolce & Gabbana liquid soap into the Jacuzzi and bathed himself and Isabel in the hot bubbly water. He dried off, dried, and put a pamper on his baby, made her a juice bottle, and she fell asleep on the bed. Since all Izzy had on was a pamper he put a light blanket over her. Just as he was thinking to text Juicy she knocked on the hotel room door.

"Mm, look at you," he complimented her with a sinful glint in his eyes as she walked past. Automatically, he could tell she had no panties on underneath her silky white loose gym shorts. She had a tank top on that he could clearly see the outline of her gorgeous breasts and her nipples looked like .45 caliber bullets ready to shoot somebody.

He shut and locked the door and stripped naked right on the spot…

CHAPTER TWO

"The truth is more sinister than that."

<u>San Diego, CA</u>

"No panties on, huhn?" he whispered as he stood there and grabbed ahold of his hard length with the right hand and his balls with the left.

She instantly came up to him, dropping to her knees and rubbing his gigantic brown cucumber all over her face, taking in his beautiful musky male scent. "No panties, Daddy. Just a steamy, hot, young pussy still wet from the shower…"

He scooped her into the living room. She was used to the taste and touch of her long-time girlfriend Ava Applez. But she'd always had a craving for the male gender. Her first time ever having sex with anyone, it was with Ava when Juicy was 13. Ava had used a strap-on dildo to take her virginity.

However, ever since Sage had fucked her mouth and when she got her first swallow of semen, her senses had been on full blast for another taste of man. Her sense had been short-circuited. He laid her down on the sofa and kissed her so deep she began to tremble. And the way he tongue-fucked her sweet mouth it should have been illegal. Her titties were firmer than usual. The pussy juices coming out of her did so like one of those old school oil lamps the way her clean-shaven vagina and her inner thighs were glistening from all the spillage, causing her to smell her own cunt scent wafting up in the air between them.

"*Sweet Mary Moses...* you got a *good* smellin' pussy! Like first walkin' in a bakery takin' da top off da bakin' cookies!" He laid her petite body across the soft cushiony sofa, kissed her French tipped toenails of her tiny sexy feet, then started eating that bald lil pussy like a gooey lil peach. "Damn! So wet that I can wash my face in it! It's like a ripe mango!"

She humped it up, down, circle and circle, up and down… then down, up, and down. Next, she did some acrobatic hoola-hoops, but only this time, she cocked her knees back and made sure that she was feeding him that slick, wet asscrack. This way his tongue, nose, and lips were sucking, kissing, and licking her brown cute little anus. Suddenly, she shook like a leaf and bussed a girl nut that came out like an entire raw egg! It tripped him out but her cum tasted real good.

He put her in missionary and found the slick wet opening

to her still orgasming pussy hole. Her pussy was extremely hungry.

"Fuck me, Sage," she begged, grabbing his ass. "Take my virgin pussy, baby!"

He felt his big thick penis slip through the entry point. She brought her little legs back far. Following six or seven thrusts, she was fully impaled with his massive nuts covering her asshole. He made sure not to leave bites but he fucked her hand. She was small but she could take a lot of dick. Even with a small tight vagina. He pulled out to the tip and slammed it back up in there. She was using all of her leg muscle power to fuck him back.

"OH FUCK! OH MY GOD! OH GOD! OH GOD! OH GOD!" she screamed when his giant balls exploded and the cum rushed inside of her. "I feel your cum in my tits!"

They fucked once more after that and it got even hotter. She let him fuck her in the ass and cum all over her neck, face, and breasts. He couldn't believe how good her pussy was and knew he'd be having her again.

No one returned for almost four hours, which gave C.H. time to bathe Isabel and call Rock's cartel contact. Liza called him and told him that Lilly would fly out tomorrow with Lupé.

By the time everyone returned, C.H. had it figured out how he'd handle questions about Shadow Warrior and Tommy Gunz being *"gone"*. He wasn't just gonna admit to killing them in fair combat. The truth was more sinister than that.

C.H. wanted Garter's Strip Club for himself. There was too many chiefs and not enough Indians back in New York.

Shit has to change. Rock's gone. *Savage Hoodz? We'll see about dat,* he was contemplating. *That goddamn VULKANY-CKACYD? I don't know cuz it's only a matter of time da fuckin' FBI gonna be onto us. Maybe it's time to take shit back out to da fucking corners, traphouses, and small drops. In other words, back to da old school way of doing things.*

"How's things at Garter's?" Liza asked C.H.

"Everything cool back East," Coldhearted told her in front of everybody. He added, "I'm getting a lil' concerned that I sent Tommy and Shadow back wit some substantial weight and all I'm getting is crickets from their burners."

He looked around. Silence.

"Deuce, Tate…nobody heard anything from Tommy and Shadow?" C.H. asked them.

"Last I heard, they were still in Chicago," Tate reported as planned.

The tall lanky Dojo made the comment, "*Chicago*? I thought once you made contact wit Rock's contacts out here, we'd pick up something in Chicago."

"Shadow and Tommy are in Chicago tryna resolve shit wit them 'H' boys," C.H. stated. "We here on 'C' business."

It was some bullshit but hopefully, it was all that would be needed. On some real live shit, Coldhearted knew most of the Savage Hoodz crew was soft and that was why niggas felt like they could step on SHZ's toes in the first place. If SHZ was established in the street like some cold-blooded *gangsters* then even dudes like Bugout would think twice about trying to lean on SHZ.

Coldhearted was a gangster for real-through and through. The gangster with the "E-R" at the end, not the "S-T-A" type talking tough with a microphone during *"Midnight Madness"* or *"Rap Attack"* on New York's Friday night radio stations. Coldhearted may have been taken out of his dope addicted mother's house half-dead, and he grew up away from Brownsville, Brooklyn, that shit was still in his heart. He knew who he was and who he wasn't. He was never a kid. He didn't get a chance to be one of those because he saw the head of his mother's trick get sliced off...

Followed by his own mother's head – at the hands of his father (or his *alleged* father) Titus "Big Kato" White. *With a machete.* And as it turned out, Coldhearted caught his first homi (homicide) with a machete and fell in love with the power he felt when he held one in his hand. He had one that he'd named "Heartless." She had a nice weight and he carried it strapped clandestinely to his back out of sight. Like a Black Ninja or something.

Now he had several machetes. He had them all custom forged by fire in the presence of an Indian named Daniel Eaglebear. C.H. called him "Indio." He had a shop in Larchmont where he made knives, swords, and he repaired these and other metal objects. One day C.H. and Liza stopped in there to see if he could make machetes. Mr. Eaglebear took an order and told C.H. to come back in a few days. The machetes he'd made also came with beautiful handmade alligator scabbards that cost $2500 each.

Liza couldn't believe the cash C.H. invested in those things. But what she did believe was that the man she loved and had a baby with was a killer.

CHAPTER THREE

"Don Armadillo"
Calexico, CA

"You're a little cheater, Lilly!" Coldhearted snapped half seriously towards his eleven-year-old baby sister.

They were now at the Doubleday Hotel just up the street from where they were at a week ago. Everyone had their own hotel room except one year old baby Isabel and Lilly. They were all on the same floor, the 16th floor, which was the top floor.

Coldhearted watched Lilly scoop up another $20 bill from the card table.

"You taught me Pitty Pat and now that I'm a winner, I'm cheating, big bro?" she asked with more giggles.

"Boss!" Double Deuce called into the luxury hotel suite belonging to Liza, Coldhearted, and the kids.

"I'll be next door – watch your money, fuckin' wit my baby sis. She'll getcha ass when you ain't lookin'!" C.H. stated as he grabbed an unopened bottle of beer and left the room, shutting the front door behind him.

"He all flustered," Lilly teased as she counted her cash boastfully.

As soon as Coldhearted stepped out of the room he was handed the Telstar Satellite Telephone or what the crew referred to as "The SP" or Sat-phone.

"Spider Monkey," Deuce's lips said in silence.

Spider Monkey was the drug cartel connect that Coldhearted inherited from Rock, but in doing so, he's also inheriting his debt. Of course, "Spider Monkey" was nothing more than a code name.

"You were supposed to meet with us a week ago," a man with a deep Hispanic accent stated.

"My apologies. I don't like giving excuses," Coldhearted told him. "But right now, we're at the - "

"We know where you are," the cartel man told him. "Come downstairs right now. Your ride is waiting. Come alone. No weapons."

The line went dead.

Coldhearted held onto the phone but went inside to rid himself of his twin machetes. He kissed Liza and the kids, grabbed a grey suitcase with a lock on it, and exited. At the elevator Deuce, Tate, Kaz, Cumba, and Ammo had concerned looks on their faces. The codename "Spider Monkey" was thought up when the men chose an animal that lived or was native to Columbia and Coldhearted had said that the spider monkey came from South AmeriKKKa - "70% sure," he'd shrugged.

"So that's it?" Tate said to him. "You da boss of da whole damn thing and you just gon' go runnin' when these crazy Mexican mufuckaz call?"

"He asked me to come," Coldhearted reasoned as he repeatedly pressed the elevator button in a hurry.

"Yeah, I don't like it either," Deuce told him. "I thought Rock owed these mufuckaz a half million?"

"Yeah, so? He cow manure. How else they gonna get repaid?" Coldhearted mentioned as the elevator car came and they all go on it. *"VULKANYK?"*

Tate and Deuce glanced at each other.

"I thought we were learning our way around the darknet so we can make VULKANYKACYD POP OFF?" Tate probed.

Coldhearted shook his head. "I thought so, too. But niggas is on there doin' broad daylight assassinations, major gun, and explosive deals, and err'thing. Why you think Tommy and Shadow gone? Just so I can have Garter's? Son, if the feds got to them they'd crack. Trust me, we need to get da fuck outta VULKANYCK and get rich on da streets."

"A half a million is a lot of debt, kid," Tate told him.

Not when you got it, it ain't, Coldhearted thought to

himself. "Somebody gotta put they nuts on the table. May as well be me," he said.

Outside, he waved his crew off and noticed a white 1981 Bonneville waiting with an older Latin man dressed in a business suit with expensive cowboy boots. He had a full head of dark brown hair that was graying along the sides. He made eye contact with Coldhearted, nodded, and opened the front passenger door for him. Not waiting for him to get in the older man got back in behind the wheel.

Coldhearted got into the car and he put the suitcase down on the floorboard before putting his seatbelt on. The man didn't talk so Coldhearted didn't talk either. The driver looked as if he were headed to Tijuana, Mexico at first. But instead of heading towards the U.S. – Mexico border crossing he started driving East towards Imperial Valley according to the freeway signs. When they got to El Centro, Cali, they pulled up at a gas station where a black late 1970's model Dodge utility van was sitting next to two pay phone booths. Instead of going to pump the Bonneville full of gasoline the man parked alongside the van where three more Latinos- these were dressed considerably less conservatively as the driver of the white Pontiac.

They were also armed.

Two of them got out of the van with Uzis trained on Coldhearted. They pulled him out of the Bonneville when he didn't move fast enough. He was bewildered and wondered if he was being jacked. One thing he knew was that the jux could come anytime, anyplace, especially if people were running their mouth about what they had happened. That's why he never let on to anybody that he had called a branch of his own bank to count out and have ready $500,000 in one-hundred-dollar bills. The bank was strategically close to The Doubleday Hotel which he'd visited only yesterday.

Coldhearted was ushered into the van and a black hood was place over his head. He knew he wasn't being jacked when one of the men shoved his suitcase into his hands and urged him in Spanish to be quiet, to relax. Plus, after being with Liza now for six years – since he'd been ten – including being around Daphne and Maria as a child, he spoke and understood fluent Spanish. The men were not Colombian, they were Mexicano, and they were taking him to a small border city called Calexico which was a hop, skip, and a jump south of El Centro but still in California. They kept referring to a name that Coldhearted had heard Rock use before: Don Armadillo, *Bulletproof Don*. Named after the armored-skinned animal. Word had it that not many survived in a shootout with the Mexican drug lord. Hundreds of rounds were shot at him - real name Flavio Mendez Santiago - by the Lord of the Skies and not one bullet pierced him except one that hit a bottle of tequila in his inside pocket some ten or fifteen years back. Maybe more.

When the car stopped the hood was pulled off of Coldhearted's head and the doors to the van opened. Well, it wasn't the house of a Mexican drug lord. For whatever reason Coldhearted had thought the connect was a Colombian connect.

Perhaps he was or had been *hoping* to be plugged into Columbians because what the Mexicans had wasn't anything to sneeze at.

The house was a two-bedroom flat that sat on its own small plot of land in Calexico, California, right on the border near Mexicali, Mexico – also right there on the border. As soon as the men started walking across the dirt and gravel driveway towards the house, one of the three men opened a side gate. The house itself had been made with stained waterproofed cedar and gold painted stucco. Loud mariachi music from *Los Tigres Del Norte* could be heard around the back of the house.

A large black German shepherd met the men at the gate and was growling until one of the men shouted at it in Spanish: ¡*silencio!* When they turned right into the yard in the rear of the house there was a vegetable garden to the left protected from the dog by a small fenced in enclosure. To the right was the henhouse and a chicken coop. Under a large eucalyptus tree were four large Mexican men involved in a poker game while three women labored over the barbeque pit. The meat smelled good.

The poker game paused and one of the men at the table stood up.

"Sage Michael Thomas," the man said it in an almost sarcastic manner. He saw the suitcase. "How do we know who you truly are without a police record? You don't have a child support."

"Maybe cuz I'm sixteen and you still won't know who I am," C.H. answered.

"Bring em'," the man said to the three men who had brought him. They walked into the chicken coop via a solid oak door. It was a small room where they slaughtered the chickens for dinner.

There were feathers and chicken blood all over the concrete floors and on the stainless-steel sink. The man ordered Coldhearted to hand over the suitcase and to strip naked. No one had ever asked him to do no shit like that. It was humiliating.

"Avanca," he was told to hurry up.

When he just stood there, one of the henchmen readied his Uzi for shooting.

"Man, I don't give a fuck 'bout no bullets!" Coldhearted stated indignantly. "I ain't no fuckin' cop, mufucka!"

"No search, no business," the man giving the orders said.

"Aight. But this some funny shit," Coldhearted told them.

"Funny? No funny?" he said in English with a deep Spanish accent. To demonstrate, he barked an order out of frustration because it was so hot inside of there that they could barely breathe.

Each man in there started stripping along with Coldhearted who undressed, turned around in a circle, and burst out laughing. *These Mexicans some crazy ass mufuckaz.* When they all put their clothes back on Coldhearted opened up the suitcase.

"Now, *who* are you?" Coldhearted asked.

"Armadillo." He was older than the rest of the men but not a day over fifty. He was in top gym form. Just looking at him one could tell.

"Don Armadillo." Coldhearted nodded. He gave him the cash. "This the half million we owe...well, inherited it. But I'm not Rock. Anyone in my Mob not a killa will be killed. And that online darknet store?"

Armadillo gave the money to one of his men and they walked. "VULKANYCKACYD darknet?" Armadillo said.

Coldhearted nodded. "Yeah. I'm shutting it down and burnin' out all hard drives and devices Savage Hoodz Records, offices, and individuals ever been linked to."

Armadillo frowned. "If we do consignment deal, how will you pay? VULKANYCK makes a million dollars in a week."

"For *you*," Coldhearted pointed out. "And that's just the coca. I want heroin, too. Garter's strip club is one-hundred percent mine and I'm muscling in on the northern Bronx and south Westchester County narco lands. Because of all the heat on Vulkanyk, I know the Feds are getting' close. I also know all the drug customers I wanna fuck with."

"Sounds like soap opera," Don Armadillo stated. "What can you handle?"

"Ten a week in raw boy, twenty in that raw girl," Coldhearted requested, ordering ten kilos of heroin and twenty cocaine. "Lone as it ain't that boy that's killin' fiends."

"You mean horse tranquilizer and phenobarbital—okay, we not put," Armadillo assured him. He was thinking about something. "Your store, the online deep web VULKANYCK-ACYD. Is it easy to show me how to get inside of it and take it over? For a price. A *very great* price."

"Well..." Coldhearted hesitated. "It's not a simple snap of the fingers. You ever order from one of the anonymous users on the site?"

"Guns, *si,*" Armadillo replied, nodding.

"Well, it's not a dot com site," Coldhearted explained. "You'd have to buy some computer software, and then one of us will have to train you. But I really need to warn you against it... unless it'll be based out of the U.S. federal authority jurisdiction. That darknet site has become a massive crime underworld – where even an assassin can be bought with five hundred to a thousand dollars. Because of us, if a man wants to wiggle out of paying child support...or if he wants to keep half of the marital assets – no matter how bad he may have treated his wife – a hitman can collect as low as five hundred dollars for her demise."

Armadillo let out a raucous laugh. "Maybe she had it comin', eh?"

"Maybe. But did their kids?" Coldhearted showed him a video that was hidden on the deep web. "Only I can access this video... that's me in diapers. My father with the machete..."

Armadillo also saw when Big Kato went Kamikazee on the cops outside and the attached newsfeeds about the wounded child. "Sage Michael Thomas," Armadillo said with a different tone of voice now.

"The kids are innocent in their parents' bullshit…" C.H. explained as he showed the Mexican drug lord the video of his first beheading. "Until dat innocence is long gone."

Armadillo scratched the hair under his chin and nodded. He barked an order to one of his men and the henchman went inside of the small house. A minute later, the man returned with a fancy machete which was encased inside of a black leather sheath.

"My gift to you," Armadillo said, taking the machete and removing it from its sheath. *"Muy bonito.* She's yours."

"Thank you," Coldhearted stated.

"So, not even FBI expert can locate those videos?"

Coldhearted shook his head. "No way. They can try but all that'll happen is that they will destroy the files. The firewalls are built up or encrypted with a complexity that'll only self-destruct and kill the entire file."

Armadillo cursed in a slang dialect. "If I buy VULKA-NYKACYD…how will I learn?"

Coldhearted thought it through. "You'd have to come to New York. In a couple of weeks I'll have -"

"Me in New York?" Armadillo shook his head. "I have my daughter. She is computer smart. You have a Puerto Rican wife, huh?"

"Puerto Rican- Dominican," he corrected.

"How much to sell the secrets of VULKANYK?" Armadillo inquired.

Coldhearted had decided. "How 'bout nothin'?" he proposed.

Armadillo stared at him as if a snake was wrapped around his neck. "Nothin'?" the Don asked.

Coldhearted nodded. "Except. Whenever we do biz I never have to come here again. And the previous deal for the coca and the boy…bring it down."

"First, for you and me," he stated, pausing momentarily. "For the cocaine, it's the 'Animal Food' for one kilo, since I own a dog food factory. More than one kilo is *Bags of Adult Dog Food.* And for the heroin, it's *'Puppy Food'* for a kilo and for more than one, it's *Bags of Puppy Food.* Your partner was paying twenty-four for animal food and forty-eight for puppy food. Those are consignment prices because of my risk. He picked up the bag or had his men do it. You're asking *for* consignment price to be lowered *and* for delivery three thousand-plus miles across country. That's not good business. Not over the long run."

Coldhearted ran that through his head. "I only need the consignment price this time because I'm repaying Rock's debt with my own cash. After this, we kill the consignment price – the price drops how much?"

"Four thousand for the animal food and five thousand for the puppy food," Armadillo started. "I'll tell you what. We deliver as far as Chicago, no consignment fee, our best product."

"Twenty K animal food, and forty-four puppy food," Coldhearted negotiated with the murderous drug lord. Armadillo had long black and grey hair, a mustache and beard that grew into a natural goatee, giving him that *Norteño Mexicano* look. Looking at him Coldhearted went on: "And, I cook the animal food with the best of them so I'm not tryna drop a quarter of that shit is bake or cut. So, tell your Chicago peoples that I'm takin' random bags of the adult dog food and Imma test the shit on the spot. If its shit, I'll take another half million to the Colombians."

The drug lord scowled. "We are Norteños. When we give our word, the word of a man is worth more to me. But I see you do cautious business. That's brains. I respect a man who *thinks*. Test all you want! *Es puro chico! Los dos!* Both! Ninety-five to ninety-eight percent pure quality. Hold on."

Don Armadillo told his men in Spanish to make the arrangements and to prepare a good clean vehicle for Coldhearted to drive back to New York. And to outfit it with twenty-five kilos of cocaine and twenty-five of heroin which was an enormous consignment load. While that was being done, Armadillo and his security team piled up in two different very nice pick-up trucks – one a Dodge Ram extended cab and a Silverado – and the drivers ferried them to another house. This one was another ranch – or La Finca was what the Mexicans called it in Spanish.

There was no hood put over Coldhearted's head this time. He rode in the back of the pick-up where two grey wolves were tied up. When he and another henchman got in, the henchman poured cold water into the wolves silver water bowls. In his pocket Coldhearted had some unopened beef jerky which he had fun feeding to the large, beautiful animals.

Coldhearted read the signs along the way but he wasn't certain where the ranch was. Probably in Niland, California but very close to the Salton Sea. When he'd been adopted by Daphne and Armand – and then living with Maria – he read everything. He kept a book in his hand. Encyclopedias, animal atlases, National Geographic magazines, he studied computers, bodies of water, island nations, etcetera. His brain had sucked it all up. *But*, he thought to himself, *I didn't know the United States had a fuckin' 'sea' in it but there it is. The Salton Sea. I'll be damned.*

They got out of the trucks and Coldhearted saw a nice two-story ranch house, a barn, a bunkhouse for the help, and a few other outbuildings, including two small guesthouses. Coldhearted noticed several curious-faced horses that trotted over close to the railing. Being a city boy his whole life he'd rarely had the chance to see such amazing animals.

The wolves were set free, and they ran off towards the tree line in back of the vast property. The horses seemed to calm down and Coldhearted walked across the dirt road there and climbed up on the first aluminum rail. One of the horses, an Appaloosa mare, was not shy. Coldhearted extended his hand and she walked up to him in order to have her face caressed and her long neck scratched.

"She likes you, Seco," a woman's voice said from behind him. She had a Northern Mexicana accent.

Coldhearted turned around and saw a lovely woman with the longest, curliest, and bounciest natural red hair he'd ever seen. She looked like the classic Irish redhead. She even had a light peppering of freckles across her nose. She was twenty-two, a recent college graduate from US's computer science and technology program.

"Seco? What's that?" Coldhearted asked as he greeted her with a warm hug.

She smiled. "My dad said you spoke Spanish."

"Oh, you mean s-e-c-o. Someone strict, indifferent, cold, and severe." He paused and shrugged. "Well maybe that does describe my *apodar*. My nickname."

"Hmph. Not maybe, it does."

She was cute. She was wearing an expensive $500 sundress from Bergdorf Goodman's so she knew how to dress and would love the "Big NYC." She wasn't short but she wasn't tall either at 5 feet 6 inches. Standing next to Coldhearted she looked short because as he approached seventeen, he was really stretching out. He was six feet tall now and 189 pounds. She wasn't skinny either, but she also wasn't as thick as his baby's mama Liza was.

"What's your name, *Red?*" he teased with a smile as Don Armadillo came over to them.

She frowned. "If you want your balls sliced open with a scalpel and your fuckin' throat slit…call me Red."

"Oh, I forgot to tell you she *hates* when people call her Red," Don Armadillo warned Coldhearted. "When she's in New York she'll be Daniela Esmé Vallillo *La Colmillo."*

The Sting – of a serpent or scorpion defined what *colmillo* was.

"Why a sting of a serpent?" Coldhearted wished to know.

The three of them sat on cushioned lawn chairs underneath a seventy-year-old maple tree which shaded them from the sun. Beers were served by a female maid who came out of the house.

"Flavia Naomi Santiago was given my first name and last name by her mother who's an Irish-Mexican woman. That's why Flavia has the red hair. Her mom didn't but that's how she came out. Her mom was a dancer when I'd met. My wife came to me one morning and said a woman came by and said: *'Tell your Flavio that I can't raise no baby on my own.'* Left her right here. My wife was pissed…she gave me three sons."

Don Armadillo paused to drink.

The story was interesting. Coldhearted was all ears. "It was just me and my men. I slept in the bunkhouse. Kept staring at Flavia to see if I saw resemblance. First day, second day… then she was a baby who needed raising. Didn't think about it no more. She drank goat's milk. A week or two later my wife came and told me that Flavia's mother overdosed on sleeping pills, sliced her wrists – a real mess." He sighed. "Very sad, *very* sad. Flavia grew up right here; she rode horses, roped in bulls, trained with my men on target shooting, sniper rifle systems, she learned a lot. But I knew she was too smart for the ranch, so I sent her to school. Then to college which brings us to you training her about VULKANYCKA-CYD.onion."

"Aight, cool, but her nickname," Coldhearted reminded him. Don Armadillo had been drinking tequila and Corona beer all day. The sun was not setting.

"Huhn?"

"Her name. The Stinger. *La Colmillo*. Did she kill your wife for keepin' you in the bunkhouse?" Coldhearted laughed at his own joke.

"No, Señor. Somebody else," Don Armadillo stated and left it at that. "Deadly poison. She can bump into you and inject you with poison, say I'm sorry, and be in her getaway car before you are even affected. Right, *querida?*"

"Si, Papa," she nodded with a pure sweetness.

Coldhearted stared at her through dark shades without her even knowing that he was staring at her. Her harmless little red-head innocent act had him fooled. "So, I'll be goddamned...How you Mexicana and look like you from *Doubling*?"

That made her burst out laughing.

"*Double* what?" her father asked, puzzled. "Where that?"

"You mean *Dublin*, Seco?" she corrected him.

He was laughing with her, saying, "Whatever Miss *U-S-C*. Her computer science degree large like one of those big ass dummy checks charities make for the TV cameras and shit!"

She loved a man who could make her laugh. And Cold-hearted – in Spanish, she like to say *Seco* – was funny as hell. Plus, his muscles rippled. He was *jacked*. Obviously, he worked out, had excellent teeth and dimples. He dressed to kill and his cologne was very nice.

"It's your car coming right there," the Don pointed as a brand-new black Chevrolet Suburban was pulled into a parking space behind the other cars. "Daniela Esmé Vallillo… get used to that name. *Querida*, compadre? Seco, here. Tell her to really make him feel comfortable, okay?"

The young murderous scoffed and walked away.

CHAPTER FOUR

"Las Colmillo"
Calexico, CA

"It's cool, sweetie, if it's aight, just ask La Colmillo to come for a second so we can go over tomorrow's plans," he told the "maid." She wasn't no maid but a whore the Don kept around looking like a maid – until important guests arrived. Her job was to pole dance on the stripper pole installed inside of the guesthouse bedroom. And – after dancing – it was supposed to be on to the fucking and sucking…

Coldhearted was already showered up and lounging around in pajama bottoms and a wife-beater. A half hour had passed and he figured out that the "poison assassin" with the red hair wasn't coming. He called Liza.

"I was *worried*, Papi," she said, sounding relieved.

"I'm sorry, Mommie, but you know I'm cool," he assured her. "I gotta run somethin' by you. I made the decision to shut down or wash our hands wit da dark site."

"The web thing?"

"Yeah." He was flipping through TV channels with a handheld remote as he spoke with her. "I included the site in a huge deal. Part of that deal is with Rock's plug's daughter. I agreed to train her and provide full access."

"So you gotta bring her to *stay* with us?" Liza wanted to know.

"Yeah."

"She even computer savvy *at all?*"

"Graduated USC's Computer Science and Technology program so..." he trailed off.

"What's she *look* like?" Liza inquired. "She cute?"

La Colmillo appeared suddenly in brand new white short-shorts and a bleach-stained burgundy halter top. She had no bra on underneath it. Her nipples were so erect and her breasts throbbed with need. Those short shorts she had on were so small that her hands could only go in the pockets halfway. From where Coldhearted sat in the living room he could see that she had on no panties under those short shorts either due to the way her vaginal line was indented so deeply up inside her.

"Sage?" Liza had to call him again.

"Yeah."

"I said what's she look like? Is she pretty?"

"She's beautiful, Liza," he admitted. "She has this thick *Irish girl red hair.* A sensual body. Freckles on the nose. She dressed really nice. Her perfume smells really good and expensive. Her breasts…"

"Have you fucked her?"

"No! I haven't fucked her. I remember what we talked about," he returned. "Why fuck up what we have when we can be fuckin' these babes together?" he reminded her.

"I don't think you realize how horny it makes me to see that big brown cucumber slicing in and out of a tight squirting pussy other than mine. Is that girl Mexicana?" Liza asked as Coldhearted snapped a photo of Colmillo who'd taken a seat across from where he sat. He texted it to his wifey.

"She is. She's mixed on her mom's side," he explained. "I sent a photo to your phone of her."

Liza didn't know it but he had put his cellphone on speakerphone. Colmillo was listening closely, with a mischievous smile of interest.

"Y'all get home," Coldhearted told her.

Liza was looking at Colmillo's photo. "She looks gorgeous. All I'm sayin' is to hold off. Let's feed both of our hunger."

"Aight. I promise. Be safe," he wished her well. "Kiss my daughter and little Lilly for me."

They ended their call.

"Is that your wife?" La Colmillo asked.

He nodded. "Yep."

"Damn y'all have a really hot sex life. Lemme see a picture of her."

He showed her family pictures, the video of him chopping the head off of D-slice, and then a truly hot and scorching XXX-rated amateur porn video of him and Liza. By this time they were in the bedroom. She was laying back against some pillows propped up against the headboard, laughing. He took off her slip-on *Vans* sneakers, placing her little feet in his lap. Her entire foot was so small that his big hands dwarfed them.

"I'm smiling and laughin'… but the truth is y'all are so hot and brave," she observed. "She's thick and curvy like the big butt magazine girls in *American Curves* and *SHOW GIRLS LATINA."*

Her toes were painted up all pretty in yellow, green, red, orange, white-all sparkling colors. She had a diamond platinum ankle bracelet on her left ankle and a hold toe ring with diamonds emeralds in it on her left middle toe. The bottoms of her feet were baby soft. As she watched his freaky pornographic videos he was rubbing her feet and doing a delicate massage to each of her cute little toes… causing her legs to fall apart… making her comfortable.

"Damn, Seco, that feels good!" she moaned, turning off the cellphone. His touch dampened the petals of her love lips.

"The prettier the feet the better the massage," he informed her.

"You have foot fetish for pretty feet?" She smiled pleasantly as she asked, closing her legs because she could smell her own cunt.

He nodded.

She placed both feet alongside his face and pinched his ears playfully between her big and middle toes.

He shook his head, grabbed her ankles, and kissed both of her feet. "Your feet smell like the rest of you. Like lotion and your expensive perfume. Too bad I can't suck on your toes and lick all in between them… 'til that little pussy's leakin' all into them panties."

"Not wearing panties…and why you can't suck them? You know how hard it is to find a man to do all the shit I saw you do to Liza in those videos?"

"C'mere." He pulled off her halter top and took in her lovely titties first. "God, your breasts are gonna make your babies so happy! Them nipples are perfect! You got a baby?"

"No! You are so funny!" she stated, laughing, horsing around with him.

He removed her shorts and laid her on her belly. He took two fingers and ran them from her clit through to the top of her buttcrack. As she watched him, he put those same two moistened fingers under his nose and deeply inhaled. He laid down next to her and pulled her smaller body into his chest. *UMM!!* He nodded.

"Let's sleep and hold off," he said to her. "We gon' have mad fun when we get to New York. Let's wait for Liza. If not, it'll be like walkin' into your surprise party already knowin' they're in there waitin' for you."

"You and her are real tight, huh?" she inquired.

"Yeah. That's my baby," he declared.

"Y'all always do girls together?" she murmured sleepily, smelling the recently showered male scent of him.

"From time to time," he admitted. "Damn yo pussy and ass smell good!"

"I can tell you know how to fuck *and* make love. You don't just have a big dick for nothin'. And you're only fuckin' *sixteen?* You're a *man*. All these muscles, you're tall, hairy… I *love* that hairy shit."

They fell asleep talking.

But the next morning they were up early dressed and headed to New York. Coldhearted drove with her. Daniela Esmé Vallilo AKA La Colmillo loved to get away from her father so that she could be *free*. Like most daughters of rich and powerful men she wanted to be a slut. Colmillo had never been fucked by a black man, so she admitted this to Coldhearted.

"Even at USC!" she said laughing. "So please forgive me ahead of time for becoming a black man's Irish freckle face slave!"

They burst out laughing.

"I said that because I know the white gringo is so racist he *cringes* at the words *white Irish slave* for Mandingo big dick Black boy!" Daniela kept laughing until tears came out. "And I know I'm not White. *Soy Mexicana.* I also want to be ass-fucked…and I wanna swallow cum from Black dick and be breast fucked."

They woke up having a time of it all morning. She was so likeable and funny as hell.

CHAPTER FIVE

"Niggas is Wolverines"
Mt. Vernon, NY

After arriving in New York four and a half days later, Coldhearted drove straight to their newly renovated house in Mt. Vernon. Just prior to crossing the northern Bronx-southern Westchester County border that led into *"Money Earnin' Mt. Vernon,"* there was a massive police/first responder presence on White Plains Road and 240th Street where there was a line of popular nightclubs on each side of the street. In the parking lot of the infamous *"Skate Key"* and inside of a blue, big body Mercedes were several dead bodies.

"Looks like two dead in the Benz and one or two more the

cops are tryin' to cover up," La Colmillo observed along, pointing towards the Skate Key parking lot.

Coldhearted just kept driving. "The night didn't end well for them."

"Maybe it did for whoever did it."

"Maybe."

They drove on up to Coldhearted's house where an electric gate had now been built. La Colmillo was all eyes and what she was seeing about this youngster was incredible. She had learned about his back-story, and she'd seen his father's crazy suicide video, the beheadings-*everything*. And she was drawn into his wild world. Now, she was looking at this beautiful house, the gates that surrounded it, the well-lit front yard with its nicely landscaped lawns and gardens.

"Yeah, they *been* back," he said as he pulled the sleek new SUV into the 4-car garage when Liza opened it for him from inside. "We just had some upgrades done on it and all of our stuff was packed and put into storage. They been back so Liza had movers put it all back. C'mon," he said to the drug lord's daughter.

He put security locks on the garage doors so no one could break in. Liza, Lilly, and Isabel came out. "What's up, my babies??!" he excitedly hugged Lilly and kissed his wife and baby.

"Everybody meet Daniela Esmé Vallillo," he introduced them. He brought his and La Colmillo's bags and luggage into the house.

"Mucho gusto," La Colmillo said to Liza. "I feel like I met you already."

Liza stared at her. *"¿Porque?"* (Why's that?)

La Colmillo shrugged, grabbed Liza's hand, and off they went into the house to get acquainted.

Coldhearted couldn't stop kissing on the baby, little Isabel. And Lilly was telling him about some little boy who'd tried to kiss her.

"Did you like it?" Coldhearted asked her.

She just shrugged.

"In California?" Coldhearted probed.

She nodded.

"You too pretty to be playin' around wit boy, Lilly," he admonished her. "Liza!"

Liza brought him a plate of shrimp enchiladas sofrito. She took the baby and La Colmillo came out into the living room to eat on the sofa as well.

"Some boy tried to kiss Lilly out in Cali?" he asked Liza.

"Your men had some of their folks come since they wasn't doin' shit at the telly," Liza explained. "Some of them had wives and girlfriends' wit kids. We had the whole floor. There was a cute boy running around behind her."

"See why she need to watched?" Coldhearted was murdering Liza's enchiladas as he spoke. "Damn these shits is bangin'!"

"I was watchin' her. She was teasin' him," Liza explained. "Messing with his ego. Lilly's mean."

Coldhearted looked at his little sister. "You mean?"

"You tell me to be," Lilly stated.

Coldhearted put his hand up and she high fived him. "Lilly, don't make me have to kill somebody over you. Aight? Stay away from boys cuz you don't know nuttin' about them."

He wasted no time taking a shower and crashing out with Liza snuggled all up against him, trying to suck him off, but he begged for sleep first…

AT 6:30 AM he was right back up, ready to remove the fifty kilos he had brought from California with him from the secret stashes built inside of the Chevy Suburban. He came out of the bathroom and noticed that Liza had also arisen. She was sitting on the side of the bed drinking some sweet soft drink prior to standing up and stretching in a short baby doll nightie. When she stretched he could see that she had no panties on because he could see her clean-shaven cunt peeking from under the white lace that line the entire bottom part of the cute nightie. He hugged her and kissed her.

"Lemme pee, Daddy," she said. He watched her walk past him and almost had to bite his fist at seeing her creamy phat ass as it jiggled in plain sight under the nightie. And she looked backed at him to let him know that she knew what she was doing.

He got undressed and followed her in the bathroom to

watch as she peed and washed up. She brushed her teeth and gargled. "Look at you," she accused and teased him.

"I love you," he said, standing there. "You are so beautiful, mommie. I still find it hard to believe that someone so beautiful would molest me at ten."

She laughed, "We were kids!"

"But look now. You're the prettiest thing ever," he declared, pulling her with him into the bedroom and onto the bed where he removed her nightie. "You gave me a baby, you married me, and Imma put a baby girl in it next."

"I love you, Sage. It's all because I'm crazy in love with you. I'm Latina. Boriqua y Dominicana. My blood is thick… my loyalty runs deep. It's really for life for women like me, baby."

He was on top of her, smelling her breasts, nuzzling them, and staring at her gorgeous mocha nipples. Grabbing both of them and sucking them, causing her pussy to lubricate. "Me, too, mommie. Nobody gon' rock like we do. Truss dat shit. Here…open then phat ass thighs. P-H-A-T phat. Pretty, Hot, And Tasty. Don't be shy, lemme smell da hot pussy cream leakin' and fillin' up the room wit your sweet, musky, horny scent. Look at it. I ain't even touch it and it's dripping, all hungry to be sucked, nibble on, and made love to. You want this big ass dick in there, don'tchu?"

Her pink lips were in a wet snarl as she listened to all of his dirty talk. That shit had her vaginal walls contracting. "I do. I always do. I be withdrawing without my Papi. Smell it, daddy. Go 'head. I wanna show you somethin'."

He slid down her body. "California tanned you. Look at your shaved pussy." It was shiny wet around the puffy vulva, her clitoris was erect and pulsating right before his eyes.

"What do you smell?" she asked in a small voice.

He inhaled her aroused cunt and shrugged. "My baby. Liza. Pretty, thick ass Liza. Don't you lose this baby weight either…you hear me? Tell me what I'm sniffin' on? Chanel new scent?"

She giggled. "Papi, whatchu don't smell is *you.*"

"You mean after I spurt it all up in that belly?"

She nodded. "I know you don't like it but the next day your nut still be comin' out. I put my fingers in it and smell it. I *love* smellin' that shit. That's my husband. Right now, I just smell my own sugar pack."

He dived headfirst into her sweet honey pot. "I be withdrawin' without you, too." His tongue licked along the outer lips until finally he parted her little "*innie*" to reveal the angry dark pink flesh inside. Her soft moaning as he sipped and consumed her juices caused her monster pole to throb relentlessly. It got so hard it started to ache where he had to hump the bed a little to relieve it. He licked her soft pussy lips, first up the lips of the one on the left. He intentionally ignored her thumping clitoris which she was trying to force him to give attention to by humping that tight cunt into his face. He licked down the length of the other lip and harshly commanded her,

"Open up that thick phat ass, mommie! Gimme that lil asshole too!" Liza bussed it open and displayed her clean hairless anal orifice.

They didn't know it, but they had a voyeur in the hallway watching them. La Colmillo stood there with white t-shirt and baggy gray sweatpants – with no panties on underneath – and no socks on her little feet. The bedroom door was only slight opened. The fiery red head already had her right hand thrust down into her sweatpants, frigging her excited, wet, clit in slow circles. Her other hand was cupping her right breast, squeezing the firm fleshy orb, and pinching the nipple. Even in college she had never witnessed two fully naked people doing it. And here she was, her cunt cream soaking her hand, as this sexy boy-man was between the legs of his strikingly beautiful wife, talking filthy, slurping, and licking Liza's asshole and pussy.

"Top drawer, Papi! *Hurry* before Isabel wakes up!" Liza begged.

Coldhearted reached into the nightstand drawer and removed a black motorized butt plug. He was about to use the AstroGlide lubricant but Liza stopped him. "Uh uh! It'll slip out. Just tongue that ass and spit in it. Spank it while you doin' it."

She turned onto her belly, got onto her elbows, and opened up her knees, bussin' that tattooed ass wide open. C.H. didn't hesitate to continue eating that thing from the back. The sight of her was so sensual and sexy that she almost made him cum without even touching him. Liza was just built like that. Her beauty was always on "10." But after Isabel was born she seemed to put on even a little more weight and he couldn't believe how much more attractive that made her.

He had his face and tongue smashed into her warm, wet pussy and ass slice, making her whole body come alive. He licked and poked his tongue in and out of her anus, spitting inside of it. "Yeah, baby, fuck me with your tongue. Spit in there again! I like that. Ooouuu, damn, my clit 'bout to buss!" It was as though tongue and nose were hard cocks the way she was throwing her soft, big, sweet alabaster ass in his face.

She skeeted and soaked his face with her sweet cunt honey. Then she flipped back over onto her back. "This how I do it when you ain't here. Watch me fuck my tiny asshole," she whispered. "Ooouu! Ohhkay…?"

She took the buttplug and eased it slowly into her ass from the side but then she had to put its round base onto the hand below. Using her own weight and a series of grunts and moans she swirled and twirled her hips downward until it slowly and gently was pushed into her. In the center of most any buttplug, it looked *fat* so when the entire dildo was inside of the anus, the contraption can't slip back out. Her anal ring held it in place around the smooth slender neck of the buttplug which was closest to the base.

"This is a remote control for it," she revealed in a gasp.

"Like the ones I bought from *AdamandEve.com* that time.

I know what this is," he said with naughty grin, watching her squirm with sensual delight.

"Damn, I walk around with this thing in me – you just don't know what pleasure in my ass does to my titties and my pussy," she moaned as he turned the remote on vibrate, volume one, off. Vibrator on, volume three, off.

"Tell me!" He started to kiss her wet, hungry mouth. He could feel the perspiration breaking out in a gleaming sheen all over her body. "Mmm, baby, I love you. I love our family. Tell me... what it do?"

"My breasts get really firm. I start sweating like real bad. I was in Walmart and was reaching for my debit card and turned it on by accident. That fucker made me sweat bullets. The cashier guy asked if I was cool. All I could do was nod yeah. My clit started doin' jumpin' jacks like its startin' to right now! Umm, oooouuu, Papi, fuck me! Please – bang that big black dick in me. Please!"

He could literally *feel* her need. Her hungry pussy was always resistant to the length and thickness of his cock, so he didn't bang it in but thrust it through until his orange-sized testicles were draped firmly over her perineum. Because of the buttplug she never lifted her feet up off of the bed. He could feel the vibration pulses from the buttplug that was implanted deep inside of her ass.

"Sage, ooouuu, Papi, oh fuckin' shit, oh fuckin' shit, I'm cummin' on my daddy's big ass dick! Ummm, mmm, oooouuu, fuck your Liza Garcia Thomas. Make me have a baby again, Sage. Huh? My man so hard…Liza so soft…she wet, sticky…"

He was turnt up now. With her whipping that sweet pussy in wild circles around that big dick had him grabbing her long black hair to where her soft neck was exposed. He humped up and down hard, fucking her like a madman, slamming that tight pink pussy. He grabbed both breasts and bit down so hard into the left one that he drew blood, turning her on even more.

She took the buttplug remote and turned it up so it not only vibrated but it "shook" like crazy inside of her, causing her to yelp and bite the shit out of his right shoulder. One moment they were fucking like newlyweds, the next vampire cats, where they we getting off on the taste of each other's blood.

In the doorway La Colmillo had never witnessed a violent, wild passion like theirs. They were not acting like a couple that had been together, in love with one another, not to mention having a baby, for six years. They had the lust of wild animals for one another with the biting, the scratching; it didn't feel good unless half of it hurt.

"Mm… I love this pussy!" he declared as he licked her left ear and under the neck.

As soon as one orgasm dissipated in Liza, another started to build up. The remote was back down to volume one. They were kissing and making love. His dick was having awesome control. Staying power.

"Damn. Goddamn," he murmured as he fucked her harder.

"You want me in that pussy while somebody else fucks your asshole? You want to be double penetrated?"

She shook her head. "Just you. I just want Sage,"

"Damn, I love my Liza." He kissed her, fucked her deep. "It's okay to fantasize. You a bad bitch so I know you look good. I know this hot asshole you got or this sweet pussy would go crazy for some strange big dick fuckin' it. You want him to be Black? Latino? A big dicked Italian?"

She got hotter and hotter. He knew she was thinking about sucking on a brand new big black dick or perhaps even craving multiple men at one time. Coldhearted wasn't naïve. Even teachers, policewomen, doctors, and powerful female lawyers, judges, and politicians fantasized about being secret sluts. Church women were the lustiest of them all. All females had hot blood pulsing through their veins. They wanted hot and nasty sex behind closed doors where they can do what they wanted and be what they wanted with no questions and no judgment. And their desire was to have the most nasty, slutty, and satisfying sex as possible before tomorrow came and they had to hide their true selves from family, friends, their employers, and every other "judge" out there. Women didn't have the luxury of easy sexual gratification like a man did. She didn't have a dick or a scrotum. The dick had tens of thousands of erogenous sexual nerve endings that caused climax. A man's scrotum also had thousands of these nerve endings. A woman's chances of sexual gratification were way less. Men were almost always guaranteed orgasms while women rarely even knew what a man was packing in the meat department until it was too late. So, she was left unsatisfied.

This was why women tend to "fantasize" about their gratification more often. They often wished to be "slutty" in fantasy more than reality because in masturbation sessions, this fantasy produced stronger orgasms. No female actually wanted the "negative" reputation of being a slut but it damn sure was a turn on to fantasize about being one.

"Oh god, um-hm," she nodded as she now was riding up and down on her man's big brown cucumber. Her phat breasts were flailing up and down as well. "I'll suck on one while the other one fucks my ass."

"You'll take him deepthroat? Like you do me?" he asked her.

She nodded again. "*And* swallow all his cum."

"In your ass…you want it small or big?" he asked. She was gasping and sweat was flying all over him as it streamed down her face. Her long black hair was matted to her wet skin. Her long neck, breasts, and belly glistened with it.

"Not that big! Smaller than yours so it won't hurt. Maybe seven or eight inches." She whimpered as she squeezed her titties and pinched her nipples real hard. She was actually picturing C.H.'s head of security pushing his cock into her ass, boning her slowly with it; she started to hammer her pussy down onto his stiff pipe almost unable to breathe she was so turned on!

"Um-hm, um-hm, oh god! Oh god! Oh god! It's too good,"

she shivered and her cunt exploded. Her anus was quivering with need. "I smell that love-honey aroma!"

She reached down to her pussy and wiped her cunt juices beneath his nostrils so that he could have a whiff of her frothy cunt crema. After, she collapsed on top of him as he removed the buttplug. They lay together kissing and whispering endless words of endearment.

"We obsessed with each other," she said.

"Yeah, this ain't normal," he agreed with a smile. "And I though we was waitin' to have another kid."

"Huh?"

"Put another baby in me," he mimicked her.

"You misquotin' me," she said, pulling her hair back, fanning her face with her hand. "I was fantasizing about a double fucking!"

He went to find some work jeans and a T-shirt. "I ain't even botherin' wit a shower. I'll be in the garage."

After he dressed, he went into the bathroom, and she closed the door. "Papi, she was watchin' us fuckin'."

"I know. How you know?"

"It's a creak in the floor right outside our room," she said, smiling. "I can tell you ain't fuck her either."

He nodded. "I know you can. That's why Imma really take this shit serious. You my best friend and why do anything when we can do it together?"

"Or get permission, man," Liza said.

"You, too," he told her. "A double fucking?"

She sat on the toilet. "You'd really let me act out my fantasies? Fantasize is one thing. But to *actually* bring another man around? I'd call the cops I'd be so petrified."

He took a deep breath. "It's like six billion people on the planet. Me and you wasn't even teenagers when we started foolin' around. Look where we at six years later and we only sixteen and eighteen now. Of course, I'm a jealous man but I don't wanna be a deceived man. And you hot as fuck. To think one man going to satisfy a woman all her life is me lyin' to me. I mean I don't want to participate but if you want some extra spice or excitement at a male strip club then go for it. For me, it'll be exciting to hear 'bout it' - even more if I can see it."

"Wow, I never expected that," she said, wrapping her arms around his neck. "I am one-hundred percent happy with us as-is but that's good to know. I like girls though so lucky for you, if mama needs spice, it'll be from a female and we can share her. If you ever want a bitch bring her home."

"Ok, babe. Have you can checked out Garter's and the bank books since you've been back?"

"Garter's is cool. Management got it under control."

"I need a location for a thrifty-junk shop," he told her, sitting on his bed to use the Sat-phone. He called Tate. "Hello?"

A female answered. "Hi."

"Tate close by?" Coldhearted asked.

"Hey, C.H., he in da shower. Want him to call you back?" she asked slowly.

"Tell him to bring some tools, a toolbox," C.H. said. "I'm at the crib."

He called Juicy P. "Hello?" she answered.

"Ayo, who was the best when it came to Vulkanyck?" he inquired.

"We all helped Rock set it up," she reminded him. "Hey, where's Shadow? Him nor Tommy is answering their phones. Everybody looking for 'em."

"Yeah I know," C.H. feigned some empathy. "They shoulda *been* back from a pick-up they were s'posed to make with cats Rock was plugged into for some boy. I handled the half one million out to the Mexicans. Out in Cali, I went alone wit a black hood over my head down to Mexico and made it back. I thought I was a dead man at one point. Shadow and Tommy shoulda been back, runnin' Garter's."

Liza looked at him with a puzzled look.

"Look," he went on into another subject. "I just got back, come over."

"Shadow and Tommy missin'?" Liza asked.

"Them Chicago niggas are wolverines. They eat the meat and the bones, baby. You know how this game go," Cold-hearted said, opting not to tell Liza shit, just because he was crazy for this bitch... he wasn't *that* crazy. "Babe, thrifty-junk store location."

She heard Isabel crying. "And the rooster crows."

"Late ass rooster."

"Don't be talking 'bout my baby," Liza said before she showered. "Go get her and bring her in here."

Lily was already up. She brought Isabel into their room. As soon as she saw her daddy she started kicking her feet and stretching her arms to get to him. He took her, removed her shitty pamper, trashed it, and handed her funky little butt off to Liza in the shower.

"I'll be in the garage," he told her.

"You didn't even eat," Liza yelled.

"I smell food," he said back. "Daniela out there."

"Oh. How long she stayin'?"

"Coupla weeks maybe?" he guessed. "Her dad's buyin' the dark site so we gotta train her on each aspect of it."

Moments later he walked into the kitchen where Daniela have prepared something exquisite. They discovered that the young woman could cook!

CHAPTER SIX

The Drug lord's Daughter
Mt. Vernon, NY

Daniela - alias La Colmillo - had went into the bathroom after coming all over her fingers while watching Coldhearted and Liza fuck, bite, and scratch each other like animals fighting over a mate. They were so hot and sinful to watch and listen to. The bloodsucking Liza fantasizing about three men penetrating all three of her holes... they were way too much!

La Colmillo put on her red shorts and a pink USC T-shirt and big red and gray winter socks before hitting the kitchen. There was already some beef charque that was thawed out in the refrigerator, so she knew exactly what to make. Her grandmother had always fed them real meals to start the day off so she chose *Mexican Majao*: a pound of charque, 2 cups of rice, 1 large red onion (chopped fine), 1 large tomato diced, 2 teaspoons powdered red chili pepper, 2 cubes beef bouillon, 5 plantains (but must be yellow), and 8 eggs.

First, she boiled the pound of beef with 4 tablespoons of salt for 10 minutes. She made sure not to throw the water out. She took the beef out of the water, set it aside, and let it cook. Then she shredded the beef with her hands. Liza, being Latina, knew what charque was. It's almost like a beef jerky. She choose the onion, put it in a little oil, and cooked it until it was transparent. She added in the diced tomato, the powdered red chili pepper, and cooked it for five more minutes. She added a cup of the water - in which she cooked the beef - to the onion and tomato, alone with two cubes of beef bouillon.

Then, separately, she added three cups of *fresh* water to the three cups of water she boiled the beef in (which was now six cups of water in the pot). Then she added the onion/tomato/pepper mixture from the pan and the shredded beef into the water. She boiled the rice in the same water with everything else.

And while that was cooking, she peeled the plantains. Grabbing a knife, she cut them lengthwise into strips that were about a half-inch thick - certainly not too thin. She fried the plantains in hot oil just until they were toasted on the outside. She never used green plantains because they're dry and tough and lack flavor. The yellow ones were kind of sweet when making Majao, they weren't supposed to be crunchy like a potato chip. When her grandmother showed her how to prepare them they came out bendy and soft (almost like a sliced pickle).

Once the rice and beef were cooked she fried an egg and set it in the center of the main meal. That was the moment that Coldhearted entered the kitchen with his little sister Lilly right on his heels.

"Ola, Daniela Esmeralda Vallilo," C.H. greeted her as he smelled the rich breakfast. "This is for right now?"

"Mm-hm, and don't you need the extra energy?" Colmillo stated as he kissed her left cheek.

"Yeah. I guess," he retorted. "I was workin' out earlier."

"Sage and my cousin was havin' sex!" Lilly said like she was on *Family Feud* with Steve Harvey.

"Oh my god!" Colmillo was laughing. "Y'all like sunny side up or fully cooked fried eggs?"

"Fully," C.H. said.

Lilly repeated, "Fully."

"Your wife?" Colmillo asked, cracking three eggs, and putting them into a frying pan.

"Same," C.H. informed her as he pulled pitchers of milk and orange juice from the refrigerator. "Set the dining room table, Sis."

Lilly took glasses, silverware, and the juice into the dining hall.

"We saw you watchin' us. Did we disappoint?" he whispered.

She shook her head. "I don't wear panties becuz of the heat. But I have on panties - with paper towels down there, after seeing that!" she whispered back.

He pulled her into the garage and unbuttoned her denim shorts to take a look. She wasn't lying.

"I keep thinkin' of y'all and my pussy is leaking like a *faucet*!" she informed him.

They went back inside and C.H. joined Lilly at the dining room table. Liza brought in Isabel. "Something smells good in here," Liza stated as she watched Colmillo serve each plate.

"Is that Bolivian Majao?" Liza asked, surprised.

"Well...more like Mexicano, chica," the drug lords' copper-haired daughter told her. "I hope it was okay to use the charque you had in the 'fridge."

Liza ate a forkful of the delicious Latino delicacy. "Dios mio. That's good. You cook like this some more we'll keep you."

"All I gotta do is *cook*?" Colmillo smiled flirtatiously.

Liza giggled but she caught on quick that Colmillo was interested in her.

Lilly was killing her plate of Mexican Majao. Coldhearted was attempting to keep Isabel's hands away from his food as he fed the one-year-old her own meal of fried eggs and grits. But whenever she saw adult meals, that's what she wanted, also.

"It's too spicy, baby, all she gon' do is start cryin'," Liza warned as he put some of the Majao on Isabel's baby spoon and chewed it for her first. Then he spit it back out onto her spoon and fed it to her. "That won't help. Majao is spicy. Too spicy for a baby."

"Not just any baby," he said as Isabel opened up and gobbled the food down like it was her favorite cake. "This my Black/Dominicana/Boriqua *Alligator* Baby, huh, Izzy Mama?"

Colmillo, Lilly, and Liza waited for Isabel to cry from her mouth being on fire from the red pepper, jalapeños, and other hot spicy seasonings out into the meal but Izzy just thugged that shit out by jumping up and down in C.H.'s lap with her tiny little pink baby Timberlands on, giggling and laughing as though she understood her father's jokes.

"I'm in here drinking a swallow of orange juice after every three bites and she over there cheesin' wit two little baby teeth on the bottom," Liza complained. "And what's an Alligator Baby?"

"You know, an alligator *belly*," C.H. bragged. "Talkin' 'bout my daughter. She inherited her daddy's belly. When I was a baby I ate rotten tuna outta the trash can…toilet paper dipped in ghetto Kool-Aid to fill me up…I used to drink the whole jar of spaghetti sauce and the can I canned onions. Nasty stuff. I starved as a child. Have nightmares 'bout not havin' food. I rather be dead than ever be hungry again. You had to have an alligator belly to get where we got. Food poisoning was welcome. At least it was somethin' on ya belly."

"This is an absolutely beautiful house," Colmillo complimented as everyone stuffed themselves. "The mortgage high?"

C.H. chuckled. "This me and Lilly's house. Fully paid for. Our parents died in a fire. My adoptive parents. Lilly's blood parents."

"A house fire?" Colmillo asked.

Lilly and C.H. nodded.

"I'm very sorry," she offered.

"I'm not," C.H. admitted. "Lilly is."

"No, I'm not," she countered.

"Dang. Y'all both cold," Liza said, shaking her head.

"They was tryna have my brother locked up!" Lilly explained to Colmillo. "My father ain't like him."

"Lemme guess. They had life insurance. *Very good* life insurance," Colmillo gestured with her hands, indicating the house.

"And house insurance. It was demolished and rebuilt. Their mom, Daphne, was my mom's sister," Liza informed her.

Colmillo paused for a moment. "So…you married your adopted cousin."

"Been in love since I was twelve and he was ten," Liza boasted.

The buzzer to the back gate went off. C.H. looked down at his watch. He checked the monitors and saw Juicy P, Tate, and

Deuce. He buzzed them through and opened the door to the back deck. He embraced them, introduced Colmillo to them, and seated them at the dining room table to feed them some of the Mexican Majao she'd prepared. Liza took off to the home office/study so that she could use the house phone and computer to speak to a local real estate agent about store locations.

"Damn, who's the bad *Red* babe?" Tate asked C.H. after they were alone. "The new cook, cuz?"

Colmillo was sitting right there and took what Tate said as disrespect. "No. Because I'm Mexicana? You have no idea who I am so why disrespect me?"

"Man, nobody disrespected you, Red," Tate told her.

"You called me 'Red' when the boss told you my name is Daniela Esmé Vollillo alias La Colmillo," she declared eloquently and courageously. "And do I look like *anybody's* goddamned *cook*?"

Tate just ignored her. "I don't know where you find 'em at, cuz."

"Well, you was a little outta line even after she nicely called you on it, cuz," C.H. told him. "She don't like bein' called Red. She cooked for us, you hear her Mexican accent and say that cook shit… it was *racist*, homie. And she wit me so you know she official, nigga."

"Now I'm racist?" Tate questioned him.

"The *'is she the new cook'* comment was," Coldhearted

said, getting mad because the nigga was playing dumb. "Do da fuckin' right thing and we done wit it."

Tate thought twice about fucking with Coldhearted because he saw the young boy's work. He wasn't afraid of blood, pain, killing, or dying. He turned to Colmillo to address her in a respectful voice. "I was bein' an asshole to you, Miss Daniela. Forgive me… it won't happen again," Tate apologized.

She nodded.

"She can cook her red-headed ass off though!" Deuce joked to lighten the mood.

"Imma pull her to the side to talk deep web, Bitcoin, cryptocurrency, TOR, and VULKANYKACYD.onion," Juicy P told the boys.

"Who is she anyway?" Deuce asked.

"She da plug's daughter," C.H. told them. "Grab that toolbox and c'mon in da garage."

The trio went to work removing the kilos from the truck.

CHAPTER SEVEN

How to Steal Drug Dealers Data
Mt. Vernon, NY

It was only a two-hour job.

There was a hidden hydraulic button that dropped back the entire front dash where twenty bricks were stashed. Then they had to use a power tool to remove the seats where fourteen more kilos were. Inside of the spare tire they discovered eight more. Last, underneath the vehicle, they located the extra gas tank. They used a hydraulic jack to hoist up the rear end and once more they had to use the power drill to remove nuts and screws and take the tank completely off. Tate used an electric handsaw to cut it open and that's where the last of the kilos were located plus a bonus three pounds of "Pasto" marijuana.

"No more VULKANYKACYD," C.H. stated. "We quittin' while we ahead."

"You sure 'bout that?" Tate asked, sweating like hell in the hot garage.

"The feds 'bout to hit if we don't," C.H. warned him, bagging up the cocaine in black bags and the heroin in red plastic trash bags, five in each bag. He kept out a kilo of cocaine and a kilo of heroin. "How y'all get here?"

"I came on my new motorcycle," Deuce told him. "Tate came in his ride."

"These go to Farnum Road to get bagged up and cooked," he told them. "Cook it wit three hundred grams of baking soda. I'll be through there if not late night tonight then tomorrow."

Tate whistled and shook his head. "Son was dead serious 'bout da takeover. Twenty-five and twenty-five?"

"We at a truce," Coldhearted stated. "The town still hot 'bout them boombastics. But only thing we stoppin' is da bullets and C-4 right now. I'm opening up a coupla thrift shop-junk shop stores where the most important thing is the electronics section. Daniela may be takin' the dark site off our hands but Imma fuck wit Juicy P and Diamond Girl on the cellphones we sell to Bloods, MS-13, and other hustlers."

"Like what, riggin' 'em up?" Deuce asked, not understanding.

C.H. nodded. "Once word get out that we fix tablets, cellphones, computers, and sell used ones for cheap, mufuckaz gonna fuck with us. And we gonna install spy programs on they devices. We gon' move on they clientele and they ain't even gonna know how…If we find a local connect we bury 'em. Simple as that."

"How you come up wit this shit?" Tate asked, loving the idea. "Not killin' they drug connects, da other shit…"

"We hacked into a lot of Bugout nem folks before and… that's basically how," C.H. revealed. "So, on the way back from Mexico I was thinkin' of how to steal data, get into drug dealers' computers and devices with the least amount of attention. Mufuckaz would love clandestine, cheap, services in the 'hood."

They were ready to leave.

"Take a pound of that weed with y'all and stick it in the Farnum Road safehouse safe," C.H. told them. "Whenever y'all smokin' and shit, be smart… have them super long incense burning all day all around the block so it's in the air. Police use any excuse, though Farnum's a fine block and neighborhood. Let the niggas smoke for free."

Deuce and Tate took off.

CHAPTER EIGHT

The Streets Named Me
Mt. Vernon, NY

Coldhearted had returned to Mt. Vernon, a one-hundred perfect block official Rollin' 60 Neighborhood Crip – made official in the presence and by OG Bobby Tate and others. So, all that Savage Hoodz shit he wasn't even reppin'. They didn't stand for strength. They just wanted the money but when real niggas like Blood Bugout and his homiez came through, they were the superior crew. And C.H. wasn't feeling it. The sad part of it was that he was a young dude. Younger than all of them. And very few of Savage Hoodz were willing to kill to keep the money. That's how the AmeriKKKan government set the example: *take from the African everything and make him a corpse*. The Ameri-

KKKa C.H. knew took the money and the land and they kill daily in the name of "freedom" to keep it from being taken from Russia and China.

There was a lot to do. On Liza's end, she acquired leases on a dozen small business locations in the hood sections of Mt. Vernon, New Rochelle, Yonkers, the Bronx, and Brooklyn. She also leased a warehouse located in the Bronx on Baychester Avenue and East 233rd Street. Inside of the warehouse were two cargo vans and three fourteen-foot trucks. She filed for an LLC/Limited Liability Company certificate and business license with Bronx County/New York Division of Corporations which came in the mail within a few days. And the Department of the Treasury/Internal Revenue Service issued her an Employer's Tax Identification Number.

"Your job is to fill up the warehouse and use what's in da warehouse to put on store shelves," C.H. coached Liza. "You will up da warehouse by goin' to storage auctions to bid on abandoned lockers. The name of the game is to buy smart."

"How the hell I know what I'm doin'?" she asked.

"You don't, that's why you go in and watch other people," he told her. "I saw this cute white girl with a phat little ass on the Internet doin' it named *Mary Padian.*"

"If she so cute, find her to do it, asshole!" Liza shot at him.

He chuckled when she slapped him in the back of the head. He showed her the growing number of storage hunters online and when she actually saw MarysFinds.com, she agreed about Mary. "I see why you like her. Even I'd try her little ass," Liza joked.

From there Liza studied everything she could about the business. She saw a video of a guy who bought a large freight/shipment container locker that was cluttered up front. At these auctions no one could touch anything; they could only look so it was a real mystery of what was stored in the rear of the locker. The bids went up to $3500 but stopped there. The guy who'd won the bid had his work crew empty out the locker. In the rear of it was an original 1967 Camaro SS, fully restored, showroom condition for classic late 1960'S cars. He later sold it for $36,000 to none other than car lover *Jay Leno*.

And that was only one example of many.

"Rock's mom could use work if we got it, she a real smart lady," Coldhearted mentioned. "The Savage Hoodz dudes keep questioning me about Shadow and Tommy disappearance. Got me not wanting to fuck wit 'em. So, fuck them niggas. Don't even answer no phone for 'em, no questions, don't volunteer shit. I'm Rollin 60 Neighborhood Crip now."

"So, they banged you up to bang you in. Is that what you was all fucked up for?" Liza demanded answers.

"You da wife of a gangster, bitch. You have a strong mind cuz youse a strong ass bitch. I can't fuck wit no weak ass niggas. Next thing you know these niggas gon' be tryin' on panties." C.H. said angrily. "A real woman respect strength and leadership outta her fuckin' man. These bitch ass Savage

Hoodz niggas is weak and they were led by the women. How you think Rock got his top popped? He ain't make no real show of force when the Almighty Black P. Stones went after Orca. Not only that, he wanted the money, but he was scared to squirt lead into them fuckers. Coldhearted is a name I *earned*. The streets named me, them niggas named themselves."

"What about Juicy and them?" Liza said as she braided her man's hair. He sat between her legs on the floor in their office.

"The bitches we keep," he told her. "They your employees. And fareal, fareal…they was the real master hackers anyway. We lost a couple to college, moving outta state or whatever – fuck it."

"We gotta worry 'bout any of day boys?" she asked.

He was dismissive about them. "No."

She sent a text to Diamond Girl that stated: *Need you, Sonja, Alejandra, Shay, Joyce, Blue Eyez, Bhad Barb, Sunnie, Ava, and Juicy to come over ASAP (tonight) if y'all want money in ya clutch.*

"The emphasis on these businesses is *electrics*," he informed her slowly – with authority – so she understood. "Like I told Deuce and Tate… we gon' repair – for cheap – computers, tablets, cellphones, and whatnot. Our targets are drug dealers, Blood niggas, MS-13 niggas, even other Crip niggas. We jackin' clientele for coke, heroin, ecstasy pills, percocets, oxycontin, oxycodone, weed, we 'bout to kill it in da Dirty Rotten – word ta da mutha. I know you want a Lambo and a Phantom, dontchu?"

She had butterflies in her belly. "I'm fine with our Cadillac truck. And by the way…it's *electronics* not *electrics*."

"Be truthful, bae," he urged her. "When you be seein' bitches like Remy, Lil Kim, and J-o in videos, on TMZ and shit, you don't want that life?"

She kissed the right side of his neck. "Not if I haveta lose this. Our life now. Plus, Remy 45; Kim 55; and J-Lo 65! C'mon now."

"Why you think I've surrounded us by *real* killaz?" he inquired. "That increases our survival. Weak niggas and fake hoez decrease our survival. Now, if we can have big dough, don'tchu want it?"

Liza nodded. "Hell yeah – like da Kardashians?"

He chuckled in that sinister way he does. "More. Fuck that comparison. They keep surroudin' theyself wit weak mufuckaz. First, Bruce Jenner wanna be a woman. And not a young one but an ugly old hag – at his age! Then, all these other clowns. They got bank but they weak. Amber Rose outted Kanye when TMZ.com reported that she was finger poppin' him. Then the Kayne fans were surprised when he wore the dress when he performed. He was tryna come out but Amber Rose fucked his moment up!"

"You funny as hell." Liza was cracking up. "A girl finger up her man booty don't make nobody gay either. I lick yo ass all the time – And you cum *harder*. You cum more."

"Lickin' is different from stickin'," he explained.

"We both do a lot of reading. We watch porno videos. Don't act ignorant. The male has a prostate gland which surrounds the urethra at the base of his bladder that controls… *urine release from the bladder and the prostate secretes a fluid which is a major constituent of semen,*" she was reading out loud from something she'd pulled up on her cellphone. "Understand?"

He nodded. "I get all that," he stated.

"Baby, we *eloped.* You my husband. I'm your wife. What a man does with his wife makes him heterosexual." She paused, staring at him. "Private bedroom stuff is private."

"Right."

"Whether it's my tongue or finger. Listen to *my* words. M-Y F-I-N-G-E-R. It's *mine.* I'm a *female.* The finger came from your *wife.* So, if you and I discover that the prostate has a *colossal* amount or erogenous nerves…" she just shrugged. "We doing what feels mad good."

"Erogenous nerves?" he looked at her blankly.

"Erogenous is gettin' sexual pleasure from," she described for him. "You act like if I'm deep throating him and I spit all over your balls…so he a *battering ram,* ball tight, you been eatin' my pussy but I can't concentrate. And youse a hairy ass nigga which I love about your chest, underarms, belly, arms, legs even balls, cock, everywhere. But you know if you want *my* mega-mouth it has to be clean-shaven. Anyhow, picture it all

being sucked…wet and warm, I'm ready to make it *explode*. My fingers have been on your asshole a million times. So, just cuz I wanna massage my husband's prostate, I'm takin' your manhood? That one act between a woman and her husband makes him gay- or homosexual?" Liza questioned incredulously.

She had him stuck. "Well," he said, thinking it over. "It's a heterosexual act."

"The marriage bed is a sanctuary between a husband and wife," Liza mentioned as she wrapped her arms around his shoulders and gently offered herself to him. "Amber Rose is standing in with all the rest of the scornful in Hollywood. When she wagged her finger at Ye he prolly shoulda told her *'you felt like a mannequin every time I hugged you!'* Fuck that fake bitch."

Juicy P called them to the living room. Diamond Girl, Barbie, Ava Applez, and Blue Eyez showed up. Siting at the bar was Tanya Taylor and a dozen other women that Sage didn't know. Everyone took seats and put to use the massive new U-shaped leather sectional by *DANE DECOR*. There were also several leather ottomans with three matching overstuffed leather recliners.

"Okay, ladies. I'm Sage. My friends call me C.H.," he introduced himself to about a dozen women that he didn't know.

"Bertha," a slim, brown-skinned Black woman offered. She couldn't be any more than 26 years old.

Sage had an evil grin on his face as he lifted up his shirt. "You ever think about shootin' the person who named you?"

Bertha burst out laughing. "No! But I should've, huh?"

"That's a fat, mean, *grandmother's* name!" he said, shaking his head.

"Sage! Boy if you don't -" Tanya playfully scolded him. She was 54 now, even-toned flawless brown skin that she took care of. Men half her age attracted to her tallness, her large juicy lips, and those prize packages that most men liked: ass, hips, legs, and breasts. She had some extra belly and a little bit on the sides but it wasn't unattractive or scarred with stretching. Tanya was one of those older women who loved hours and hours of oral: she had a beautiful face and lovely lips, so it was very easy to desire her mouth.

"My bad, Ms. T.T." Sage embraced her. As usual she smelled good: CHANEL. Small, tasteful jewelry: VAN CLEEF & ARPELS: The strong dainty chain was from their Lucky Spring Collection. Pendant, rose gold (like the chain) carnelian and onyx. She had finally gotten rid of Chubb and Rock's father. He was a loser. Thankfully, Rock had made her a part of what he'd create with SHZ LLC or else she would have lost the house. "Matter fact, lemme pull you to the side a sec. Then I'll leave y'all, Ms. T."

He followed the older woman into his office-study and as she walked ahead of him he couldn't help but to stare at her full round buttocks in the gray khaki-style pants. Something he and other boys and done with her ever since they were much younger. Tanya Taylor had been the #1 MILF. Inside the office Coldhearted laughed.

"What's so funny, Sage? Is something in my hair?" she smiled back.

"No. Your butt," he chuckled. She stood up wiping it, stroking it up and down, making it jiggle.

"You-" he stood in front of her. "You was kidding."

"I was." He locked the door and cracked the office safe.

"Asshole! Whatchu want?" she asked him as he removed several safety deposit box keys. "Chubb said y'all had cash problems."

She started to say something. "I'll figure it out."

"Don't be proud!" he scolded her. "I had you open a *box* here. Is $100k enough to get you out of debt so your heart and mind is clear to run the Bargains Galores business. Liza said she hired you at B.G.'s."

She took the key and tears pooled up in her eyes. "Thank you."

"After all you do for Liza, me, Lilly and Izzy." He hugged her close to him and it felt good to show some emotion for a while.

"I should get back." But he put both arms around her waist and pulled her even closer.

"We getting' rich out here, Tanya. Anything you want from me you can have." She felt the hardness and the heat of him, his great cock pressing right there at the top of where her female heat started...Her nipples hardened. Pussy dampened.

"But you're like my son!" Tanya whispered as her nose was caught up underneath his chin, smelling his spicy scented Burberry cologne.

Tanya was *STACKED*. She knew it too. Never in her wildest dreams did she ever think she could have such a fine boy who was such a man! The forbidden fruit nature of it all...

"LIZA! Oh my god! NO SAGE! I'm losing my mind. Do you want this key back?" she asked quickly. "I don't want it if -"

"To the safety deposit? No!" he said it indignantly, taking her small hands and wrapping them both gently around his long, thick, dick...and his hot balls. "Just...wanted...you...to feel that fuckin' pipe."

There was a knock on the door. He opened it and saw Bertha. "Tanya, they ready."

Tanya exited and Sage called Liza. When she came in he asked her. "Babe, you got panties on?"

"I-I don't know." She hesitated as he locked the door and stripped naked. "I need you...*bad*."

"They startin' the meeting on the locker units and stuff." But even as she was saying it she was stuck as she shed off her boots, socks, and jean suit.

"C'mere." He pulled all of the sofa pillows off and laid there with his battering ram standing there as if it was about to start shooting flames. She got on top of him and looked him dead in the eyes.

"Which one of them got you sparked up like this? Or did

you take one of them blue pills?" she asked as she trapped the plum-sized knob at her Honey's Gate and buttered him up. "Bertha? Every shirt she wear, you can see her nipples staring atchu like headlights."

"None of 'em," he gasped as she started to take more of his flagpole. He suddenly took himself out and went down on his Puerto Rican-Dominican sweetheart.

He made sexy moans and slurping sounds as he licked her.

"Papi, I gotta confess somethin'," she said as her hips writhed in ecstasy. "Just promise you won't flip out?"

He paused to look at her.

"Promise me you'll still love me and eat me and fuck me?"

"What it got to do wit that?"

"Anyway, I was at Lupe's house while she was out shoppin'," Liza started telling him. "Daniela was wit me. We fooled around a little, kissing. I was really horny and I needed to getchu, Papi. So, I clean Lupe house, got sweated out, so I jumped in the shower. Lupe got shampoo it's like battery acid. I'm cussin'… my eyes is burnin' so I rinses it out. What I do? I wash my face but this shit smell mad good so I wash all over."

"I've done that," C.H. admitted as he continued to kiss all around her wet creamy center.

"Mmm," she whimpered as her clit became trapped between his teeth and lips – not biting it – but the tongue was savoring that baby. She cried, "Finger my asshole while doin' that!!"

C.H. did exactly that. "Keep talkin'. I'll keep suckin' your clit and fingering your-"

She keeps talking. "The bathroom door opens...the shower stall. So, I'm thinkin' okay, Daniela. She makes me massively horny by soaping up my breasts. I let my fingers dance over my clit. She fingers my asshole, my eyes are closed, masturbating. No conversation. Then I feel she's went and strapped on the dildo because I feel it's hardness against my backside. I'm getting really into it. Her arms go around, clutching my breasts and kneading them eagerly."

"So, Liza, you mean..." Coldhearted stopped and watched her.

"Don't be mad...Please suck my clit!" she begged him. He watched her get scorching hot. "Fuck me. I see that hard monster!" She watched him: "One of his hands moved down, and I removed my own hand from my crotch so his could replace it. I was moaning like a slut, Papi...as I felt one of his fingers go into my cunt while another found my pulsating clit and caressed it in little circles. I humped my crotch against his hand. My breath getting ragged. I had to brace myself against the shower wall to keep from falling as the passion overwhelmed me, and I came with a cry of joy."

She stared at her husband who was listening while still nursing a gigantic boner, which she reached for, and it leaped happily forward in one and then both of her hands. She kissed him lovingly all around the glans and then took him halfway into her throat.

"As much as I wanna kill him, baby…" he picked her head up and kissed her. "That shit got my dick ready to break prison bars!"

"Baby!" she cried. They kissed. "Oh my god, C.H…um – I -"

"Chubb's mom, Tanya," he told her. "She was in here. She thick as all fuck. She smell good. She made my dick hard as hell."

Liza smiled. "You wanna fuck her?"

"One day," he said. "I wanna see you get fucked, mama."

"Want me to finish the story?"

He nodded.

"He was kissin' on my mouth, then my neck," she described. "He was sucking my nipples. I reached for his hard cock and next thing you know, I was on a soft rubber mat sucking on a big ten-inch horse-hammer. He was the next-door neighbor boy Brandon. His big dick oozed a steady stream of pre-cum, too."

"Liza, I been wantin' to fuck you so bad! I, I mean you're any man's dream come true! Please, I am beggin' you to let me fuck you!" he kept on and on. "And you and me have already acknowledge, right Sage…a new partner revs up the sexiness like crazy."

Sage nodded as Liza slowly gave him a handjob.

"So, I compromised," Liza said. "I tell Brandon: fuck me in the ass…fuck my pretty little asshole, SAGE!"

That's when she got onto her knees and elbows, spreading

open that creamy alabaster tattooed body of hers and resting her face into the cushions. C.H. found a bottle of Astroglide in the desk drawer and lubricated his cock and her asshole. She described the ass-fucking that Brandon gave her whole Cold-hearted delivered his own.

"Sage – I felt the big head of dick pushin' into my asshole and thought it wouldn't fit, Papi!" she moaned, pushing her ass back. She moaned uncontrollably as he moved into her inch by inch. "Oooouuu, shit – I *love* ass fucking! You fuckin' me just like he did! You make me feel so filled up! He was just longer."

"Oh shit. Fuck mama! You feel my balls on your clit?" Sage was up in those intestines he was like an octopus. Sage made women crave and thirst for the fucking he gave them. When he was buried completely inside of Liza he grabbed hold of her breasts and that's when they truly started to fuck. Liza's sweet cries could be heard by the other women and unbeknownst to Liza and Sage, all of their vaginas were moist. Their clitorises woke up, a little sweat made them steamy-warm, and their nipples hardened.

"C'mon you guys!" Tanya whispered.

The women loved the older woman. She was supposed to be their supervisor soon. The new dozen or so females Tanya had got together had worked for Tanya in the recent past at the New Department of Labor & Unemployment AKA "The Labor Office." Tanya had gotten fired for insubordination when arguing with her white female boss one too many times. Rock and Chubb's father had divorced her for the Pastor's younger daughter – ShaQueena Patterson years before...

But that had neither been the secret – nor the funny part. First, ShaQueena ("Nay" for short) was damned near 250 pounds. For a 5-foot 3-inch woman of 20 years old, that's fat as fuck. Then, come to find out, Nay was pregnant. She had given birth to a baby girl and a couple of weeks later was when Rocky, Sr. found out that his "Lovey Dovey" was all over *Pornhub.com, BBW.com* (Big Beautiful Women) and, to top it all off, she was on *eBay* selling pussy. Rocky, Sr. and Tanya had fallen out of love long ago but raising their sons in a $469,000 house, nice school, and decent neighborhood had kept them together.

Sexually, the two never had any problems but the emotional destruction caused by the loss of love was as damaging and hurtful as the death of a loved one. Love may not have blood in it but it can be blood-stained. Loss was loss. Tanya had been sought after by other men almost each day of the twenty years she'd spent with Senior and he'd had three long term affairs. Because she had boys, that's the only reason she'd never let a man penetrate her vagina other than her husband. But, often left in need of sex, she'd bought a secret cellphone and made a *AshleyMadison.com* (e.g., a clandestine cheating-on-your-spouse account).

Senior had a small dick, so Tanya's *Ashley Madison* account specifically sought after men with what she described as *"the perfect dick and balls."* She'd wrote there (it's taken down presently):

> *I don't mean to take men down.*
> *Sorry if I sound like that. Only*
> *interested if I can see it erect. I have*
> *a very lovely pussy. I've never shaved*
> *because of chaffed skin – it can*
> *darken after years of shaving. I*
> *am nearly hair-free anyway.*
> *I'll show myself first (no faces*
> *but I have a gorgeous face!)"*

When she'd posted that, by the next time she checked, she had 198 messages. About half of them came with the nude photos she'd requested. She clicked on nearly all of them when she found *Randy Brannum*. He didn't use oil or lotion to pump when he had an erection. He was sitting on a cushioned weight bench – harder than the streel barbell he was using. In another photo he was standing sideways. That dick he had – Tanya Tayla, who was in her early or mid-forties around that time, had decided – was *the perfect dick and balls.*

That was what – or *who* – Tanya was thinking of as she witnessed the little boy that she used to know, transform into a *man*. He didn't just "have" Liza…and Liza didn't just "have" him. Their love was aesthetic. He possessed Liza. And she him. What he was doing to her right now, somehow it looked like something only the Devil would do…

He'd produced a dog rope. The kind thrown around a dog's neck, put through the built-in loop, and pulled it. "Whatchu doin', man, oh my god, ow! My employees out there! I need them to respect me. Ow!" He slapped her sweaty, buttery, buttcheeks.

He dug into the cabinet – where the Bose music system and speakers were – and found the chain and handcuffs. "You ain't goin' nowhere 'til I get all da nut gushin' outta you!"

"Those are real, bro!" she pleaded as he cuffed her hands together so that her breasts scarped up against the sofa and he cuffed her to the brass rings on the wall. "When'd you put up rings in here, Papi – oh my fucking – *ow!*" she cried. "What was that?"

He had taken a tiny pen-scalpel and sliced open a half-inch cut on the back of her shoulder. "C'mere, bitch, come to yo Daddy."

They barely missed a beat. Sage always threw the most exciting curveballs at her, so what they did privately (or publicly) was never predictable. He was sucking the small droplets of blood dripping from her cut and then they were sharing the most loving kisses. She was handcuffed so it frustrated her not to be able to play with his long, thick ass, cock. She badly wanted to get to it.

"Daddy. You my Daddy, mm! Fuck me! My ass… aaanghhh!"

He was lubed back up and he was looking down at her phat sweaty ass. "You still want me to fuck you in the -?" He teased her with the tip, bumping her clit.

The chain had about a foot and she used it all. "Get that big shit in my ass. God, Sage, please stop teasing me! Daddy...oooouuuggghhh."

He rubbed his enlarged dickhead all over her sweet cunt lips and that angry ice cream pink pearl. Then, back inside of her, her sphincter is "popped" through, and she emitted a prolonged whine as he burrowed down deep inside of her. This was what his audience observed. Coldhearted hurting it so good...

The faucet of perspiration made their youthful, energetic, bodies glow like a beautiful sunset. "Oh, Liza...fuck! Obsession! Obsession, baby! I love this ass, these fuckin' tatas, my sweet wet pussy! Was it good?! Did he suck the blood outchu like this?"

Where he'd cut her open at, he sucked the trickling blood, something they both got off on.

"No!" she whined, pulling on the chains and handcuffs, wishing she could touch him. "No, he couldn't make me cum like this... we never sweated like this. Obsession, Papi! You my Daddy! Nobody has our love, Papi! Since we was little kids, I fuckin' know you was mine forever!"

To Tanya, the bloodsucking, chaining her up – your own wife – it was only something the Devil would do. *But, oh my god!* Tanya thought, as she saw Sage's huge balls cover up

Liza's entire pussy like a curtain. He had that gigantic bone buried MOBB DEEP up in that sexy tattooed ass and he stopped to *grind* it. As he did so, he cut his inner forearm with the scalpel.

"Suck it." He didn't even need to ask. She sucked the forearm like a big cock and worked her ass to the left as he kept up the deep grind. "You love suckin' it like you loved suckin' that boy Brandon?"

"Yes." She nodded as he grabbed her waist tighter and – still buried to the hilt – he winded his hips, and that's what the girls out in the hallway were viewing with huge eyes and soaking wet cunts. Several of them were so turned on from what they were monitoring that they couldn't help but grab onto their own breasts and caress their pussies through their clothing.

"Show, me, Liza," her sexy husband commanded.

"How I sucked his big hard dick?" she asked breathily as their wet, sticky slamming sounds filled the office.

He stuck two fingers into her mouth, and she sucked and sucked. "Mm, like this?... Mm, oh my god Brandon... I love this long, big dick." She kept showing him as he hammered her hairless asshole in and out.

"Uunh, Jesus, Liza," he moaned, licking the perspiration off of her sexy neck and ears. "You're so sexy, baby."

She threw her phat ass back because she sensed that the rock-hard power in her man was slipping from his grasp and she knew that her hot sexy body could take it away from him like a bullet took away a life. Right now, Sage had awakened a new spot inside of her ass that had it orgasming.

"Imma, we gon' build a room, Daddy!"

He had her anus doing flip flops and there was literally an *anal* orgasm totally separate from the (A) *vaginal* orgasm and (B) *clitoral*. They were both 1000% certain because her anal tunnel leaked a clear foamy white froth that helped keep the passage lubricated profoundly well. Half the time he kept his fingers away from her clitoris during the anal sex because it felt so good fucking her that she demanded: *"More!"* and *"Deeper!"* then, *"Harder!"* and *"Okay stir it slow, Daddy!"* Also, *"Now grind that shit hard, Papi!"* It was astonishing to see such a tiny hole take suck a big dick.

The women didn't notice Juicy P slipping away from the door and coaxing Ava Applez away on the right wing of the house to "talk."

"Nah, I ain't come back here to have sex witchu either, Juice." Ava shook her head. "You think bitches ain't tell me you was fuckin' Sierra in Garter's. And don't think I ain't hear of y'all at the Hip Hop Gala. Y'all in the picture wit Diggy and Angela Simmons."

"We donated to a kid's charity Angela behind. Anybody who donated five hundred or more got a picture with Angela. Diggy was just there," Juicy defended her actions. "And if you don't want me around, what I supposed to do? I care about you but I want sex with other people. If I could take a pill to turn off my sex drive…we'd *never* argue! I'm just sorry not to have been more honest sooner. I just get so horny…"

"You horny right now?" Ava asked in her small voice.

Juicy walked up to where Ava sat, pulling her capri pants down mid-thigh. Ava gasped. "Girl you're *soaked*! My god, it's all down your thighs and in your jeans! You can't walk around all day like that."

"Ava, if you saw what we saw… The way Liza and Sage fuck?" Juicy shook her head. "He got a *nice* big dick. And he ass-fuckin' her like he was just released from prison. Sweat drippin', they cut each other and blood suckin'! Oh, I heard her admit to fuckin' a neighbor boy and she tellin' him how she sucked his dick and he steadily deep stroking the shit out of her…Like he loves to hear about her extra-marital…"

Back in the study the ass-fucking got harder. Liza was staring at him and still sucking on his fingers. But, suddenly, he froze. "Stop movin', Liza. You better not fuckin' move… *Don't*."

He ripped his T-shirt. He fold it over and over and then used it to blind fold her. He eased his huge dick out of her. He caught his breath, uncuffed her, but ordered her to leave the blindfold on. He opened a cold beer and gave it to this lovely wife.

The refrigerator was close to the door. He played it off like he was returning to the refrigerator and pulled the door open with his index finger to his mouth so all the "Peeping Toms" knew that they could stay but they had to be silent.

"Papi, come on," Liza urged him. "I wantchu to cum inside my ass."

"I'm not Papi, your husband ain't here. It's your secret lover – Brandon." He got on the sofa after putting all the cushions back. He wrapped his arms around her waist. "Can I call you Mrs. Thomas?"

She nodded, "Whatttaya want, Brandon? My husband gonna be back in an hour."

"Well… I couldn't stop thinkin' about how good you looked and smelled." He started sucking those pretty nipples and licking around the areola. She smelled hot but feminine.

With the blindfold still on she moaned and reached for his face. "Brandon, you need to stop!"

"But these titties are so pretty!" he murmured.

She pushed him back on the sofa. "Okay… I'll suck you but you can't fuck me. I don't wanna get pregnant…"

"Ooh, ohhh-okay, no pregnant," he murmured as he turned to watch the women who were watching them. He stared right at Tanya when saying. "You have beautiful lips."

Liza's head game was *ill*. She was already warmed up from so many orgasms already. She was able to take his long, thick penis deep into her throat and let him feel her swallowing muscles go to work in a way similar to her vaginal and anal muscles. On the way in she was showboating what her pharynx and larynx could do.

"You love that big new dick, dontchu?"

She nodded and moaned while his giant cock was awash

with her saliva. She was a savage and a ferocious cocksucker, and she understood all of the superpowers she held with these amazing talents. If she could be on AmeriKKKa's Got Talent and corner its judges one by one: Simon, Howie, Sofia's pretty ass, and Terry included, Liza would get all them "gold buzzers" and take home the half million dollars. (It's actually $1 million in prize money but anyone who's not part of AmeriKKKa's Elite 1% will pay about 50% to those crooked, thieving, motherfuckers at the IRS.)

"C'mere, Mrs. Thomas. Gimme some of that sweet Spanish pussy you got. Please?" he begged.

"No, I told you! I never cheat on my husband."

"Okay." He laid her on her right side and he draped his arm around her mid-section. She felt the hardness of his cock hit her in the back and he lifted her left leg so his long hard penis was up against her clean-shaven pussy.

"Oh my god, Brandon. He's on his way..." she whined, horny for his dick to enter her leaking passage. He fingered her and she moaned when he squeezed her clitoris.

"You smell so fantastic." He snigged his fingers and put them underneath her nose to sniff as well. She licked them and he rubbed his glorious meat all along the wonderfully scented labia majora which she rubbed firmer and firmer, against him until the inner pink of the labia minora was opening along her inner cleft and juicing him all up and down his stiff obelisk.

"Fuck...I have to cum, okay?"

He was ready. He slid his already lubed up monster inside

of her and they almost instantly turned into animals. The sofa was a large one so there was plenty of room to spoon-position. Then he let her take over. His feet on the floor she screamed and pushed her titties in his face, while he grabbed her yummy ass and pulled it open.

"Fuck me Brandon. Fuck me like my husband **don't**. You fuck me so good and make me so fuckin' wet!"

And it was true. The blindfold had her believing she had a different dick because she went buck wild. Sage's cock was sending Liza to heaven and she screamed as she came. She was so overcome with ecstasy at that point that she could not even think about anything but the "new" man she was fuckin'. And it was the same cum, the same screams, *three more times* until she burst open like a water balloon.

"Liza!!! Fuck! Ohhh, shit mammaaaa... I love you!" he screamed, squeezed her breasts, and fucked her super-hard.

"Te quiero mucho, Papi, mi amor. Oh my god!" She collapsed on top of him and removed the blindfold. She looked down and giggled. She was shaking like a leak. "Oh, I made a mess. *Disculparme, Papi.* I squirted all fuckin' over! *A cada muerte de un obispo,*" she whispered.

He smiled. "Once in a blue moon? Uh uh. Liar. Once a week!"

"No, once a *month*. You can't give me ten orgasms, hand-cuff me, suck each other's blood – especially buttfuck me and roleplay with a new man's dick! You knew Brandon was fake... Didn't you motherfucker?"

He smiled at her. "Baby, I check all the camera footage. Even if a camera blacks out, there's a backup system – on batteries – for thirty hours. Of course, I knew. You was mad into it."

Liza got up but was weakened by the session and then it ended with her squirting everything. "I was but in actual reality...I'd probably be a disaster. Please never try to girls. The right ones are like... bringin' ya wifey a tussie-mussie. But a man? Never try that."

"A tussie-mussie? What's that?"

"A bouquet of flowers," she said, looking at the door while getting dressed. "Baby – the door's open!"

"Well," he said then shrugged it off. "What's done is done."

Liza left to take a shower.

Deuce arrived and followed Sage into the workshop. He dumped the cash and they checked it meticulously against the financial ledgers. The money was counted via digital cash counters. Then, they literally washed the scent of narcotics off of the cash inside of the bathtub. Then, the cash would be divided by denomination, put inside of nylon laundry bags, and dried on "Light Head" in four different dryers in the laundry room.

The process was slow but Sage wasn't taking any chances when it came to the cash. Police dogs were getting more and more sophisticated. Once dried, the cash was placed inside of industrial plastic sheaths, air vacuumed out and then hermetically sealed.

Once that was all done they locked up. Deuce went upstairs and Sage locked the money up in underground safes as well as the narco-stash. Nobody else needed to know where he put those big-ticket items at. He called Deuce back down to the "Boom-Boom Room" so they could mix it up. (Boom-Boom Room = Game Room).

"Son, we gave out a thousand dollars samples to all the fiends on the 'target list' and when we opened up shop, they was lined up from Elm to Post Road!" Deuce recounted the street events. "Mad cats is tryna cop weight.. Tate's bussin' off eight balls for a buck twenty-five. They want boy weight." ("Boy" = Heroin).

He just gave Deuce a brief look. "Wassup then?" Sage shrugged. "Lemme calculate some weight prices first. Ask me in two weeks. We ain't in a rush."

"The boy was in a drought so this shit made us instant street kingz. The rock that been out, that is good, they sellin' one rock for a dime. Our shit's twice the size and the shit is boos. So we makin' eighty dollars a gram off the rock. You know we cook one of two kilos at once. We getting' about three hundred grams in extras back which totals thirteen hundred grams a brick."

"That means a hundred four thousand a brick," Coldhearted (or Sage) calculated. "Just be sure each dealer hands a money slip in with his name and how much he or she hands in each time. What kind of packages that you givin' out. And what's the dealer's cut?"

"We hand out five-hundred-dollar packs and they keep a hundred," Deuce told him. "And we ain't cuttin' the boy. Each brick we baggin' about a hundred fifteen grand. Our stamp is *'5-stars.'* The shit is high-po…so the baggies is a little smaller. You put more than that, the fiends'll bang the whole bag, cuz."

C.H. was thinking it over from a business and street takeover aspect where his whole team profits. He spent $44k on each brick of boy. $115k for one brick of boy, retail, "sounded good" but it didn't. Fit in with his street takeover plans by putting "small dime baggies" out on the block.

"Deuce, check it, son," Sage told him seriously. "I said use a McDonald's coffee stirrer to scoop da boy. The *whole* scoop- don't shake it. If they O.D., you think I care? A dead O.D. is good advertisement my nigga. Them other niggas is usin' horse tranquilizers and mufuckaz is bein' *killed purposely*. The DEA know da fucking difference. They've labelled it 'fentanyl poisoning.' I specifically told our connect *not* to gimme that. Shit cuz I read newsfeeds day and night. Ever read *Generation Kill* by Even Wright?" Coldhearted questioned his lieutenant.

"Nigga, you da big brains in da mob," Deuce mentioned as he followed C.H. out of the game room and into the garage. "Never read it but I'll see if it's on urbanaintdead.com. They'll order anything and link us the audiobook, too."

C.H. placed another key of boy in Deuce's backpack. "The

Mickey-Dee's coffee stirrer (Mickey-Dee = McDonald's). Full scoop. No shake."

"Aight." Deuce strapped the backpack on and checked the rounds in the 9mm prior to re-holstering it.

"Hit the city-wide radio and group texts…" C.H. ordered. "Err'body need to be here."

C.H. went out into the living room where the women were still having a meeting. "Y'all need anything regarding the new business?"

"We were discussing budget at each auction." Tanya said matter of factly. "Liza said you guys have found or signed a dozen leases for a dozen thrift stores. The warehouse is really huge. Two vans, three trucks. A very nice start."

"You seen it?" he asked the beautiful mother of Rock and Chubb.

"Just blueprints," she admitted with an unaware lick of her lips.

"Here's what I learned," C.H. rationalized to the ladies as he, coincidentally, held a black alligator skin attaché case filled with drug scratch thus far collected from Double Deuce. "We gotta know a lot about products – old, new, whatever. Right now, y'all gotta focus on fillin' up da shelves of our warehouse. Far as budget three to five g's for each auction."

"Cash only," Tanya state with certainty. "Those are the rules. And there will be times when we must go all in for a unit. Particularly when it's a shipping container, a car, or something. Don't just show up with three grand is all I'm sayin'."

C.H. opened up the attaché case, handing it over to Liza. "From the trust fund, Flaca. Bueno Suerte (good luck) with your business."

"Um, your daughter number two'd," Liza alerted him,

"Ya aunt, none of 'em here?" he inquired as Isabel reached for him. "She too happy to know she got a stinkin' ass."

Everyone laughed as he took her away, let her splash and play in the bubble bath, dressed her in bed clothes, and fed her dinner. Izzy fell to sleep next to him. At 11:00 PM, Elizabeth and Lupé arrived. Lupé looked aglow as if she'd been getting some lately.

Lupé had this ultra-straight long black hair with a lot of gray in it. She was beaming about it being dyed all black now. Her eyebrows were thinned and trimmed. And her face was small and happy. Lupé was darker than her sisters or Liza's. If one had to draw a comparison Liza's skin was like that of superstar Jennifer Lopez and Lupé's was like that of *Chicago PD*'s Lisseth Chavez.

While Lupé primped on how she got her sexy back, C.H. showered and got Liza, Daniela, and Juicy ready to hit Garter's and a restaurant late that night.

He zipped up her expensive black Christian Dior party dress. He thanked Liz and Lupé for watching the kids. He wore blue Jordans, a $500 pair of True Religion blues, an 80-inch all gold and diamond Cuban link chain, a Rolex

Submariner watch, a gold and diamond lower grill in his mouth, and a black wife beater. Liza saw the black and blue bullet-proof jacket he put on before he slipped on the new blue New York Yankees cap and on expensive blue special edition *New York Yankees Half of Fame* T-shirt with all the top Yankees baseball greats on the front and rear.

"You look mad good, Papi!" his wife told him as La Colmillo stood behind her, finishing her long black hair.

"Thank you," he returned. Juicy P sat to the side of where the master bedroom mirror was positioned atop a dresser. She inspected the sexy Prada strapless silk and leather peach colored dress that Liza had on. *"I see a lady tonight that should be having my baby, baby,"* C.H. sang the Notorious B.I.G. song lyrics to let Liza know how good she looked. Her ass was like something in a bakery that made a person want to squeeze on it, smell it for freshness, savor it, and eat it.

C.H. couldn't help but to run his hands over that round, soft, thang. "Damn," he murmured.

Colmillo looked at Liza's hair, an up-do. "That'll do it, but I can tell you got panties on."

"Take them off for me," Liza dared the red girl in presence of her man and friend. "C'mon now…"

Daniela paused and reached under Liza's dress. Down and off came her panties which the sensual daredevil held up to her face. The coppery red head Mexicana inhaled Liza's must cunt scent and the fruit-flowery fragrance of her perfume, increasing the powerful lust crush she had on her.

"So, are we goin' to da club or is y'all pussies about to get stretched by Sage?" Juicy P teased.

"Juicy, you just horny and freaky all the time now since Ava not takin' you to those parties no more, huh?" Liza asked, putting Juicy and her ex-girlfriend's, Ava Applez, business out there! "What? Y'all all fuckin' public wit it on Facebook and err'thang."

"Daniela smellin' all on your pussy in front of Sage means only one thing. Threesome," Juicy countered. "Ain't got nothin' to do wit my break-up, me missin' the sex parties or nuttin'. Leave me alone, Liza."

"Parties?" C.H. said. "Why I ain't hear 'bout these parties?"

"I'll tell you in the car, Papi. I'm ready," Liza assured him.

C.H. held up his hands and let Liza holstered his .45 semi-automatic handguns in his shoulder holsters. He threw on his New York Yankees jacket and they exited the house.

CHAPTER NINE

Garter's New GM
Luca Sirocco
<u>South Mt. Vernon</u>

The Italian cook was standing near the entrance to the kitchen at Garter's strip club smoking a cigarette when Coldhearted, Liza, Juicy P, and Daniela "La Colmillo" Vollillo were waived in by security to enter the already packed club. As soon as they walked in, they opted on heading straight out into the thick of the entire thing. Friday nights were usually a huge night at Garter's now that Coldhearted had taken over.

"Hey, Mexicana," Juicy whispered as they were slowed down at the west end door due to crowd congestion.

Daniela, a little taller than Juicy, said, "Huh?"

Juicy leaned up on her tippy toes and slowly trailed her hands up Daniela's thighs. "You learn anything about the dark site today?" Juicy inquired demurely.

"I did," Daniela nodded. "I also learned you broke up with your girlfriend who took you to *parties*. What kinda parties? And are you two on or off right now?"

Juicy P had several security and strippers wanting to get past, so they were pushed further out into the club. Two men were yelling at each other over a woman and the argument quickly turned into a fist fight. Coldhearted was behind the bar. He paid for a drink he called "*The Black Mama Bite:*" Bourbon, Scotch, Rum, Gin, and Grenadine with Jalapeno Pepper Juice.

The bouncers had stopped the fight between the two black men and were throwing the men out. "What da fuck y'all fightin' for?" Coldhearted asked them.

"Whose you?" the young man on the left of him asked.

"*Coldhearted*," he told him, his dark eyes piercing into the stranger's. He looked like he'd had one too many.

"Aw fuck! The owner," the other man said.

The drunk young man reached for C.H.'s drink, took it, and drained the glass. "Damn, nigga. Now dis shit here? Make a nigga wanna *slap* a mufucka cuz!"

"Take his car keys, let em' sleep it off downstairs."

"So, dis nigga can try to fuck my bitch again?" he re-accused the man with fewer words. "Nah, homie."

"You can have her!" the other man stated.

"Both of y'all can kiss my ass! I keep tellin' you that I wasn't with him last night! I wouldn't betray you or disrespect our kids like that!" she screamed at her man who everyone called "J.D.," his true name Joey Dent. Her name was Tamala Elliot, a beautiful light skinned stripper from another club, twenty-seven years old, and had two children with K.D. She did admit to cheating on him before – with a man from her club. Tamala had admitted to one time with one man but it was actually about fifty times with two men over a three-month period.

"Drive him home, okay sweetheart?" Coldhearted handed her a twenty-dollar bill, her man, and the guy he had been fighting. They all hugged C.H. and thanked him for the $20.

"C'mon, J.D., lemme take you home," Tamala urged him.

He followed his girl out of the club with his drunken swagger.

Near the brass railings that lead upstairs there was a quiet privacy booth, with a large table, opaque black curtains, the whole thing. Juicy P had already led the red-head Mexicana inside of the booth with Liza.

"Y'all never heard of '*Ava's All White Weekend?*'" Juicy P was elaborating to Daniela as they were served exotic Peach Schnapps in frosted glasses by beautiful Black females who were topless, wearing G-strings and high heels.

Daniela shook her head. "I'm not from here."

"Aight," Juicy acknowledged, as if she'd totally forgotten. "Ava Applez was my first. I was fourteen when she turned me on and turned me out. I'm half black, half Latina. My dad is Puerto Rican. Ava's chocolate. I have this fixation for breasts, I saw her in the shower stall after P.E. at school."

"What's 'P.E.'?" Daniela asked as the women in the club started screaming. Rap group *Dipset* had entered the spot and their D.J. started playing Jim Jones' mega smash hit, *"WE FLY."*

"P.E. is Physical Education." Juicy scooted closer to the hot Mexican whose red hair had been styled in a cute bun that showed off her small head, her pretty, slender, neck, making her look clean, fresh, sweet, and innocent. "Ava is called Ava Applez because of her lovely handful-sized tits. They fit in small feminine hands like mine."

Juicy was rubbing her hand across Daniela's belly, then slowly down to her right thigh. "They must be some really pretty titties to turn you on like this," Daniela stated.

Juicy nodded. "I was a freshman, Ava was a sophomore when we first saw her in P.E. We knew each other before, but nude? Not 'til that day. She was bathin' her body-holding a bar of clear soap between her asscheeks...up and down, you can see her fingers kinda inside her anus, washin' it real clean y'know?"

"Uhn-huhn," the Mexicana nodded, knowing that Juicy was not only telling her an erotic story to try seducing her but Juicy was still into Ava. Perhaps she was even a bit obsessed with her. Whatever. Didn't matter either way to Daniela because head to toe, her body was screaming out bloody murder, Mary, and Joseph for sexual release.

"What really, really got me though," Juicy continued on with the story, "…was not even her diddling and circling her hairless, tight, and pretty little brown asshole. Two things. First, she caught me staring at her pussy. She had it unshaved but the way her cunt hair grows is very light brown like.. and it was very sparse. It was the first time I seen a pussy other than mine. And she soaped it and her clit bulged out of the hood of it and she put baby oil in her hands and kept rubbing on the swelling pink marble. While she did that she squeezed her titties and pinched her nipples. She has the most gorgeous nipples in the world. We were cumming so much in there that we had to leave before we got caught."

Juicy was kissing and licking on Daniela's neck, under her ear, and then Daniela captured her soft lips on her own. Juicy's fingers were tracing their way around the Mexicana's soft pussy lips. They had the privacy of the booth with hundreds of rap music fans all around the club, for the moment, going crazy for Dipset.

"I wanna hear more about what Ava did to you," Daniela said it in a sensual Spanish. "Look how wet it made me. No panties on so pussy juice wet between my thighs."

"Damn I have to fuck you," Juicy P whispered as she caught the hot scent of Mexican-Irish cunt cream in the booth. Juicy took off her dress and Daniela felt a stringer feeling of companionship and desire for her. "Ava took me to Rockaway

Beach and we had blankets, weed, and wine. I was a virgin. She had a strap-on dildo but she didn't use…"

Daniela was sucking on Juicy's chest and titties, where there were some of the most beautiful tattoos she'd ever seen all over her caramel-colored body. There were multiple hues of red, gold, green, and black art that covered her and one could tell that each tattoo done on her petite frame was very costly. They red-head Mexicana beauty was hungry and horny for Juicy P.

"She didn't take this little virgin pussy from you?" Daniela asked as she took off her own dress.

"She had her face in my pussy and my ass – lickin' them both when her fingers bust my cherry," Juicy admitted breathlessly, as the women got into a position where they could rub their bald cunts together and fuck. Meanwhile, oblivious to their surroundings, they kissed, licked, humped, moaned, and fucked. "Fuck me, fuck me Daniela!"

Daniela bit her nipples, squeezed her titties, left hickeys on her chest and neck, and had multiple orgasms. It was the wildest sex she'd ever had. Right next to hundreds of other people. Then Juicy got on top of the beautiful Mexican girl with the batch of freckles on her nose and backed her pussy and asshole up to her face. Daniela was lusting bad for the taste and scent of another woman. Especially a Black one. Daniela was sensuously thrusting her long pink tongue inside, out, and all around Juicy P's love holes. Juicy P held the sexy

Latina's legs up and back as she ravenously devoured Daniela's sweet pussy.

In the office, Coldhearted was checking out the books while meeting with his club's general manager, Luca Sirocco, who had 18 years of nightclub/strip club experience in Miami and Atlanta. He'd been involved in a shooting case involving a former Miami cop. Luca survive in Atlanta for two years at Magic City before the same bad news had caught up with him. Coldhearted had been made aware of Mr. Sirocco's past and wanted to talk to him anyway.

"What's up wit the cop shootin' at da Casa Blanca strip club?" C.H. had asked the 50-year-old Spaniard. "You shot him at the club?"

"*Allegedly*," the salt and pepper haired tall man said in his deep, booming voice. He did have an accent that sounded like it was from Spain. "And the cop you speak of was not shot. He was *shot at*."

"First, I think that I gave you the wrong impression of me," C.H. had stated. "I don't give a fuck whether the cop was shot or shot at. In fact, I woulda hired you just for smokin' his fuckin' ass. Why was he shot at?"

"The rules were no touchin' the girls and that bastard went too far," Sirocco had explained. "One of my guys who'd bounced him shift was over. I saw him getting smacked around and we went to put a stop to it. Other dirty cops showed up and roughed us up. So, when the guy came into the parking lot, on another day, let's just say he was greeted from the rooftop with some unfriendly fire."

"They heard of this in ATL and sacked you for *that*?" C.H. had probed for more answers.

Mr. Sirocco had nodded. "Yeah. Are you guys sackin' me?"

Coldhearted had pulled out two gleaming machetes form the scabbards attached to his broad back. "Nah, homie. But we do some shootin' around here ourselves, feel me? Especially when mufuckaz get loose lips."

"I get it." He looked at the machetes. "And those?"

Coldhearted only had smirked. "I promise you – you do a damn good job for us…I mean run Garter's like she's your own, and you'll never have to worry 'bout these babies."

And just to emphasize, or maybe to show off some, he had taken one of the blades and threw it with power and finesse at the far wall near the office door at Garter's just as Tate and Deuce had arrived. The sharpened tip of the machete had hit and pierced through the wall like it was Styrofoam, causing Tate to duck and curse…

Now, as Coldhearted sat with Liza inside of the office, he pointed at the same hole in the wall. "Babe, they much be keeping shit as a souvenir or sump'in."

Liza looked over there. "Of your ignorance?"

"You a hatin' ass Puerto Rican bitch," he said laughing.

"Ya baby mama a bitch," she shot back, grinning.

"You my baby mama!" he pointed out.

She shook her head. "That's Chubb's baby."

He yawned and said, "Yeah aight. You know I'd kill ya ass... and chop Chubb up and everybody who ever shook his fuckin' hand."

"Whatever. And I'm Puerto-Rican Dominicana, nigga. Don't get it twisted," she told him. There was a knock on the door but before an answer could come, three of the club girls came in bickering like little kids.

"Where's the boss?" a short, thick, light skinned babe wearing a see-through black sarong with white flowers on it and red pasties over her orange-sized breasts asked C.H. "Well, I mean, you know who I mean. Mr. Sirocco." She smiled embarrassedly at him.

"Downstairs," Liza said, checking the girls out. Liza felt a mad attraction for the tall slender girl with probably the darkest skin she could ever recall seeing on a dancer. "You, love. They got you straight from the Motherland, huh?"

The dark chocolate honey halted and turned around like a movie star posing for the paparazzi. "Me?" she asked.

"What's your name?"

"Naiba," she chirped.

Liza looked at her closely. "You are tall and you sound cool as fuck. My god, you what they call a dime bitch."

Naiba smiled and batted her eyes before glancing at C.H. then back at Liza. "Turn around for me?" Liza asked her. The girl had a lovely ass...

Naiba's white G-string had gotten sucked up in between

her love lips so, as she slowly turned around for the owner's wife, she reached down and freed the thin piece of material from her warm cleft. Liza watched her and it turned her on so much that she gently grabbed Naiba's hand and brought them to her nose and smelled her pussy on them.

"You other girls can go," Liza said to them.

C.H. was standing next to the two-way mirrors looking around. "Look at this, babe. Leave Naiba alone for a second."

Liza smacked Naiba on the ass and sent her on her way, "What?" Liza asked. "I can't resist a clean cute bitch."

He gave her the binoculars.

She looked down into one of the booths and saw Juicy P and Daniela going at it like nobody else's business. Liza just shook her head. "Juicy a bad little bitch. I kinda knew it but… in a Garter's' curtain booth?"

"Aw fuck!" Coldhearted exclaimed as he saw Ava Applez come in. "Ava down there."

Liza looked and, sure enough, there was Ava, Diamond, Barbie, Blue Eye, and a handful of other girls.

"We don't need no in-fighting," C.H. said. "I guarantee you – one of them hatin' ass chicks down there gon' tell Ava that her ex is in da booth fuckin' some new bitch and Ava gon' wanna fight."

C.H. hurried downstairs with Liza behind him.

CHAPTER TEN

"Just like that…they gone."
Garter's Strip Club
Mount Vernon, NY

"Y'all bitches get dressed, Ava's out here!" Liza warned the two disheveled women. The sex was over but they still were half-naked, laying back basking in the afterglow, smelling like sex. "C.H. don't want no fightin' out here."

Juicy P hurriedly got dressed and was able to slip out the club through the kitchen but Daniela only went to the bathroom to freshen up, brush her hair since it fell out, apply new lip gloss, and reappeared fifteen minutes later looking like she'd just stepped out the house. Her cunt felt like an oven light bulb!

OG Bobby Tate came through with Deuce, Kaz, Cumba, Ammo, and what looked like three to four dozen Rollin 60's niggas. They caught up with their crip boss and "cousin" Coldhearted, dappin' and handshake-huggin' him. Nobody was worrying about the coronavirus anymore so there wasn't a mask in sight. Spooky and rapper Double J popped in. They pulled C.H. to the side.

"We heard you *Neighborhood* now, nigga!" the dark skinned Spooky said, happy for him as they exchanged the handshake hug and Rollin 60/Neighborhood Crip salute. "And you left the hospital."

"I'm still feelin' da damage them niggas did." C.H. shook his head. "What up wit it, cuz?"

Double J told him. "I'm done wit da 'Nutha Level' album."

"Yeah I heard it and you lightin' up Spotify, iHeart, Apple Music, and everybody wit da downloads," C.H. told him. "We about to send you out there to do some shows on the West Coast this time. I hope your stamina up."

Last call was at 3:00 AM so Garter's closed up soon after. However, C.H. had several spots in the area that sold bootleg liquor and the girls could still work well into the day if they chose. The ones that were super-bad and took down big bank at Garter's didn't bother. The sub-par babes had no choice. They hit the thriving underground strip club circuit with a vengeance where, by this time, the men were so drunk the women looked super-bad anyway. So, it all worked out for the older, bigger girls, who hated the younger, skinnier girls who didn't know how to suck a dick right or ride a dick proper. Plus, the older girls thought, "Them young bitches throw dat ass all night but still can't take a dick in it."

By the time Garter's was closed there were at least three hundred Rollin 60s there. The bartenders and bouncers were hurried out and everybody went downstairs to the basement where it was more private. The public didn't generally come down there. It was being set up as an underground casino: Poker tables, crap tables, slot machines, and a few other things were being set up in the vast basement.

"Aight- I *know* niggas is tired," C.H. said after he asked everyone to be silent. "As y'all prolly heard, shit, I'm back on track wit the connect. Look, Buffalo, Binghamton, Schenectady, Albany, Poughkeepsie, New York are upstate areas we need to be in. For the same nickel of crack we sell they pay twenty. And for the *quality* and count we have in *one* bag of boy, you make double. Anyone willin' to hit those towns the split will be fifty-fifty. That would also mean if you pay four hundred for an apartment per month – I pay two hundred. We go half and half on everything. Bring receipts."

There was a lot of talking among each other. Tate told them that those who wanted to explore going "O.T." or "out of town" holla at him and Deuce over the next few days.

"The mechanics was two-fifty girl, two-fifty boy for each in the Mob, and y'all return four hundred. This shit we got is *superior*. And it's flyin' off the shelf. Next batch you'll just return three-fifty. That's next month. Then the month after that you'll return three."

A tall man everyone called Munchie said, "They may as well drop five boy, five girl and we hand over six, cuz. I mean the mouth after next."

C.H. nodded. "Good idea. It'll cut down on trips but we'll discuss it."

"The Regency Park Apartments and White Oak Mobile Homes are at capacity," Tate mentioned.

"We havin' housin' problems?" C.H. asked Tate.

Tate shook his head. "Nah just sayin' it was a good idea. Niggas got they wives, girlfriends, kids, and shit out here. And they makin' money they wasn't makin' out L.A."

"What's the average everybody makin' each day?" C.H. asked.

"Maybe five hundred, they get hit with new packs about five times," Deuce told him. "We get no rest."

They spoke for only about another hour before the meeting disbanded. When C.H. went to find Liza and Daniela they were inside of the office with Luca Sirocco, the general manager of the club, three heavily armed security with Kevlar vests on, and the tall dark chocolate beauty Naiba that Liza had met earlier.

"Papi, this bitch has a RT 10 Dodge Viper and what do I have?" Liza asked C.H.

C.H. looked at her. "You have a fuckin' Cadillac Escalade truck, a house, *Garter's* – and the new thrift store business. Buy your own Viper…wait. What year is yours, Nai?"

"Mine's 1995. Liza's had one too many," Naiba said, taking Liza's hand. "We leavin'?"

"To *our* house," C.H. told her.

"I know! I'm not kidnappin' her," Naiba stated with s sarcastic smirk. "You ain't gon' make me disappear."

"What's that s'posed to mean?" C.H. asked as he walked with Daniela, Naiba, and Liza out to their cars.

Naiba had a bad little RT 10 Dodge Viper, shiny black candy coat with the white racing stripe going up the center, bumper-to-bumper. she opened it and threw her soiled bag of clothes in the back seat along with her Birkin clutch.

"Shadow Warrior and Tommy went out to Chicago and just like that," she said with a finger snap. "They gone. Their girls and their family members came around early in my shift askin' all sorts of questions."

"What'd you say?"

"How'm I s'posed to know? I'm a strippa. I come to make my paper and mind mine. They put in a missin' persons report."

C.H. believed her. "Aight."

They went to C.H. and Liza's house and crashed out. At least C.H. knew that they'd never find any bodies, and as far as anyone knew, Tommy and Shadow had gone to Chicago on illegal business. And they were in San Diego at hotels which the cops would certainly check. And even before they left,

C.H. had made sure their cellphone tower/GPS pinged. Tate knew that as well as Deuce. But the policy was to play dumb and then stonewall the cops.

"Just say the '*Lawyer*' and give them fucks Melissa Verducci's card," C.H. told his peoples. The whole squad had her card.

CHAPTER ELEVEN

Bargains Galore Business
Bronx, New York

Liza hired a tutor for Isabel because she didn't trust her husband's enemies. So, Isabel was nearing 18 months when she started her third month of tutoring with former Montessori school English and Math teacher Elicia Sales – a Black woman from Carlisle Avenue in the Bronx. She was a chubby 5-foot-tall woman who wore bad wigs but she was very kind to Isabel. And chubby and fat women had magical powers over babies because of all that cushion and warmth. Fat women had a way of calming babies that a thin person could not.

Liza was at the new *BARGAIN GALORE* warehouse in the capacity of General Manager. The warehouse was on

Baychester and East 2330 street in the Bronx. As soon as Diamond Girl, Bhad Barbie, Ava Applez, Blue Eyez, Tanya Taylor, Bertha, and Tanya's other one dozen hirees showed up, Liza was ready to go.

"You twelve new girls stay here," Liza ordered them. "If we need another vehicle we'll call you. Meanwhile, the place can use some more cleaning."

They drove out to *Milbrook Storage* on Bronx Boulevard where a public auction was being held. There was a crowd of people there who had seen the Bargains Galore van and truck they'd driven into the parking area out front. People were giving them the ice grill and whispering hateful things about them. Liza was dressed in all-brown leather pants, a yellow thermal shirt, and a brown leather vest. All the other girls were dressed nicely as well. To the other storage hustlers, the all-female team looked like they came to spend money.

The auctioneer team was a Black husband and wife couple from Long Island who travelled around the Tri-State doing this for a living.

"Okay, alright everybody!" the husband yelled excitedly. "Welcome to Milbrook Storage in Bronx New York! Today, we have five lockers for sale. The rules are simple: When my guy opens that door, no one is allowed to step into the locker, do not touch anything - take a Quick Look and let everyone else see it - This is a cash only sale. Everybody understand?"

The crowd hollered, "Yeah!"

"Everybody all pumped up, huhn?" Liza said to Diamond Girl.

"Girl, I know I am!" Diamond admitted as the group of twenty-five to thirty persons walked into the storage yard.

Two young Black men were walking behind the women from Bargain Galore. Diamond was definitely grabbing attention with the way that Gucci denim overall outfit was hugging her thick 5-foot 5-inch, 160-pound frame. Her long natural brownish-red hair was in a long ponytail.

"She look like a young Coco - Ice T's wife," one of them said. He was about 6'0" tall with a mustache and beard, braids that were done by a professional. He was rocking butter Timberlands boots, jeans, and a New York Giants hoodie.

Liza said something to Diamond who only shook her head. "Ice-T my boy on *Law and Order: SUV* but I do not look like Coco! She look like a ferret in the face. The ass? Yeah, but the rest… hell no. And this is all God-given, nothin' by the surgeon."

"Let's go!" the female auctioneer shouted as a locker opened.

The girls from Bargain Galore got a look at the contents. Speakers, dozens of boxes, a lawnmower, crates that held storage lights, furniture, and much more. Tanya whispered into Liza's ear.

"Look way in the back. Is that a deep freezer? If so it's expensive. It's vintage. People pay out big money for pieces like these," Tanya told her.

Liza whispered back as she stepped away. "We have a warehouse to fill. We tryna take all these lockers."

The bidding started at $200 from a white-haired man. Then another bidder put up $300. A black woman put her hand up for $400.

"Do we have five for the vintage freezer and stage lights locker," the auctioneer spoke one sentence in about two syllables due to the speed in which he spoke. "Goin' once-"

Tanya finally jumped in for $500. Right after her was $600 from the white-haired man.

"Eleven hundred!" Liza jumped out ahead, not wanting to stand here all her life.

Bargains Galore won the bid at $1100. On to the next locker the crowd shifted as Liza and the girls used their own padlocks to bolt the locker. They hit pay dirt with the next locker. It was filled with electronic devices, and it had boxes inside of it that hinted at it probably belonging to a store owner of some other kind of proprietor of electronics.

Bargains Galore won the bid again at $6500. After the crowd shifted, once again, to the third locker, Liza said to Diamond, "Y'all go 'head and bring them trucks on in and load 'em up. We gon' need all the room in the truck and van as possible. Empty out the locker, set it all in there. We can't dump nothin' here so we'll sort it all out at the warehouse."

Bargains Galore won four of the five lockers for sale. The one they passed on was full of black garbage bags. Tanya said that it was only old clothes and stuff the owner never care about.

"You'll just be paying to clean out this mess and then give the clothes to the Goodwill Store. Fuhgeddaboudit," Tanya warned.

"Yeah I ain't feeling it either," Liza concurred. "C'mon, let's go bust down these lockers."

They all got down and dirty. Liza wanted to look at what she spent $6500 on first. When she opened up the locker Ava and Barbie were with her.

"Oh, shit!" Barbie said as she cut open a box. "It's Dell brand laptops! Brand new! One, two, three… four, five, and six."

"Witcho chipmunk voice," Ava cracked on her.

"Whateva, bitch," Bhad Barbie shot back as they began pulling the boxes out. She stated to the other women, "Look on the sides of these boxes. They were shipped to this company. These are cellphones, these are widescreen Dell computers in the big boxes."

"This is exactly what Sage was lookin' for," Liza remarked as she made a phone call to the warehouse. "Hello? Who is this I'm talkin' to?"

"Monae," the girl chirped from the office telephone. She could see Liza's caller ID. "Hey, Liza. Whatcha need?"

"We're at Milbrook storage," Liza told her. "We bought four units and we need you girls to load up in the other vehicle and come on over."

"Okay, be there soon," she said and added, "I'll leave one behind so we don't have to lock up the warehouse."

"Roger that, Monae," Liza agreed.

They loaded up the van first, as super tight as they could. Diamond Girl, Ava Applez, and Bhad Barbie squeezed in up front and took off. They went back to the Bargains Galore Warehouse and went to pee first because they'd been holding it.

The warehouse was fairly large at 10,000 square feet. The vehicles could come inside and then be unloaded onto cheap but very strong oak picnic tables that were lined up in a straight row all the way to the office and bathrooms in the back. The goods were all unpacked and put on top of the tables in the best possible order: electronics, glass/kitchen items, tools/automotive equipment/lawnmowers, real jewelry/jewelry boxes/ perfumes, and so on. Sort of like a grocery store or a hardware store, like Walmart or Target.

The Bargains Galore team average about two auctions per day. A few weeks into the business the entire team hit a big box auction down in Manhattan near South Street Seaport. These were not ordinary lockers, they were abandoned shipping containers that were loaded onto huge ocean liners that had been abandoned.

Luckily, Coldhearted had already taken a trip to Chicago to pick up a brand-new load, secretly packed in a brand-new black Yukon that the connect said to bring back next trip.

Business on the streets was good so Liza had $120,000 in the war chest.

Tanya Taylor had an 18-wheeler on stand-by in case. They won a locker for $8,500 that was loaded with fifty solar panels, two new Harley motorcycles, and boxes containing thousands of rare first edition Marvel and DC comic books. Then they caught another container for $10,000 that had two real NASCARS and boxes of parts and automotive diagnostic computer equipment that would resale altogether for about $75,000 on a quick sale. On a careful sale where they put advertising on it, they'd get $100,000 easy.

"Oh my god! I can't believe we won those containers," Tanya said as she called in for an auto transport. "Those Harley-Davidson motorcycles are about sixty-five hundred each. The solar panels are five hundred I believe because they go on buildings, not houses."

Three weeks later they were already beginning to stock the first store. The warehouse was packed up real nice. Not surprisingly the B.G. team was coming across, literally, *hundreds* of cellphones. All of them were going to C.H. who had a master plan.

"I want all laptops and computers, too," C.H. told Liza. "I told you I was doin' someth'n' wit' 'em."

"I wanna see what's up," Liza told him. "Your evil ass is up to somethin'."

C.H. just laughed at her as she lay nude on top of a massage table while Naiba, also nude, massaged her with hot oil. C.H. sat on the bed and undressed, eyeing the dark-skinned babe.

"How's dat pussy, mama?" he asked Liza.

Nai just smiled. "I'm right here y'know," she chided.

"She been here how many weeks now?" Liza said more than asked as if that answered his question.

"Baby, we takin' down a half mil a week," C.H. said as he walked up behind Naiba with his hot meat growing long and thick. "I been wantin' you but you my wife's lil pet. Cuz once you feel dis dick all the way up in yo armpit…you won't want her no more. And I ain't tryna break up a happy thang," he boasted arrogantly.

He ran two fingers from her clit to her asshole and made her watch as he smelled them and smiled. Naiba laughed but her pussy was getting wet from needing dick. She wished he'd fuck her.

C.H. just went on into the bathroom.

Liza just laughed, "Crazy ass. But I love him more than anything. And I know you wanna fuck him, Nai…cuz I can smell your sex whenever he comes around."

"Hm," was all the lovely dark stripper said.

CHAPTER TWELVE

"Bout to take over the city..."
Larchmont, New York

C.H. leased a dope ass house up in the quiet section of Westchester County called Larchmont which wasn't that far from New Rochelle. He assembled a team of Savage Hoodz Girlz and Boyz who were not quite the part of what he envisioned for the streets because the truth was the truth. These mufuckaz were softer than baby shit and a Disney flick combined. However, they were computer savvy. They could be *used*.

"No more VULKANYCK," he told Choir Boy, Chubb, Sonja, and Sunny. "And what we're doin' out there? C'mon son - y'all know dem streets ain't where y'all's strength at."

"Okay, so what's the gig? Some five-minute hack job?" Sonja, a Spanish-Indian girl, inquired as they followed C.H. "How long can we stay?"

"One year or less. Y'all have rent problems, move in," he said as he closed the garage door. "No visitors. You'll be paid enough to take your boys or girls to the hotel not even a mile away. No mail. Get a P.O. Box. Internet, cable, all the connections you'll need is here in nearly every room."

From the garage there was a trapdoor that led down into the basement. C.H. said, "The gig, as you say it Sonja, is to upload spyware into each of these devises that will tell us where the owner is, is going, is texting, is calling, and I want recordings of their voices. With the computers, tablets, laptops, nearly the same. Just minus the talking part. The plan is to get these burners into the hands of dope dealers so we can identify their buyers and persuade them to cop for us. Also, can we activate the phones?"

"You mean so the person who's buyin' the phone thinks they're gettin' free service?" Choir Boy asked as he inspected the hundreds of phones. "It's not as easy as stealin' cable TV as they used to but we can do it."

"Goodness!" Sunny exclaimed as she stared at one computer in particular, pointing at it. "Do you have any idea what the hell this is?" she exclaimed.

"It's a Dell. A lil' fancy…but it's a computer," C.H. said, shrugging. "Right?"

"That's a fucking BX-32, water-cooled, baby! This is *it!*" Sunny said. She was one of those slender women with a small chest of delicious "mouthful breasts" and a small ass to match but it was a juicy bubble. And the way she walked one would never know that ass was small. "I could crack into the Pentagon and FBI with equipment like this. This is real serious shit."

"Well, we're 'bout to take over the city wit it, aight?" C.H. told them. "I'm keepin' this crew small and secret cuz that's how I need it and how y'all should, too. It's a dirty game we playin' and if the wrong people find out where we live or operate from, we're dead. They'll kill us or pay to have us killed. So don't get found out. And don't let no-fuckin'-body in this house. If y'all do get burned, there's bleach and gas bombs ready. All y'all gotta do is call in to the cellphones on the bombs, steer clear about two blocks, and blow it to hell. The lease is in a false name, false face, so it won't come back on me."

"What's the pay?" Sonja asked as she brushed some imaginary lint off of the front of his black hoody with "BLACK UNIVERSITY KINGZ" in gold lettering printed on the front and back of it.

"Yeah, follow me," C.H. told them. They all went out to his Cadillac truck. He reached inside and grabbed a brown paper bag. He tossed it to Sonja. "How's that for a start?"

All of them looked at the stacks of cash inside and it had to be at least $100,000. Sonja nodded.

"Start with the cellphones," C.H. said, starting up the luxury vehicle.

He took off moments later.

CHAPTER THIRTEEN

"P-Man was right there."
Mt. Vernon, New York

C.H. pulled up to a house two blocks away from the Farnum Road stash house and checked out his surroundings. He reached into the back seat of the Cadillac SUV for his Kevlar hoody, something he'd seen on the Dark Web they were selling for $1700 each. It beat being caught with a tactical police Kevlar and harassed about it by cops or, in some cases, being charged with a crime.

He threw a backpack over his back and removed his Elite-3000 scooter from out of the rear cargo hold of the SUV. He started it up and circled around the residence. Once he felt a safe vibe he parked the scooter in the alley out back where his pit bulls were kept. They were happy to see him and he briefly acknowledged them with light pats on their faces.

He banged on the steel gate outside and seconds later, Double Deuce opened the heavy-duty inner steel door. "What up wit it, cuz? Bangin' like da Jehovah's Witnesses and shit."

C.H. threw it up and walked past him. "What up wit den bringin' sexy back' braids, nigga?"

Kaz, Cumba, Ammo, and state were all in the living room playing *CALL OF DUTY* on an enormous smart-screen television. All of their wives were there re-twisting and styling Kaz, Cumba, and Ammo's dreads.

C.H. walked upstairs and all the men knew to follow him. They went into one of the bedrooms, closed the door, and turned on some music by Mike Knox, a hardcore gangsta rapper from Philly. Some record called "Back Block."

"Y'all the experts in the disposal biz, right?" C.H. asked the killers with dreads.

"Indeed," Kaz responded.

"What's the job?" Cumba wanted to know as C.H. gave them the backpack.

Deuce opened it and dumped all the bundled-up cash onto the bed. $125,000 which Deuce split five different ways.

"Graves," C.H. told them, pulling out his cellphone. He pulled up Google Earth/Maps. "Burners. Always use burners then destroy them. Choose areas that are remote. Use calcium oxide-"

"Lime. Industrial lime," Kaz elaborated. "Otherwise known as calcium oxide."

"It'll speed up seconds of the bodies," C.H. Told them. "I'll have one of the stores Liza rented preserved as a murder store. A *slaughterhouse*. There's a list of mufuckaz that need killin' if we goin' survive."

"You said we'd be millionaires," Tate reminded him. "But a *slaughterhouse*, cuz?"

C.H. nodded. "We will be. Actually, I already *am*. But I'd rather be dead in that slaughterhouse with my body decompin' under like that than locked up in Attica or Clinton - you feel me my nigga?"

"I'm witchu mufucka," Tate said, handshake-hugging his boss. "I love you, cuz. But it just sounds crazy."

"I respectfully concur," C.H. nodded as he prepared to roll up a blunt with a few strips of k2 in it. "But I'm tellin' you the feds is chompin' on the bit. The cops got a warrant for my Cadillac. They asked for my cellphone. I gave that to them."

"They lookin' for Tommy and Shadow," Deuce said. "They ashes, flushed in a toilet."

"The phone stays either at home or Garter's. I'm smarter than that. I know GPS is a digital footprint. Any hustle or hitta on the street stay watchin' FBI Files, The Oxygen Channel, Forensic Files, Snapped, Dateline and all that shit," C.H. kicked the Backwoods cigar paper he'd rolled up the weed in. "So, all the niggas who 'suspect' gotta go. But we need to be smart about it... cuz police have budgets for this. Solving murders instills the public's trust in cops. That's why they spend so much fine and money in solving murder and other major crimes."

Kaz pulled out a switchblade and said, "I need to cut your fuckin' brain out and put it in my head and give you mine, nigga! This an evil genius ass fucker!"

"If you give him your brain he'd be brainless, you fuckin' black bastard," Ammo cracked on him as he hit the blunt.

"Just pass day shit, ugly hairless dog lookin' ass nigga," Kaz said. "Puff, puff pass, homie."

"And where's you find a switchblade?" Tate asked Kaz. "Last time I seen one was in the first *Rocky*. *Rocky One*, like 1975."

"Online. You can find anything online," Kaz admitted. "They even smellin' pairs of Beyoncé panties."

"You buy 'em?" C.H. asked with a smile.

"Hell yeah I bought 'em. Jay-Z fuckin' other bitches now and Beyoncé … she's just perfect… she prolly jus' be in her hot tub, wit a Rabbit dildo, wit pearls in it, ten inches deep - writin' her next platinum album," Kaz daydreamed. "Kiwi Banana *Lemonade Part Two* Bitch!"

"Stupid nigga." C.H. joined the others in the laughter.

"I bought Dakota Blue Fanning panties, too," Kaz blurted.

"The little fuckin' girl from *Man On Fire*? She like five years old!" Tate exclaimed.

"She in her fuckin' *twenties* now, asshole!" Kaz reminded him.

"Oh yeah," Tate said, high as shit like the others.

"Coldhearted did this shit...wit dat fuckin' k2 in the blunt."

Deuce was laid back on the bed. "Mystique homie up north. I be sending him a page of k2 every month through his lawyer and he cashapps me fifty dollars for each stamp-sized piece he sells."

"Like a regular little postage stamp?" C.H. wanted to clarify.

Deuce nodded. "I make a couple grand extra each month. I order the highest quality bottles of liquid k2 from *spice4-fun.com* and soak a plain sheet of paper in it on a baking sheet pan, you have to be sure that the paper gets soaked. Let it dry in front of a fan once it's dried and use a flashlight from the back to see if you can see spots or any abnormalities. Then, put the paper on top of your printer and write out your legal letter, contract, will, IOU, or whatever, on your computer. Then print out several copies. Put it in an envelope and let it sit under the weight of other paper and books for a day or two. Then get it to the lawyer who knows nothing and off it goes."

"Why you gotta do all that? Why not just shoot it through regular mail?" Kaz asked, sitting down in the sofa.

"Cuzzo, some prisons use mail processing centers now where all regular mail is scanned, copied, and your man inside never sees your original document," Deuce explained.

"And y'all talked about this plan how?" C.H. wondered aloud. "Not on no prison phone call cuz they're recorded."

"Nah, my homie kept askin' me to plug him up with a bitch who was down to ride, so I got my Aunt Coco to go get the rundown," Deuce revealed. "She like fifty but she likes the homie."

"Coco?" Tate asked his nephew. "I had no idea she'd go see a jail cat."

"She yo stepsister, y'all don't talk?" Deuce stated slowly as if he was deciphering a family mystery or something. "She got the whole rundown in the visiting room and gave it to me. The thing is though, a nigga or ya chick gotta buy the right liquid K2 because some of the shit on the market is trash and them prison cats won't be fooled. So, I was taste-testing the shit wit my chicks and my nigga first. It's worth it when my dude inside can make four grand a page or more. All it costs me is a couple hundred. Do da math, homie."

"I just read a book from *UrbanAintDead.com* 'bout some Brooklyn nigga doin' dat shit," Tate mentioned a little too buzzed to remember all the details of the story. "It's entitled *HITTAZ: Get it Back in Blood... Hittaz 1, 2, 3, 4 ...* I think it could be five or six of 'em. Elijah R. Freeman is CEO. They down with Kwame Teague, AKA DUTCH, Mike Enemigo, and Suge Knight. Lou Garden Price, Sr. is in Suge Knights' *MOB TALES* book with a prequel called *SOSA: Killing Tony Montana.*"

Tate pulled Amazon up on the tablet he had on the dresser and showed Deuce. "There. Dutch even has a movie out called

DUTCH on *BET.com*. These cats is in prison makin' moves cats on the street barely dream about."

"Aight," C.H. said as he looked also. "I wanted to drop dat boy and here… the keys to da Caddy."

"To da truck? Your *baby*?" Tate said surprised.

"Dat SUV's a G-ride fareal," Kaz added.

"It's equipped wit a fly gun and drug stash, too," C.H. mentioned. "Y'all use it as a company car. I have my scooter to get back."

The team loved that.

"So, if our bitches need to go to da grocery store or get they nails done…" Kaz presented a scenario.

C.H. shrugged. "Just take care of it and do not remove The *BARGAINS GALORE* signs off the sides and rear. We have Garter's and B.G. We'll have ya looking like we're law-abiding citizens. The slaughterhouse store… I'll let you know when I'm ready. But meanwhile, take da Caddy on up to Stamford or New Jersey… buy shovels, pick axes, nylon rope, industrial plastic tarp, and five hundred pounds of cement which will be poured down over the body and line where it'll harden and keep animals from trying to dig the parts out. And I need every other thing y'all can think of for digging the secret graves. They *must* be dug in places where people just ain't walking into. We don't want the wrong people findin' it six feet deep."

He exited shortly after that.

It was already getting dark when he arrived at a corner

store bodega near his south Mt. Vernon residence. He entered the store and grabbed several packs of *Backwoods* brand cigars and one pack of *Black & Milds*. Suddenly -

"Coldhearted, thatchu?" a sexy female voice asked.

"Nah, you got the wrong one, baby," he stated very politely as he paid for his purchases. "Keep the change for the WOUNDED WARRIORS thing right there."

"Here then," the pretty dark-haired Indian cashier handed him the change. "It's an awesome charity. Mr. Thomas put it in there."

"Boy, it's me, *Seji*," the Jamaican-Chinese half-sister to Taizhan Ivone Hooks.

He dropped $100 in the Wounded Warrior box and looked at her. "Seji Elise Hooks. My bad. How you doin'?"

"Nothin', just gettin' back into town," she said as he embraced her and kissed her cheek. He noted how sweet she smelled and... how expensively dressed as well. Chloe glasses, $10,000 tennis bracelet, a necklace, niggas would chop her head off to get. A red leather trench by Gucci, a red leather dress which was strapless so her beautiful upper light skin showed off along her yummy apple-sized breasts.

He went outside and scanned the street. He observed a cream-colored Maybach double-parked up the block about ten meters with a spanking new 699 SL Mercedes-Benz that was a two-tone black up top and charcoal black underneath it.

C.H. counted eight niggas standing on the sidewalk smoking blunts and drinking straight Hennessy. A $450k car and that was the best they could buy? C.H. hit a speed-dial group text: NEIGHBORHOOD! 9-1-1 on corner of Richler Indian store! Red Alert.

"Who them fools, Seji?" he asked as he put his purchases inside of a secure compartment on the scooter.

"Just some guys we were chillin' wit up in Chicago," she told him.

"Tell me about 'em," he asked but she knew it was more of a command.

She sighed. "They some Blood dudes but they got money and me and my sister had to do a few things. The leader is P-Man, the dark skin tall one. To be honest, I ain't tryna fuck wit them. They scare me."

"Seji!" It was one of P-Man's henchmen.

"Where Taizhan?" C.H. asked as he moved his burners up to the front of his waist where he could reach them. Thankfully, a van was parked just ahead of where they were standing so it blocked his movements.

"She in the Benz, her face swollen from Bugout beating her," she revealed.

"*Blood* Bugout?" C.H. asked her. During the bombings, SHZ thought that they'd killed Bugout but weeks later, DNA reports had confirmed the male deaths as belonging to other victims. Bugout's name nor his photo had been in any of the newsfeeds. Plus C.H. had already known that Bugout was playing the incognito/truce roll. He hadn't been around much but B.P.S (Black P. Stones) were still deep in south Mt. Vernon.

The Rollin 60s started showing up. P-Man was right over there in the flesh. Hulk-like, dark skin, he had deep set beady eyes that saw everything. He had big dark lips and a look that instilled a sort of fear in anyone that came around him. He stood there, like a Zulu warrior, wanting to attack a man and buss open his meat shirt with a sword.

The Rollin 60s niggas loved their cars. Even though they were in New York on the strength of a live wire OG Bobby state and a young money-making Killa thug nigga who was before his time like the original 50 Cent and Killa Ben from Fort Greene, (R.I.P.). The Rollin 60s niggas may not have been in Los Angeles but when they rolled up in their cars, it was like *"DRE DAY - LET ME RIDE"* video from the classic Chronic album. It was a car show but the drivers weren't smiling.

These niggas had their bitches behind the wheels of a 1955 Chevy Nomad, a 1972 Chevy Nova, an original 1967 Shelby GT 500, a 1961 Cadillac Coupe Deville, a 1966 Corvette Stingray, a 1973 GMC pick-up truck, a 1971 Land Rover, a beautiful El Camino, and a 1978 Ninety-Eight Oldsmobile. Every other minute a van full of Crip niggas would show, park across the street, and lay in wait. Every one of them had AK-47s, M-4s, MP-5s, and HK-91s.

"We can toast them niggas tonight, cuz!" Tate whispered to C.H. when their team rolled up. "Look at our power!"

"Nah. Remember what we spoke about earlier," C.H. said as he turned back to Seji. "Tell your sister if she wants my protection, she got it. But if she - or you - wanna play both sides of the fence, I'll put you both in a tub of acid until you turn to liquid and then I'll pour you both right into the gutter."

He pulled out a burner phone and put the number to another burner phone inside of it. "If you want me, call me or come to my house."

"I'm no snake bitch, Cold," she said, pocketing the phone.

"We got a hook-up for iPhones, Samsungs, whatever, where you never have to pay another bill like that one I gave you," he told her. "Spread the word. I'll hook your people up since we have a truce with da Bloods and all. Matter fact gimme dat phone."

He put the number to the Bargains Galore Manager Tanya Taylor. "She'll plug you through with the phone connect."

Seji walked off after thanking him.

Before P-Man and his entourage pulled off, he walked up to the closed doors of a jewelry store to surveillance the show of power that the young gangster they called Coldhearted was putting on at spotting Almighty Black P. Stones leader, P-Man. The "P" standing for Piru or "P-Funk" which was a code for the diesel. On one hand, he could make a phone call and have six hundred Blood Hounds fly into New York and another 150 from New York, come through and smash these nigga-like termites in a monkey's mouth. But bodies scared Westchester elite.

"Mount up, niggas!" P-Man glanced over at Coldhearted and looked back.

Just like that they were gone.

There had to be at least 400 Crips crowding the block by now. C.H. knew they'd eventually attract cops so he gave the word to disperse. He just really wanted to show his crew what P-Man looked like and to also flex some muscle on him.

"Aight, Tate," C.H. said as he zipped off on his scooter and hit Garter's for an hour or so. Then he went downstairs to go home. But, again, P-Man and dozens of his men were around. P-Man waved him over.

"Me and you one day soon, let's rap," P-Man said in his deep voice. "I may not love every mufucka I run into but I see certain shit I need to respect."

"Just gimme a hollar," C.H. told him. He waved the female bartender over. "P-Man and his folks drink for free."

P-Man nodded. "Youse a cool nigga."

C.H. fist-bumped him. "Maybe. Just be sure to tip the ladies."

C.H. went on home after that.

CHAPTER FOURTEEN

Noni & Deva Honoret Garcia
Mt. Vernon, NY
12:00 Midnight

Coldhearted came home just after 10:00 PM and checked on Izzy. She was in her crib snoring. *She about to need a real bed*, he thought. Lupe and Elizabeth were both asleep on a Queen-sized bed in her nursery. Then he checked on Lilly in the next room over. She was in there snoring. For a girl nearly 12, she was bigger, thicker, older looking just like Lisa was when they'd met. And Lilly already liked boys. C.H. swallowed and thought, *Oh shit. Imma watch her ass.* He closed the door and went into his room to shower and see Liza but she wasn't there. He got into the shower, used some Dolce & Gabbana After-Shower baby oil for men that smelled banging. It was a whole box set but he didn't bother with the soap, bath gel, baby powder, hair items, nor all the other shit in there because he only likes the oil. It didn't make him smell like a bitch but that other shit did. He had a feeling that shit was made for them three-dollar bill niggas. The "funny" ones. *I ain't him,* he thought, putting on his boxers, some fly black pajamas Liza had bought for him, no shirt at all, but a live ass Ghostface Killa long black robe.

He got close to the kitchen and heard all the laughing and giggling out on the back deck and either out in the swimming pool or Jacuzzi. He heated up an entire slab of BBQ ribs and corn on the cob because he was hungrier than a runaway slave. He peeked out the window and saw Daniela, Liza, Naiba, and… two super-bad Puerto Rican girls that he was trying to place. Liza had about 1,000 bad cousins and aunts, girlfriends, and people he didn't know. Whoever they were, all of them were in the skimpiest bikinis on earth. Like a postage stamp was covering their pussies.

He ate inside first because it wasn't warm outside anymore. He killed the food in fifteen minutes, drank a beer and went on our back. He looked around before Liza saw him.

"Papi, it's hot in here, c'mon!" she called out to him.

He shrugged, put his robe aside, and took off his pajama bottoms - cat calls from the women were instant - he smiled at their playfulness and dived into the deep-end and swam the entire length of the pool under water until he reached Liza sitting on the third step at the opposite end with only her head above the heated swimming pool. It was *real* warm, too. Like in hot. Liza must have heated it all day with the cover on.

The two lovebirds kissed hotly and openly as they usually did, causing the other women to look on with envy and lust in their hearts but smiles on their faces.

"You ever meet Deva and Noni Honoret-Garcia, my cousins?" Lisa asked as he sat between her legs with her arms wrapped around his powerfully built upper body.

"Um, maybe when we was kids," he said as the other girls were still having fun off the diving board and slippery slide. They all had some fly ink all over their bodies and every time they got out of the pool, C.H. had to bite his bottom lip at how phat Deva's and Noni's asses were. And the way their pussy could be seen from the back he wanted to reach out and "fist bump" them two baby fists they had in there cuz *GODDAMN*!

Baby Fist/Camel Toe combos. That's what them bitches had.

"Baby, the warehouse is full, so we've already started stocking up stores," she informed him. "We need more bodies so Noni and Deva are down on their luck. Can they live with us?"

"If I was a fool, I'd say yes," he said so only she could hear him. "Why you think I ain't bone Naiba?"

"I thought about that."

"Cuz I'm in the stripper business and I see how foolish men can be and how dirty and ruthless bitches can be," he schooled her. "They suckin' and fuckin' like the Devil has a hot pitchfork on they neck. They always callin' out sick but it ain't a cold or flu that has 'em sick, but their pussy. Naiba hand-jobs a lot of white cats. One bought her that car she got… I heard. And she smart. Send her back to work or you'll just be her next trick. Trust me. If I bone *any* of dem hoes at Garter's, I'm da *Donkey of the Month*."

"Naiba, c'mere, honey," Liza said, calling across the yard to her.

The dark-skinned beauty sauntered over. "Yeah wassup?"

"You better hustle on back over there to the club before you get replaced," Liza warned her. "Gimme a sec, Papi."

Liza walked Naiba inside to give her some money and to open the gate for her. Daniela swam over to Coldhearted. "I love New York," she said. "Don't get to see much of you, hm?"

"Nah but you see Juicy P," he smiled.

"I need dick now. Pussy gets boring," she said. "The passion is manu, manufic – "

"Manufactured?" he finished for her.

"Don't think I don't see you or want you," he told her. "You da baddest Mexicana I ever met."

"I sent my father what I've learned about the dark site via special courier. He sent to pick up the video Juicy made," she said. "He has other tech savvy people and he's pleased so far."

Noni and Deva saw their cousin bust out the Armand de Brignac AKA Ace of Spades and two bottles of D'USSE, both from rap overloads and Hip-Hop Kingpin Jay-Z's champagne and cognac. No one bothered with glasses. They drank a while, emptying the champagne and one of the cognac bottles. Then they hit the Jacuzzi at 12:30 A.M.

"Damn, why y'all starin' at us like that?" Liza asked her cousins and Daniela.

"Can I be honest?" Daniela asked. "*Please?*"

Liza was feeling no pain and she'd lost her bikini under all of the heated frolicking.

"Be honest, Mexicana," Liza permitted, feeling C.H.'s long thick cock against her ass as he massaged her underarms and breasts all at the same time.

"A man and a woman as sexy as you and your husband and inches from fuckin' in our faces is like watchin' a movie you already know the ending to," Daniela said. "And this one ends with y'all havin' all the suckin' and fuckin' and us left on base, stranded."

"How you know?" Liza asked her as she made C.H. sit on the other wooden deck. She pulled his boxers off. "You don't know what we gon' do…"

C.H. was completely hairless down there just like Liza wanted him. Noni, 22, and Deva, 23, watched their little cousin closely as Liza skipped all the formalities and let that black python lay all across her face as she went right in for his balls. They were pulled up but big. Like a big brown onion big. She suckled those juicy pink lips of hers all over his scrotum and she worked her way up to the top of the tower where a fat ass plum-looking gland set. She took him into her mouth and was not fucking around. Her tongue slurped it.

Liza actually swallowed more than half of him in one gulp. She wished he could just bob her pretty face down one time and put that monster in her throat but she'd gag too much. Daniela had one hand on her cunt under the hot jetting water and another hand on C.H.'s right leg. Soon Liza was deep-throating that fat cucumber dick nearly to the root. She knew she had his ass but she wouldn't let him cum. She let his dick out of her mouth and squeezed it so his copious precum discharged and she smeared it over her lips and nostrils because she loved how it smelled.

"Dani, Noni, Deva… cum taste my husband's delicious black Mandingo dick," she told the other girls.

Dani, or Daniela, and Noni shared a wet kiss first and then they both took him. Noni sucked his balls and licked his asshole as the hot Mexicana deep-throated his dick. Noni and Deva were thick below the waist but they only had 34-B cup breasts with skinny waists. Liza had thickened like a motherfucker subsequent to having Izzy so her breasts were at least 34 to 36D's now. She wore milk pads and sports bras because she still breast-fed Isabel and bras were expensive. The proteins in the milk stained them and made them look old or dirty even if they were cleaned. She liked Serena Williams sports bras and other things she sold like the sports pants and shorts. Liza was a marvel to look at.

"Let's go inside. Lupe and my momz are here so we

don't have to get up," Liza said after watching C.H. coach Deva to stand up, hug the wall, and sit her cleanly shaved little pussy on his face which she did. Watching him jump up into Noni and Dani's mouths made Liza so hot that she sat on the edge and fingered her engorged clitoris and squeeze her breasts.

They hurried through the house but he had a few missed calls from Deuce. He texted Deuce: **Come on over. Bring Tate, too, if y'all tryna fuck.**

Ten minutes later Deuce and Tate arrived and C.H. had to let them through the gate. They gave him a duffel bag which he locked up and then he looked at them. "Ayo, Liza's two cousins are here, Noni and Deva. They lit as shit. They horny, sweaty, and Liza gon' let me fuck but thanks for the rescue! Go back in the guest bedrooms, shower, shave whatever. They in there eatin' pussy right now." He pointed towards his own room.

"They bad, why not fuck 'em?" Tate asked.

"I don't need the future trouble, nigga. They wifey cousins," C.H. said. "They good bitches too. Puerto Rican. Them white Puerto Ricans wit green eyes. The real emerald green eyes not the hazel green," he found important to add that fact.

C.H. went back to his master bedroom and grabbed Noni and Deva. "Com'ere. I have a surprise for you. Liza hired y'all for B.G., right?"

He opened up a drawer in the office study. He held an

envelope with some cash in it. The girls, only wearing terry cloth robes with nothing underneath, he gave them $500 each.

"My security captain and my lieutenant are in y'all's bathroom showering and whatnot," C.H. told them. "Y'all wanna take care of them?"

"We want you, Papi," Noni said, moving up on him and softly caressing his half hard bulge.

"I know and I want both of you," he told them. "But Liza's y'all's cousin. That means you my cousins. Trust me on this. I'm givin' y'all jobs and your own apartments. But you must trust me. Huhn?"

"Okay," Deva said, looking at Noni. "Let's go check his Captain and Lieutenant out."

C.H. doubled back to check out the slips of the last day's take, $245,000. *This what da fuck I'm talkin' bout!* he thought. He secured the cash and slips and went back to check on Tate, Deuce, Noni, and Deva. In Tate's room he had Deva on all fours with that big white ass bussed open so he could fuck it and smell it at the same time. Deva knew how to throw that pussy back.

In Deuce's room Noni had his young ass mesmerized as she rode his dick while he chewed on her nipples. Moments later C.H. was back in his own room watching his wife getting her ocean wet pussy eaten by Daniela who was naked and had her legs stretched almost as wide as a gymnast doing a floor exercise on her belly. *Mm, what was that Latina gymnast's name with the fat bubble booty? Laurie Hernandez?* he thought as he took off his robe. Liza's hair was out, so silky, shiny, long, and black as he watched the passion showing itself all over her from the glistening sheen of sweat all over her body to her hooded eyes, the sensual snarl of her juicy pink lips, and the way her big breasts broke out with red goosebumps. Even her hardened mocha nipples were standing up at attention with goosebumps circling her areolae. And her toes were curled tightly.

"Papi, she's so good!" Liza whimpered. Daniela was clutching her phat asscheeks so she could pull them open and "shot-lick" Liza from her asshole to clitoris.

"Uuuuuuuuggghhhhh!! She makin' me juice all in her pretty ass face! Oooooouuuuu!! C'mere, lemme suck dat big juicy dick."

He put his feet towards the headboard and his head toward Daniela who got the picture and soon, they were in a 360-degree Daisy chain where only the sounds of slurping, licking, and sucking could be heard bouncing off the walls of the huge master bedroom along with the deep breathing and moaning sounds. There was most definitely something different to each and every female when it came to the taste, texture, and even the aroma of her sex. Every vagina was not the same except for the fact that they were called vaginas as C.H. came to learn. Daniela's was muskier when aroused and that was an intoxicating scent to men who loved the aroma of a hot, aroused cunt. It wasn't dirty or unclean. No one liked that. It was more Daniela nutted that aroma of musky steamy pussy filled the room and caused C.H.'s man-piece to pump wildly with blood and turn into granite inside of Liza's mouth.

Liza broke the chain, pushing C.H. away and riding him reverse cowgirl style. Once she had a slow up and down rhythm going - with her hips spinning and winding - Daniela watched her go buck wild on C.H's dick and she saw her clit standing out there more pronounced. Liza was getting close to a huge orgasm. All the signs were there. C.H. held her with his big, long muscular arms wrapped around her waist and the other around her titties.

Daniela saw her frothy coochie cream flowing over C.H.'s huge brown balls and he looked like he was about to buss nut all up in her beautiful belly. When Daniela jumped in Liza's cries and whimpers got louder. The Mexicana focused on Liza's pleasure: her clit and breasts. She licked and sucked her clit like Liza liked to have it done. Every woman had a left side of the clit they liked stimulated or a concentration on the right side. Some preferred that tongue flickering on the top or bottom. A women's body would always talk if the time was taken to observe what she *needs* to get her over into the promised land. And Daniela took her there.

"Oh baby! Oh baby! Cummmmmmmmmmminnnnn' all over y'all! Oh, Imma die! Imma die! Imma die! Imma die!" When Liza came big, she really came big - her pussy blew up Welty.

She shoved Daniela away and C.H. and all she wanted to do was curl up like a little baby, suck her thumb, and go to sleep. "That fuckin' shit was so good," she whispered, sweat soaked. "Lemme see you fuck her, Papi. And I mean really fuck her good."

C.H. retrieved a cold juice beverage out of the mini-bar refrigerator first. "Sendin' Noni and Deva back on the other side of the house with Deuce and Tate was a survival move. Y'all Spanish bitches woulda put me in a coma."

Liza and Daniela bust out laughing. He passed them drinks as well and got back into bed between them. Daniela laid next to him and he turned to her, and she only had to open up those legs and kiss him while the huge plum-sized Corona missile kissed her slick love lips. She had to hold her breath while he blazed that pipe into her Mexican soul. Liza watched as her man pleased Daniela and while he did, Liza kept her distance at first. He fucked her slow at first but then he started fucking her harder and harder.

But when he put her on all fours with her face into the pillows Liza kissed Daniela very intimately and played with her clitoris. Watching both of them set off C.H. and he grabbed Daniela's sweaty asscheeks as hard as he could, jackhammering her deep.

"Fuuuck! Ohhhhhh!" he gasped and she could feel hot spurts of cum buss off in her tight clasping pussy as she, too, spawned and butted hard on his dick while still tongue kissing Liza.

"I like how y'all sent that stripper away earlier," Daniela mentioned.

"Yeah?" Liza murmured while stroking her back.

"Mm hm," Daniela said. "Sage - can I call you Sage?"

He nodded. "I'd prefer it."

"Well, Sage here has a strip club with no bottom bitch," Daniela stated. "Since I been in New York, I been over there three times. Those women are supposed to give the house twenty percent in tips. The club pays them a paycheck for five or six hundred a week. But those women are takin' y'all for a ride."

"We do fifty thousand a week in alcohol sales and another fifty in our tip cut," C.H. said. "Whatchu mean? They're stealin' from me?"

"Yeah. Well, your age only allows you so much leverage." Daniela turned her head towards him. "In my experience, if you allow those whores one inch, they'll take a mile. You need a mean bottom bitch in the locker room. She'll smack them bitches in line, search their shit, their pussies, everything. Garter's has no real security except men. Those chicks are beauties. Real cute. Bet anything that those women are using their nuclear-powered pussy on some of those security."

"You know this from a coupla visits?" Liza asked.

"Sage ain't stupid." Daniela said.

They fell asleep after that but Tate knocked on his door.

C.H. threw on a sweatsuit and came out.

Tate looked at him. "We gotta collect cash, homie. Good lookin' on the Puerto Rican babe. Felt like I was in there fuckin' J-Lo when she was the *'In Living Color'* Jenny From Da Block."

"Nigga, I'll be seventeen. She seventy. What da fuck you talkin' 'bout?" C.H. asked with a confused look.

"Netflix, dummie. J-Lo was a dancer on the show *In Living Color* when the world found her, Jamie Fox, the Wayans brothers... like *Marlon Wayans*?"

"Imma look it up just for you old ass nigga!" C.H. laughed as Tate went in the room to get Deuce.

Minutes later C.H. let them out. The day was breaking. He closed the driveway gate and went back inside to sleep with Liza and Daniela who were both knocked out.

CHAPTER FIFTEEN

Can't Be Caught
The Slaughterhouse
Mt. Vernon, NY

Kaz, Cumba, Ammo, and C.H. were in an empty store space on Grant and Pittman in Mt. Vernon several weeks later. Kaz was chewing on a toothpick as they checked the place out. Underneath the store was a storage area that was about as large as the entire store. Along the left-side wall were two deep freezers that measured 8-feet in length, 3-feet in width. On the right side were two deep freezers that measured 8-feet in length, 3-feet in width. On the right side were two walk-in units. One was a refrigerated unit, the other a freezer.

"Y'all gettin da message?" C.H. inquired. He turned on the freezer.

"Hell yeah," Ammo stated. "Freeze the mufuck in here for however long we freeze 'em for. Nobody'll know we got 'em here. And freezin' a body fucks up the time of death if he's ever found."

"In a trial they *gotta* know dat," Cumba said. "Cuz police need a timeline and they gotta put you wit 'em at or around dat time, or else how'll they convict you?"

"Long game. Always think long game," C.H. told them. "Come in here each day during daylight hours, put on rubber boots and gear…break out da electric saws, chop 'em up, dump 'em in da acid drums, let 'em liquify…no more bodies."

"What to do wit da liquid?" Cumba wanted to know.

"Pick a drainpipe. Any fuckin' gutter. The Hudson River." C.H. shrugged. "Just don't get caught dumpin' cuz the cops'll get suspicious. You just CAN'T BE CAUGHT. Feel me? Everything has to be sprayed with a power-washer…"

C.H. took them to an area up front where he opened up another room. They turned on the light and C.H. allowed the three assassins to take a look.

"From da power tools, lime, rubber boots, vinyl suits, and two big power washers, bleach, ammonia, caustic acid, boric acid, industrial detergents, rubber gloves, ropes, zip-ties, and all the other shit y'all bought," C.H. informed them. "We stacked right."

"We'll bring it," Kaz stated. "What's up wit that store space upstairs?"

"Can y'all run a T-shirt shop?" C.H. looked at each of the Rolling 60s assassins. "Da streets is watchin'... da fuckin' feds is watchin'. Niggas need w-2's. Run a simple shop. It's a big office up there. Let ya chicks run it. T-shirts, beaters, socks, draws, thong panties."

"Lingerie?" Kaz asked.

"Don't matter to me," C.H. told them while looking at the time on his cellphone as they walked upstairs. "Tell wifey to research lingerie manufacturers even though it's more expensive. Yea, do T-shirts. Cuz when it's time to burn da operation, this whole buildin' lights up in an inferno."

It made sense to the hittaz.

"It's all kinds of T-shirt bulk manufacturers online and down on East 28th Street and Broadway," Kaz mentioned as they locked the basement door and exited the premises.

"Let's blow this spot, ya heard? I'll get that list to y'all and we'll talk about how to get it done," C.H. proposed.

"Why don'tchu give us da list and take ya fam outta town for a week or so *after* we set the store up, dog?" Cumba counter offered.

"I can do that." C.H. trusted these dudes. They were not careless killers. They were assassins.

They dispersed.

. . .

Daniela leased a $2.6 million dollar mansion in Eastchester, also located in Westchester County. This kept her away from Mt. Vernon but C.H. was good with that because he didn't need anyone figuring out who she was and why she was staying with C.H. So when he got there, Liza asked him to come meet her at one of the Bargain Galore stores in Mt. Vernon, she wanted him to see the store and what was parked in front of it.

He drove over there and parked behind an old black car. "Baby, you see it?" Liza asked as an old white man stopped to look at it as he passed by walking his Irish setter.

"Yeah, mama, I see it. Why da fuck you buy it?" he asked her, knowing it wasn't her style. "It's a Bentley or Rolls I believe."

"That's a 1969 Rolls-Royce Silver Shadow, son," the older white man said. "Only the rich had them back in my day."

"We found it in a locker," Liza told C.H. "And no, I don't want to keep it. But wouldn't it be cool?"

C.H. nodded. "Yeah I guess."

He walked into the store and checked it out. "This is cool. C'mere, babe."

Liza followed him back to the electronic section. "See how everyone just seems to be-line back here? It's like havin' a pawn store without havin' to have a pawn broker's license."

The Rollin 60s had these "Forever Burner" phones lighting up stores sales like Black Friday. Anyone who saw the Master P classic *"I Got The Hook Up"* movie understood the value of having such a device. And they weren't being sold to just anyone. The mob was only interested in selling to hustlaz. Niggas on the street gettin' money from coke and smack deals, pills, k2 for the most part because Sage had a team of bright young analysts and hackers that were collecting information in the form of: (A) Who those hustlaz were calling; (B) Who was calling them; (C) Who they were texting; (D) Who was texting them; (E) Who was talking in G-code or "street code" and who was responding - particularly in texts. Since everything was being hacked/stolen from *AT&T, Sprint, Verizon, T-Mobile,* and other such companies, cellphone, towers, and databases, these were mostly printable-readable files. They could get voice messages as well but those were time-consuming and overwhelming to even attempt listening to.

With forever burners, even hustlaz let their guards down some and spoke openly in a lot of instances. Either way, whenever Choir Boy, Sonja, Sunny, or Chubb had a new list of clients C.H. would have his folks swoop in. Usually with an invitation to Garter's if it was worth it. Nothing like sweetening up a deal with some bad ass females hired to screw a niggas' brains out and leave him with a beautifully sore manpiece.

That evening an auction house curator came and picked up the 1969 Rolls-Royce Silver Shadow. C.H. was holding his daughter when the car was being loaded onto a flatbed.

"I knew you wasn't keepin' it," C.H. smiled as they got

inside of the Chevy Suburban. "Tell you what, whatever you get for it, let's go on vacation for a couple weeks."

Liza's eyes lit up. "You're a liar! You serious?"

"How'm I s'posed to be a fuckin' liar and be serious?" he asked as she secured Isabel in her car seat.

"Okay where we goin'?" she asked as he drove them home.

They couldn't decide on a destination until they got home. Noni and Deva were there with Deuce and his cousin - rapper Double J. C.H. pulled up to the mouth of his driveway and rolled the window down.

"Niggas," C.H. greeted them. "Bitches."

Liza smacked him in the back of his head. "Your daughter!"

"Oh," he looked back at Isabel. "She got headphones on watchin' *Dora The Explorer*. Hit me again, Imma spank dat ass pink!"

"Promise?" Liza teased and mushed him in the face.

He looked over at Deuce and J. "What up with it, cuz?"

They all threw it up.

Liza opened the gates with an app on her phone. Then C.H. drove up the driveway, parked inside of the garage, and met everyone inside of the house. Deuce and C.H. disappeared downstairs into the basement for a minute.

"Nice motorcycles y'all got," C.H. told Deuce.

"Caught 'em online," Deuce said of the pair of Suzuki

motor bikes. "Double J makin' money on da road, so he went in wit me. Thirty-five hundred each."

"C'mon," C.H. stated as he took the money and looked at the slips. Frustration came over his face "Why these niggas Junior and Casino keep comin' up short in this cash, son?"

Deuce shrugged. "That's twice… *in a week.*"

"Niggas takin' my silence for softness, huh?" C.H. dumped the cash out onto the workshop table and put it through the money counting machine. "Three hundred and one thousand."

He looked up the money. "These niggas 60s or recruits?"

"Recruits," Deuce informed him as he watched his boss remove his shirt and strap on his two heaviest machetes. He had them sheathed in black alligator skin scabbards.

C.H. only wore a black T-shirt and a black bulletproof hoody, B.A.P.E. jeans, and black desert storm boots.

"We'll be back, Flaca," he said and kissed his woman. "Dominican Republic. Let's visit out there and buy a mansion there. Think about it."

Her eyes got really big at that announcement. She ordered out from a steak restaurant that delivered. She'd tried their food and loved it so that's what she did.

CHAPTER SIXTEEN

"Junior Had No Ear"
East 233rd and Carpenter
Bronx, New York

C.H. headed down to the Bronx where Junior lived on East 222nd Street and Carpenter Avenue. It was only 8:00 PM and New York didn't have many people that were out and about.

C.H. had on a black demon mask which a lot of New Yorkers happened to trend towards in the pandemic months. So it was not unusual. He parked the Chevy on Bronx Boulevard which was a one-way street pointing north. This way, if anything were to happen, he could hop in it - and be in the Bronx River Parkway North within a minute or two.

He'd given Deuce a re-up for him and Tate to distribute

and sent Deuce on his way. Deuce, who was the same age as Coldhearted - 17 now, both of their birthdays having just passed - had warned C.H. to wait for him and the other enforcers to accompany him. But C.H. being who he was, strapped up tight, and now here he was riding up the elevator to the 6th floor where Junior lived and had a trap house.

As soon as the bullish-sized Coldhearted exited the elevator he turned right and it sounded like a party was going on or something. There was a few couples outside of the apartment smooching. They didn't even look grown. Maybe fifteen or sixteen. They saw C.H. but went on with their ass groping and face-sucking.

C.H. passed the staircase which was in the center of the building. There were about eight apartment units on either side of the stairwell. More teens, they were clearly black door dealers, were chilling in the stairwell, smoking what smelled like some expensive kush and drinking that Eightball (*"Olde English 800 Malt Liquor"*) straight out the 22-ounce bottles.

C.H. clocked a tell-take bulge in the jeans pockets of one of the young blacks.

The feds is watchin'/niggas plottin' to get me/ will I survive/ will I die/ c'mon let's/ picture the possibility/ givin' me charges/niggas clockin' my grip/ people say I was raised wrong and that's why I blaze shit/ was hyper on the scene always as a teenager/ packin' hunneds in my draws/fuck da law/bitches I fuck wit a passion/ I'm living rough and raw...

. . .

Tupac's lyrics were bangin' inside as C.H. approached the open door where Junior's big black ass stayed at. Junior wasn't no young pup either. He'd been in the game since he was twelve and was now thirty-three. He was a well-known heavy hitter in the area and C.H. was definitely aware that he may have walked into a hornet's nest.

As soon as C.H. entered the party he smelled a thick haze of smoke from all the marijuana being consumed... and whatever else they had up in there. Maybe some K2 which used to be simple to purchase in some stores. Now there was a ban of the product by the State Governor and laws he signed off in. That's because light-weight amateurs were having "epps" or episodes off the shit because they weren't built like the stoners of the 60s thru 80s.

Amateurs fuck it up for everybody, C.H. thought at one time.

A girl came up to him. She was cute, her breasts fat, ass like a donkey. He removed his mask and she smiled flirtatiously at him and wiggled that ass up against him. He held her hips and scanned the living room where many others were dancing to some Drake cut now which the women liked. It seemed as if all eyes were on him but this Boogie Down Bronx crowd was out of their minds. High as a Chinese spy balloon hovering over a U.S. nuclear facility.

C.H. pushed the girl away and moved on through the

apartment with its cherry wood floors. He put on his black leather gloves and walked into the kitchen where a dark-skinned woman in her thirties was washing dishes while talking to another woman a little lighter than her but still dark skinned also. He walked on down the hallway and bumped right into Junior.

Coldhearted immediately shoved Junior back inside of the bathroom he just came out of. A tall brown skinned girl was in there washing between her legs but C.H. didn't care. Junior was a 6'2", 305-pound fat motherfucker but he was no pushover.

"What-mufuckin'-punk-nigga?!" Junior said as he punched C.H. all up on the cheekbone, top of his head, and his ear.

But C.H. was working with the strength of a chimpanzee the way he threw down. He could take blows others couldn't take. He was like a ghost from the dead. He fought like he had nothing plus everything to lose at one time. The girl screamed, naked from the waist down.

"You think you'll get over on *me*?!" C.H. said roughly as he crashed Junior's brain plate into the porcelain toilet when they both fell to the floor. Coldhearted took the toilet top off and beat Junior with it until it broke.

"Yeah, bitch nigga!! Coldhearted mufucka!!" C.H. got up and removed both machetes. He pointed at the female. "Get dressed!"

She left the thong panties on her ankle and pulled her pants up quickly. C.H. handed her a stack of cash and he took her Macy's credit card. "This you?" he asked, also checking her driver's license.

"Y-yes, th-that's m-m-me," she stated, afraid.

"You stay your fat ass on the floor, nigga!!" C.H. shouted. He said to the girl. "*Breathe*, Tania. Deep breaths. Nothin's happenin' to you, baby. We're friends."

She did as he said and stopped shaking. She even got the thong panties off of her ankle and stuffed them into her jeans. C.H. had her open the large window.

"That a fire escape?" C.H. asked her.

She nodded.

"I know who you are and where you live," he threatened her as someone knocked on the door but it was locked. "Go! You, too, Fat Fuck! Get up! Out the fuckin' window! Move! Now!"

"I got the money, nigga!" the huge dark-skinned man told him. C.H. jigged him with the sharp end of his machete named "Heartless."

Junior climbed out onto the fire escape and C.H. was right behind him. The girl was scaling down the steel flights of stairs like a Koala bear on steroids. Junior and C.H. were right behind her.

Several minutes later they were out on the ground behind the building where all the dumpsters were. It smelled like the dead back there. Junior kept trying to turn around, looking for any opportunity to rush C.H., but those machetes were terrifying. Junior was already bleeding from one small poke of the blade earlier.

C.H. shoved Junior up against the wall and searched him after sheathing one blade. He kept the right blade against Junior's ear as he searched him. And then, just like that, Junior had no ear. C.H. had cut it clean off except for a piece of skin beneath it that had it dangling like a sick Halloween mask.

While Junior yelled and fell to his knees in pain, C.H. told him, "Only reason I don't kill you is because your body's too heavy to move and burn, nigga. Next time that money come up short… I'll kill you myself. I like killin'. Shut yo fat fuckin' baby ass up! You want me to chop off your thievin' fuckin' hands?"

Junior got quiet and held his ear in place. Choking back the desire to moan and cry out in pain.

C.H. wiped his blade off and made his way back to his vehicle walking as thought nothing had happened. He was on Bronx River Parkway – North within a minute which was when he checked his cellphone. Missed calls from Tate and Deuce. He texted them back: **En route** and that was it.

CHAPTER SEVENTEEN

"Who Ear You Cut Off?"
Mt. Vernon, New York

Anyone that knew any history about Hip Hop knew long ago that New York City was not limited to raising up the only New York rappers. Westchester County, one of the richest counties in all of USA, was comprised of many towns or townships within the county. Mt. Vernon just happened to border the Bronx as did Yonkers. So, it's no surprise that Mt. Vernon blew up on the Hip Hop scene when Heavy D & The Boyz came out and enjoyed commercial success. Behind them was Pete Rock & CL Smooth who were more embraced by the streets.

In Yonkers, especially South Yonkers, with all of its white affluent people in the north, their lines were clear-racial and socio-economic. That's what eventually squeezed out Mary J. Blige and DMX, both being iconic superstars in Hip Hop, both plagued by drug use that began in their poverty. DMX lost his battle while Mary J Blige had thus far been winning. Also from Yonkers impoverished side of the city was The Lox (they were first "The Warlocks" – hence "The Lox").

C.H., Tate, Noni, Deuce, Deva, and Liza were at Big Mama's soul food restaurant which had literally hundreds of photos of these Hip-Hop Legends from Westchester County. The owner of Big Mama's, a thin, six-foot tall, brown skinned man with thick glasses and wavy hair who appeared to be in his forties but was 60 years old, stopped by their table.

"Everyone okay?" he asked politely.

They nodded.

"Man, those pork ribs, my god!" Liza beamed. "And the sweet potato pie – mm delicious!"

"And the Hip Hop lessons right in the menu," C.H. said. "Soon as I saw the name Grand Puba Maxwell, I was like that's a cool ass name so I went on Spotify, can't wait to bang his music in my ride."

"Oh yeah, Puba, his wife, and kids come in here often," Mr. Jake Harris told them. "All those guys you see are what paved the way for the new peoples in rap like Gunna, Young Thug, N.B.A. Young Boy. – and people like that," he stated in his southern accent.

"Look at you, a Hip Hop *Pop*," C.H. said and everyone laughed.

"First, I hud o' that one but I take it," the older gentlemen said. "Just look at them like… our African ancestors. If they didn't go through what they did, include da bein' born bad part…we wouldn't even be in existin' y'know what I'm tellin' ya?"

He shook everyone's hand at the table and went on…

"The *bein' born bad part*…" C.H. mentioned as he called the waitress over. "I know a little 'bout that."

"He meant slavery," Tate interpreted.

"I know, OG," C.H. said as the waitress came over. C.H. handed her $100 and another $200. "Just get the check. Keep what's left."

They left the restaurant knowing more about Hip Hop music than before they first went in. As soon as they climbed into their black Cadillac SUV, which they'd loaned to Tate and Deuce, C.H. had Tate play Grand Puba's music including the music of his old group brand Nubian.

As they drove past Mt. Vernon Park C.H. pointed at the Pelham Avenue Bridge. "Pull over and park right behind that Buick," C.H. directed Tate.

"Ain't that where all the bums be?" Liza asked.

"Yeah, lemme show y'all somethin'," C.H. said as they all got out of the car. "No heat. Stash err'thing cuz da cops be around here."

Tate and Deuce took C.H.'s double Glock 45's and put them in the custom stash behind the dash. They then had to walk all the way down a fence line to where the aqueduct was.

There was an opening in the fence where the homeless people squeezed through and walked about 100 yards to where the bridge was. Underneath the bridge there were makeshift tents, cardboard boxes, and sleeping bags where people actually slept.

"Don't be snide to these people," C.H. told the girls. Tate and Deuce already knew what Coldhearted was driving at.

"Ayo, who goes there?" a white lady with a rough smoker's voice yelled as they came nearer.

"Da boogeyman," C.H. said. "Fuck you think it is?"

"Ah, shit, met him, did him in, he don't want none of this!" another woman said. "Oh that's them L.A. Boyz and Mr. C. Who the pretty ladies?"

"Our women, be nice, Veronica," C.H. said as they all seemed to come out. Dozens of homeless people. "This my wife, Liza, and her cousins, Noni and Deva."

"Where Butchy at?" Tate asked Veronica, an older Black woman.

A black man, who wore three pairs of pants and two different jackets to keep warm said, "She locked up for disorderly conduct. Them fuckin' pigs always fuckin' wit us!"

"That's his wife," Deuce told the girls. "His name Gil."

"I don't get it," Liza was saying, trying to figure out the relationship.

"Nothin' to get," C.H. said as he rubbed his hands together. "These are my folks. Most of 'em look out for us on perimeters of the traphouses and they get fifty dollars a day, some crack to smoke, dope to shoot, food to eat. And they tell us what the cops are askin', who they askin' it about. Ain't that right, Meg?"

The white woman who spoke before nodded. "My feet are cold, Mr. C." Meg informed him.

"Y'all know where da Bargains Galore store is off Richlee by the post office?" Liza asked her.

"We know where dat mothafuckin' Garter's is!" Veronica burst out with.

"They're a few blocks apart," Liza told them. "Free clothes and shoes for all y'all."

"There's line and blankets in the Goodwill laundry bags," Deva recalled.

Liza nodded. Of all the auctions they go to, although they are required to clean out any locker unit they buy – that same day – they come across a lot of junk not even worth putting in their stores, so they trash most of it. The clothes? They keep the best – such as designer clothing – and what they don't want to they take to the Goodwilll Store to donate. If not the Goodwill then Salvation Army.

C.H. passed out $100 bills to everyone there. There had to be at least 30 of them that they could see. "Y'all see or hear anything y'all know what to do," he said prior to leaving.

"Ay, um, Mr. C?" the Black man stopped him.

C.H. turned back around. "Gil."

"Butchy…" he trailed off. "They got her way up in da

Westchester County Jail in Valhalla on disorderly and it – I thank she has some trespassin' fines from jumpin' da train."

"Butchy gon' be alright," C.H. told him. "We'll get her out and pay her fines but now y'all owe me. Owe my family. Police be askin' questions…da Bloods be askin' questions. Y'all might see something' thatta save our traphouses, Garter's, Bargains stores, Tate, Deuce…"

"We know," Gil conveyed. "Her name: Lakeisha L. Cartright."

"Aight." C.H. and the others made their way back to the waiting Cadillac. "Tate, drop me and Liza off at the crib. We gotta pick up my sister and Izzy. Y'all go get Butchy out for me."

Tate looked at his watch. "We can just go to da bail bondsman for dat."

"Y'all need her, right?" C.H. asked as they pulled off.

"She keeps them other fuckers in line I tell you that much," Deuce agreed. Butchy was a big woman, ghetto as all hell, funny as shit. It had been Tate's idea to use the homeless/"street people" as lookouts, runners, maids, handymen in the traphouses and so forth to make the drug operation run more smoothly.

"Find out from her if any of them bastards tried to find out anything about us from her," C.H. ordered.

Tate and Deuce nodded.

"You'll trust her?" Liza asked.

"She still sittin' in jail, ain't she?" C.H. stated as proof of

Butchy's loyalty. "Poor people hate the cops as much as we do. Bailing her out and payin' her fines buys her loyalty and shows everyone that we look out for our own."

"I'd say *cements* her loyalty not *buys* it then," Noni said.

"Indeed," C.H. concurred. "Oh yeah, T… that shoppin' list we was workin' on for party peoples?"

Tate knew he was talking about the hit list. "Yeah. You ready?"

"Almost." It only took five minutes for them to reach the house. "Before we go to the Dominican Republic it'll be. We got a lot of shit to do first."

"Uh uh, you know my phone blowin' up," Tate told him, showing him some texts he got with a big ass smile on his face. "Da homiez sayin' Junior had his peoples runnin' up here with dat cash he owed."

Deuce read through all the texts. "You cut his ear off?"

C.H. tried to shush him so the girls wouldn't hear but it was too late. Liza, Noni, and Deva had already stepped out of the Caddy inside of the garage when Liza heard what was said. She came back to the charcoal black SUVC with her cousins.

"Ooouu, lemme see, who ear you cut off?" Liza asked with a glint of excitement in her eye.

"It's a *text* baby not a photo," C.H. said, shaking his head. "She thinks it's on Facebook or Instagram. I don't even have none of that bullshit."

"Who ear though?" she demanded.

"Big three hundred somethin' pound black nigga in the Boogie," he said, referring to the *"Boogie Down"* Bronx. A term made famous by Hip Hop Legend KRS-ONE and *Boogie Down Productions* (BDP) when him and his brother Scott La Rock (RIP) started killin it in the late 80s early 90s with classics like *Criminal Minded, My Philosophy, Still Number One,* and hundreds more. "Owed us over then grand. Nigga's lucky he was too big or else he woulda been fish food," C.H. said, still pissed off at Junior.

"C'mon, we gotta go," Liza told him. "Crazy ass. I should cut your ear off."

"Aight my niggas," C.H. told his men.

Tate and Deuce took off with Noni and Deva.

Liza got Lilly and Izzy ready while speaking with Elizabeth and Lupé. "Somebody at least could've had Lilly's hair done, ma!" Liza yelled as she brushed out Lilly's long, thick, black hair. "God your hair is nearly at your butt!" Liza complained.

A half hour later, they were all inside of the Uber transportation van they'd called, headed up to PRAY AUDI/MERCEDES dealership up in Stamford, Connecticut. The ride took an hour to get there due to traffic on the I-95 North. Once there, Liza spoke to C.H. for a few minutes.

"Nah, I don't trust no fuckin' Uber driver wit my baby sis or my baby, don'tchu watch da news?" C.H. was saying. "I don't care how long we'll be, baby."

"But Lilly likes WWE; its right down there and they have

tickets," Liza argued. "Plus, they wit my mom and *mi tia*." (My auntie).

"Y'all don't care 'bout going to WWE SMACKDOWN?" C.H. asked Elizabeth and her sister.

"Y'all have fun," Elizabeth told them and they left with Lilly and Izzy.

It was only 4:00 PM when the couple hit the very first *PRAY* dealership. It was cool out – not cold – and there was still sunlight. They held hands and went on a leisurely walk, hunting for two vehicles.

CHAPTER EIGHTEEN

Life Wouldn't Let Him Sleep
The PRAY Dealership
<u>**Stamford, Connecticut**</u>

Liza had her sights set on bigger things and Coldhearted was behind her on anything she wanted. As long as that want didn't come back to haunt them. She'd just started up a new business, he was explaining to her as they walked down to PRAY Rolls-Royce on Stamford Boulevard together.

"I read like an English major, mama," he told her. "And I talk to our lawyer a lot. You had to spend a lot of the drug loot to stock a dozen stores…and y'all got real lucky findin' fancy cars, diamonds, and rare paintings. Y'all even found a shitload of wind turbines that cost five figures."

"I never knew there was so much that people left behind," she mentioned, referring to the many dozens of lockers and shipping containers B.G. had purchased since their beginning earlier in the year. "Wowwww. Look, babe," she said while pointing at a Bentley Continental GTC Supersport.

"That shit purple or somethin', too," he mentioned. "This bitch a convertible. How much da B.G. stores and inventory worth again?"

"One point three million," she recalled. "You said we was filing the LLC as a S-Corporation next year, right?"

"I'm not, our tax filer is," he reminded her. "Nobody knows every item you bought in those lockers. So, the play is… say you got a dinette set on sale for two hundred. *Every item you sale, be sure we have a receipt fifty percent or higher.* The more income we can claim filing as a corporation, the more tax breaks we can get on the corporation in order to keep payin' employees. You know – *creating jobs*."

"So whatchu think, Papi?" she asked.

"It says $229k…" he shrugged and pulled her to him.

She was wearing almost all Balenciaga. A white silky one-piece black dress with a black catsuit underneath it to fend off the cold, black suede Moschino shoes, and a trendy warm leather jacket by Saint Laurent. Liza knew how to dress. He looked at the car and she couldn't resist nuzzling his neck. "I'd drive this shit."

"Okay, so one down?" she asked him.

He nodded.

The deal was that they purchase two cars and they must agree to like each other's choice so that – if they wished – they could drive either car without a problem.

"We really buyin' a house in D.R.?" she asked.

"I don't dream of bein' a dope dealer all my life," he told her. "I dream of bein' mad caked up like Snoop, Jay-Z, and Fifty Cent, then – before anybody know it – we skip town for our mansion out D.R."

"What about whatchu told ya Crip homiez? I mean makin' them all rich and everything?"

He took a deep breath prior to answering. "Every mother in the world tells they son he gon' be an astronaut or doctor… or her daughter that she'll be a Supreme Court Justice or Miss AmeriKKKa if she set her mind to it. Moms be comin' from da right place but she *lyin'*. Son turn out average or a bum. Daughter prolly smart but she won't win that rigged up shit they got goin' – til she get her cock-eyes fixed!"

Liza punched him and bust out laughing. "You so fuckin' stupid!"

A white female came walking their way and C.H. whispered, "Like this big nose heifer. Miss AmeriKKKa a car salesman I bet," he stated sarcastically.

"Sales*lady*," Liza corrected him, her nose red now from the dropping temperatures.

"Hi!" the woman greeted them. She saw how they were dressed and knew she had potential buyers. "You guys lookin' to buy, thinkin' about it – what?"

"All the above," Liza spoke for both of them. "We want to walk away with two purchases tonight. We've settled on the Bentley SS convertible. It's purple?"

The woman shook Liza's hand first and then C.H.'s. "My name's Joan Goldberg. Call me Goldie."

"I'm Liza Garcia-Thomas and this is my husband, Sage Michael Thomas… Liza and Sage is fine," she introduced them.

"Finance?" Goldie asked them.

"Lemme ask you somethin', Goldie," C.H. started slowly as he cracked open a black leather carry-on suitcase to show her the cash. "Now I'm certain that y'all have had rappers, NBA players – people like that come here and spend a million on one car. That Bentley Continental GTC Supersport we want is marked at $229k."

"Okay." Goldie just nodded.

"We're payin' in cash and I'm sure we'll add between twenty and thirty grand in custom options," he told her. "Problem is I'm not buyin' that car unless I can get it for $200k. C'mon Goldie, it's pre-owned."

Goldie saw him eating her commission away. "Well, you said you want two cars. How about we discuss price when you buy your second car?"

"For now go get that Bentley pulled around out front because it won't take us long," C.H. informed her. "C'mon, bae. Goldie, it's the plum colored GTC we want."

They walked together and checked out a line of Mercedes-

Benz Maybachs. They settled on an obsidian clearcoat black S-580 edition with a $288k ticket price. They entered the front of the dealership where they met with Goldie. They told her about the Maybach and she had to look at it first so she'd know which keys to grab.

After discussing it with her boss she came and sat with C.H. and Liza inside of her office. She checked their licenses and asked if they wanted to test drive the cars. They agreed to do so and Liza drove the Bentley first with C.H. upfront.

Twenty minutes later they switched and C.H. drove the Maybach. "I know one thing…this shit goes straight to ya fuckin' ego huh, mama?"

"Yes it does!" she agreed. Liza giggled. "Know what I'm thinkin'?"

"What?"

"Not to get a convertible cuz of me and Lilly's hair," Liza laughed, causing Goldie to laugh with her. "I'm picturing leavin' the salon after paying two, four hundred for both of us and that convertible bein' down!"

"You don't want it?" C.H. asked her calmly.

"I do," she told him. "I just haveta put the top up. It's automatic, right?"

Goldie answered, "Yes. Fully automatic."

Back at the dealership, in Goldie's office, she was able to re-work the numbers. "Okay, $229k on the Bentley and $288k on the Maybach is $517k. $494k is my best best."

"Aight, let's do it," he told her, pushing the carry-on case across a clear section of her desk. "I want bullet-proof windows and paneling."

"In both?" Goldie asked.

"In both," he said. "But I – nevermind. Bullet-proof paneling and windows."

Liza spoke to him in Spanish, saying that it made no sense to spend money on the Bentley when it was convertible. That she also liked the same kind of Bentley without the soft top which bullets could pierce.

Goldie paused.

"She's sayin' that she liked the Bentley GT Speed a couple cars over – the bluish one," he told Goldie.

"Show me," the saleswoman said.

They went back outdoors and she went and got the keys to it. They opted not to test drive it. They returned to her office.

"Armored cars," Liza commented.

"Shid, I wish," he said. "*Armored* is like Level Five, Level 6 like what the President got. Each of those cars are at least a million dollars. They can stop anti-aircraft rounds and the tires on it will roll for a hundred miles after a piercing. They'll never be on the roadside flat. The paneling I'm askin' for, they can do for fifty grand a car. Can't have you, my baby sister, and the baby hit by a stray bullet just driving to Walmart."

Goldie nodded while typing behind her computer.

"Can we borrow a loaner until our cars are ready?" C.H. asked her. "On your website it said -"

"Of course," Goldie told him. She sent an email for a car. "Just you two, right?"

"Five adults and two children," Liza told her. She added, "My mom and aunt has our small toddler and his twelve-year-old sister and my cousin with them. They're at Smackdown right now."

Goldie looked at Liza strangely.

"His *adopted* sister is my cousin," Liza said, with a raucous laugh.

"Glad you cleared that up!" Goldie grinned. "Um, I have a Mercedes-Benz Sprinter Ultimate Limo. A private jet on wheels, six passengers in the rear, two recliners with swivel options, and a 32-inch smart TV. That's what the guys out back emailed me. That okay?"

"She's good, man!" Liza told C.H. "She want us to buy a Sprinter."

"What?!" Goldie smiled. "That's what it said! Not my fault the company made it sound like an ad!"

"That's Ma callin' now." Liza stepped out with her cellphone.

Twenty minutes later, Elizabeth, Lupé, Lilly, and Isabel were at the dealership. Lilly and Isabel had warpaint on their faces.

"Who put warpaint on Daddy's baby face?" C.H. asked as he picked her up. Isabel was happy as a spring chicken. Her little ass looking like she was ready to fight.

Goldie couldn't get enough of Izzy.

She handed C.H. and Liza the documents and titles of their cars after counting and recounting the money inside of a money counter.

"We'll call you when the vehicles are ready," Goldie assured them. "Let us know if you'd like to buy the Sprinter! Ha! Ha! Ha!" she joked.

"Take care," Liza hugged her.

They piled into the sleep pre-owned Sprinter.

"Damn!" C.H. said, looking around at the dashboard and everything. "Look like da spaceship enterprise up this bitch!"

He figured it out.

They hit the road after that.

"It just takes gettin' used to," he stated as he pulled onto the I-95. "Babe…this joint nice!"

Liza went into the rear with everyone else when they had a hard time turning on the TV. "I know…"

As soon as they got home C.H. hit the showers and fell asleep with his daughter and Liza. They were all worn out. Plus, with C.H., sleep never lasted long. Life wouldn't let him sleep and his soul could never find rest.

CHAPTER NINETEEN

Sage Saved Who He Love: Lilly
Sage's House (O.G. Talk)
Mt. Vernon, NY

"SAGE! Sage!" Liza was excitedly shrieking from the home office.

He came bursting from downstairs carrying his MP-5 with the scope and laser beam, ready for combat. Deuce and Tate were right behind him with the HK-91 and Tate had ad 12-gauge riot gun full of tactical rounds.

"Shit!" Coldhearted cursed when he heard her inside of the office laughing. He handed the MP-5 to Deuce as they all entered the office. "What?"

"Remember the Van Gogh sketching we found in the locker out Woodbridge!?" she asked, still going crazy.

"Yeah, I think," he replied. He wasn't even mad anymore. Her excitement was infectious. "*Van* what?"

"Man fuhgeddaboudit." She just waved him off.

"He a famous artist," Deuce said.

"It was ten sketches, eight were reproductions," she said, nodding at Deuce. "Eight were fakes."

"And why're you happy 'bout them odds?" he inquired.

"Two are original, dumbass," she told him.

"They better be worth twenty, thirty grand each wit all dat yellin'," Sage remarked.

"More. Way more!" she was nearly in tears.

He sat down, smiling now. "A million?"

"I wish. A hundred grand! *Each*!" she shrieked. Then, looking at Tate and Deuce. "Guns. Why y'all got guns? Y'all gotta get those the fuck outta here. I have people comin' over to pick up the sketches from the New York Museum of Natural Art & History. They wanna take my picture. And then we'll leave for the auction for the Rolls Royce, the Winnebago bus, umm… Italian art, and a couple more cars – it's some big ticket and smaller ticket stuff."

"The museum won't take the art?" Tate asked her.

She shook her head. "Nah, I had all of them tested. A Mosaccio…" she went to a file on her desk and showed them 8" x 10" clear glossy photographs of the art. "A Mosaccio, Donatello, Leonardo da Vinci, and Raphael's *Galatea, Madonna* and the fresh *The School of Athens* which was his most famous. They're not original but they were done in the

14th and 15th century time periods. I'm hopin' for ten grand on each painting."

"Aight, baby, I'm real proud of you," he said, kissing her. "I love you, too."

"I know. Imma have our next baby," she dropped on him. "So get yo broke ass a job. Nigga."

"You always fuckin', right?"

"You never know. You don't wear no condoms," she said as she wrapped her arms around his neck.

"You be havin' periods, bitch. I'd know." They stood in the doorway and kissed like newlyweds. He whispered, "You wanna fuck now?"

She shoved his hands off of her ass and said, "Hell no. Mama 'bout to make these checks."

Downstairs in the secret underground "Boom Boom Room," the trio returned to scheming, counting out cash, cleaning guns, and talking about the hit list.

"Remember the video of me choppin' the nigga D-Slick up?" C.H. mentioned. They nodded. "Well it was this bitch with him named Rozetta when Slick was snatched up. She a loose end."

"Damn right she is," Tate agreed. "But…"

They had washed the cash in detergent and rinsed it in cold water to wash the narcotic scent off of it so dogs couldn't detect it while stashed. C.H. dried it on "low" in the drier he had down here. Once dried, they repackaged it into all of the denominations it should be. Then, high bill first, created

$1000 stacks. Using a machine they vacuum-sealed in plastic $10,000 rectangular packages of cash.

"But what, son?" Sage pressed him.

"This plan of yours is flawed," Tate dared to say.

"What the fuck?" C.H. scrunched up his face. "That's the first you ever -"

"It ain't dangerous enough," the dark-skinned muscular OG Crip told him. "Say you take out Rozetta, she disappears. She got a mom, a dad, mufuckaz who love her. Just like Shadow and nem folks put out a missin' persons report. What happens when the FBI is called out in full force over these disappearances?"

C.H. knew he had a point. "Kill the entire family?"

"Bingo," Tate quietly answered. "If not that...make her kill herself wit the P. Stone's dope and leave the bag under her bed..."

"Juicy P, she know way too much," C.H. informed them as the cash count was complete: *$1.7 million*. That was for the next load. "Daniela might handle her for us when they go to Mexico next week."

"That'd be perfect," Tate mentioned. "Daniela's pops is a billionaire. They could spin some sort of elaborate plan."

C.H. rounded out the list. "HK, Mac-11, Orca, Dojo, Bugout, P-Man, Papo, and Maria."

"Liza's Maria?"

C.H. nodded. "Maaan...listen. I ever told y'all about the fire here?"

"Nah, just that there was a fire," Deuce said. "And how your adopted parents died in it."

C.H. texted his wife to come down a minute.

She did. "Babe."

"We was talkin' 'bout the fire," C.H. told her as she came up to where he was sitting on an overstuffed leather recliner. She was wearing a beautiful gray leather Prada dress, with a lovely silk black and white blouse with bingham patterns on it. "You look like an *executive*. A beautiful one."

"The fire. Why the fuck you talkin' 'bout the fire?" she wanted to know.

"Cuz I want those closest to me to know how much you, Lilly, and Izzy mean to me. Without y'all nothin' means nothin'. And now Tate and Deuce – y'all my family too, right?"

"Don't ask stupid shit, nigga. Fuckin' right we are," Deuce said and Tate echoed it.

"I was twelve, he was ten on Christmas," Liza recounted. "Christmas Eve or Christmas – I forgot. But a lot of my cousins were there and we was all little – so we played the kissing game, in a closet while the adults was drinkin', playin' dominoes, whateva. Me and Sage were already really likin' each other, though we was s'posed to be cousins through my Aunt Daphne and her black husband adoptin' him when he was a baby shot up in the hospital."

Sage made her sit on his lap so she wouldn't be so emotional. But she cried anyway. He wiped her tears.

"Anytime she remembers the hospital photos and that video, she falls apart." C.H. said. "Go 'head, mama."

Tate sat forward as Deuce lit up a blunt.

"We start havin' actual sex in da closet and he's big. I was small so I was tellin' him to stop. That's when they caught us," Liza revealed. "My mom, his mom – there was this big deal made about him rapin' me because I was tryna appease my mom and all the adults firing questions at me. So things settle and my mom is like let's go home. I felt so bad and guilty because I been in love wit Sage since we was in 5th and 7th grade. They were tryna get me to say to the cops the next day that he raped me and he didn't."

She paused.

"Next thing I hear is there was this huge inferno up there," Liza continued. "Well, *here*. Sage save who he loved: *Lilly*. Daphne and Armand died. Sage did it. He won't say *how* but they were tryna jack him up in the state system as a rapist."

"It could be the White House, a Children's Hospital, or my own house but for those I love, I'll burn it all to the ground," C.H. vowed. "For Liza, Lilly, and Izzy, the Freedom Tower would be the Death Tower. I'd burn a *billion* people down over those I love most. With myself inside the shit if need be."

Liza had to go.

"Ten years old? You *Mike Meyers*, nigga!" Tate told his young boss.

They carried the cash upstairs and – on the way to the

garage – Tate snatched up an entire pan of fried swordfish saying, "I'm hungrier than *three* fat boys right now!"

Deuce grabbed a six-pack of beer. "Who drinkin' Molsen's homie?"

"I think Daniela put that in there," C.H. stated.

In the garage, gone was the Chevy Suburban that was loaned to C.H. months back from Don Armadillo and in its place a black 1989 Ford Bronco with a fully restored body and brand new 700-horsepower engine. Don Armadillo had had his Chicago people switch up vehicles. The sales price in the Bronco ballooned to $170k due to upgrades.

"Ayo, cuz," Tate said once the cash was secured. "A couple thangs. First, we need to switch our safehouses out Mt. Vernon to da Bronx cuz Butchy heard crackheads sayin' how they knew where it was."

"You head of security. Make any move you think is necessary. Beats bailin' niggas out," C.H. said, as the three of them jumped into the luxury Sprinter to eat the expensive swordfish and drink the six-pack of Molsen's beer while watching the SCARFACE movie on the big smartscreen. "Deuce, start it up and turn up the heat a little bit. Crack the garage door all the way open for the carbon shit -."

"I got it." Deuce did as he was asked.

"Imma plug youse right in wit my forged document cat," C.H. told Tate. "I see y'all fuckin' wit Liza's cousins real heavy so use them to rent whatchu need rentin'. They look like two rich girls. So…what else?"

"My mom need a house," Tate told him. "She finally gonna move to New York and … my sister's kids, Deuce brother…"

"I'm not payin' you enough to buy a house?" C.H. asked him.

"I just moved into mine but I'm not talkin' about me, I'm talkin' 'bout my momz and my family," Tate stated. "I just started this thing wit Deva and man, I ain't never had no woman like that."

Sage shot up, staring at Tate. "You in love, bitch!"

"Yeah, she got me, man. I thought we was just gon' fuck but she got me," Tate admitted.

C.H. slapped-shaked his hand. "I thought it was just Noni and Deuce…Aight, I tell you what. The K2, oxycodone, molly, Percocets, how they doin' by the month?"

Deuce answered that. "Nuttin' like da girl or boy but Imma guess a hundred grand profit-wise."

"That business is yours," C.H. told them. "Keep your own books. As for ya mama's house, you need a private buyer who'll unload a house to you for all cash. And you and Deuce need to get used to comin' in SHZ Records each morning at 8:30 AM. You need job titles and make it look like you're working. You can't be havin' all this cash and think a hater won't see it."

"How you do it?" Deuce asked him.

"I have a legal trust fund that was invested wisely so, on paper, I have a mill or two of legit money," C.H. said cautiously. He never admitted to how much he really had. "Me and Lilly's mom left us life insurance and with all the upgrades on our house here…shid, we can sell this shit for a cool mill or two and be straight. Garter's is another mill. SHZ Records is to be announced. And the B.G. inventory is at a million. Insured for more than that."

Tate and Deuce respected that.

"Now look," C.H. explained to Tate. "I just gave you a lucrative business cuz y'all been loyal. But you can't be stupid. Go to work every day. Show me you can run SHZ Records and you can have it. Or I'll sell it cuz the shits exhausting to me."

"Goddamn," Deuce smiled, looking at his uncle. "Spooky be rollin' wit Double J and nem on tour in Houston, Little Rock, Seattle, Cleveland, Atlanta, Delaware – K2, Molly, Oxy, Percocet…Spooky be so cash – loaded he gets $500 money orders and mails them back to me."

"*Murder Inc., Ruthless Records, Roc-A-Fella Records, Bad Boy*… they were all drug labels before record labels," Tate added with a nod. "Hell yeah. We gon' do it. Is the record label doin' bad?"

"Breakin' even. But I'm usin' forty percent of my Garter's' cash to keep it stable, the other fifty percent comes from dope cash and ten percent from record sales, shows, shit like that," C.H. conveyed it in an almost exasperated tone. "Let's shoot to Chicago."

"Now?" Tate asked.

"Now," C.H. told them.

C.H. didn't even pack a toothbrush.

"Deuce, ride with me. Leave the Caddy keys on the hook by the door, Tate you take the Sprinter," C.H. directed them.

On their way out Noni and Deva arrived. Noni hopped in the Bronco with Deuce and Deva travelled with her squeeze Tate.

CHAPTER TWENTY

"Danger did come."
Bronx, New York

Kaz was down in the Bronx on Fordham Road store-hopping with his main chick Amris when they got hungry and stopped inside of Burger King. For some reason, the heavy snows had eluded The Dirty Rotten and so February was just a crispy clear cold day out. The tall good-looking couple was able to find a sweat in the back near a window. As he was eating he sat with his back to the front door so he could keep alert for any danger.

Danger did come across the street, at Costco's when a metallic gray Land Rover-Range Rover HSE Westminister pulled up and honked his horn. Three black male passengers stepped out and a female ran out from the store to say something to the front seat passenger: BUGOUT.

"C'mon, baby, bring dat shit witchu," Kaz told Amris. "Five fifties in da midst."

Kaz shot a text to Cumba and Ammo who were also out on Fordham shopping. The three of them were parked on a side street a block away on Bainbridge Street. They put their goods in the back of Kaz's pre-owned Alfa Romeo Giulia Quadrifoglio and sent their three women back up to Mt. Vernon.

Ammo was driving one of the crew mini vans. They'd brought it along because it held a lot of groceries but that part of the trip was cut short at the surprise sighting of Blood Bugout. They ended up tailing him north up the Hutchinson Parkway and into Westchester's Croton on the Hudson.

"They just sittin' in da fuckin' car, dog!" Cumba said from the back seat. "Imma get out and hit da nigga Bugout cuz he in da front passenger seat, jus' lollipoppin'!"

"I'll cover fire from the car on the left," Kaz assured Cumba as he attached silencers on his trusty .40 caliber Glocks. He already had on a white and black demon mask, hoody pulled over his dreads as he shoved the pistol into his right jacket pocket. "We *can't* miss this fool so empty the clip at his head, nigga!"

Cumba heard him and jumped out of the car. He slid the door back shut and started off in the direction of the luxury vehicle. As he approached he heard them banging Gunna's new shit, so they weren't hearing much.

"Go, nigga! Move dis shit!" Kaz barked as he readied two of his own silenced pistols.

Ammo mashed on the gas pedal just as Cumba was approaching the idling SUV. As he walked past it he began to wonder if Bugout had armor or bullet-proofed glass on the top-of-the-line Land Rover – Range Rover luxury vehicle. However, he was talking on the telephone and smoking a cigarette with the window cracked open.

That was all Cumba needed. Counting on his fellow assassins to have his back he was on Bugout's ass like ashy skin. He had the foreboding barrel of his suppressed firearm pressed so close to Bugout's brain that the flash from the two bullets burned his skin. That was all it took for Bugout to be cooked. His brains were hanging like President Kennedy's…

As Kaz had promised, as the van drove by, he was aiming and squeezing off rounds at the others as they attempted to jump out on Cumba and attempt fate. Kaz hit 'em both!

"Stop, nigga!" Kaz ordered. He got out and finished all them niggas off with twin cannons!

"Ride mufucka! Let's ride!" Kaz stated as he jumped back inside of the van.

They turned the corner and Cumba leaped inside. They hit the parkway several blocks away and drove all the way down into the Bronx where they parked the van inside of an indoor garage near Castle Hill Projects.

From there they opted to take the subway back uptown to

East 233rd and Laconia Avenue where they were picked up by Amris in Tate's tricked out obsidian black 1961 Riviera.

"You got what I asked for?" Kaz inquired as she drove South.

"Trunk," she stated with a nod.

They went back to the Castle Hill garage to retrieve the van. Cumba removed the stolen plates and together, they emptied out the entire vehicle. Amris Brazil Heighlon was a 29-year-old, 5 foot 5-inch, brown skinned woman originally from out of South Central, Los Angeles that Kaz had known since the both of them were in Elementary school. Kaz had seen her being bullied by other boys when she'd been in the 2nd grade; teased because of the big black framed glasses she'd had to wear.

When Kaz saw her crying, subsequent to her hair being pulled and her glasses being broken, it angered him. Then the other girls and boys were in the sand box out in the playground laughing at her – the majority of them had been boys: some White, some Black, others Mexican-AmeriKKKan. In short, Kaz had bloodied the nose of the main bully and won the "big-eyed love" of the ugly duckling: Amris Brazil Heighlon at school back then.

Shortly after that her family moved to Orange County, California and they'd lost contact for nearly fifteen years before she found him on Facebook. She'd kept trying to remind him of who she was, the skinny girl with braces, thick eyebrows, short nappy hair, and other features.

You were my hero in second grade, she messaged him online. *I told a million people the story of this boy standin' up for me when you punched a bully in the nose for me.*

He'd messaged back: *Punched a lot of them. But one girl I never forgot cuz of her smile and she lemme kiss her. My first kiss. Oh, and she got a funny name.*

That was when she'd sent him a school photograph with her name and it had been unmistakable: *"Amris Brazil Heighlon."* The middle name was supposed to be *"Basil."* The hospital had misprinted it and when it was discovered her parents, they'd agreed to keep it instead of having to pay a $10 correction fee to The Department of Vital Statistics for California.

Amris had shown Kaz hundreds of photographs and she'd directed him to see her on Instagram, Twitter, Snapchat, and so forth. The ugly duckling had grown into a beautiful swan. And not just any swan but the loveliest one out of all of them.

"I'm just gonna be upfront," she had grabbed his attention just around the time Kaz had agreed to roll out to New York and work for Sage. "I've done nudity. And I mean inside of the sleaziest magazines."

"Aight. If we gon' roll together I ain't wit it," he had reciprocated honesty with honesty. "I don't share my bitches," he'd told her over dinner when they first met as adults.

"We'll, lemme put it all on da table, baby. Niggas can't always handle what I did in my past," she started. And because of the comfortability she'd felt with Kaz the truth seemed to pour back then for her. "But this how I roll, man. When I was doin' magazine work I was mortified and alcohol ain't do shit. So I got hooked on zanies. Second – different shit. Once I was high I was Oscar – worthy in front of cameras like the best bitches in the game: *Morena Baccarin, Jessica Parker Kennedy, Carmela Zumbad, Dona Chaplin, Joy Bryant, Regina Hall, Haley Bennett, Gugu Mbatha-Raw, Teyana Taylor, Carmen Aub, Genesis Rodriguez, Lisseth Chavez, Nathalie Emmanuel...*"

She'd taken a moment as he'd waited on her to continue.

"Well," she'd went on. "Once you do the mags, in comes fresher faces, out goes the old. So now I'm stuck with a pill habit, a mortgage, and a two-year-old son whose father can be anyone's. But I'd give my life for him. He came about when I started doing triple X-rated adult entertainment with Pinky's company. I did six men total while in the industry and nearly quit when they were tryin' to get me to do anal and take ten, eleven, twelve, and even one dude with a fourteen-inch dick."

Kaz had been trying to wrap his head around it when he'd burst out laughing. "I thought bigger is better. Ain't a man I know don't want a fourteen-inch poker."

"He'd be a dumb lonely fucker," she'd said seriously. "Women have little pussies by nature – for most of us. We may be able to give birth but that's why it takes nine months... God stretchin' us *slowly* open. Getting' all the pieces to work right, so the baby can come. The average dick on a black man is about five and a half, six inches. A bitch get a five incher that's wide enough around to rub our walls – *we good*! A seven incher is a heaven sent, big dick as long as it's about as round as a ping pong ball or golf ball. Bitches is fightin' each other for a seven incher. An *eight* incher is not normal. Ask any Black or Spanish woman – an eight-inch cock ping pong/golf ball around? Keep it completely shaven – your bitch gon' wanna suck on it like a lollipop, she's gon' wanna suck your balls, your asshole, and even if you got ugly feet, she wouldn't mind at least kissing them because there's something so beautiful and marvelous about such a huge 8-inch dick."

She'd had Kaz laughing. "Damn. You seem pretty sure about cock sizes. And knowledgeable."

"Martha Stewart, Gail King, Oprah, Jennifer Hudson – none of them would lie about that," Amris had tried to joke. But she sighed. "I was afraid to be stretched out, sore all the time so I nearly had to quit porno. I had a heart-to-heart talk with the boss – Pinky herself – and I was offered lesbian porn and oral… breast fuckin' is one of my favorites and they did a lot of toe/foot worship because my legs are nice and my feet small, pretty, and dainty."

"Dainty?" he asked her as they shared a laugh. "Is that your word or theirs?"

"Pinky's!" Amris had blushed. "Anyhow, that's my whole truth…oh! Well, I'd signed a contract with Pinky for eight films, twenty-five grand for each, not knowing I was pregnant. I'd been in an orgy film *Keepin' Up Wit Da Carblackians*. It was wild and even fun… but only God knows who my son's father is. One of them bastards nutted in me and the pill ain't work."

Their dinner date had not been a disaster. Kaz had tried not to sleep with her although she'd stayed the night as his Los Angeles apartment. He had learned that she had given up the business, had no AIDS, Herpes, Hepatitis C, or anything of the sort. He'd went online and saw literally dozens and dozens of films she had either starred or co-starred in.

He dug the shit out of her and her little son, Maseo. He had these almond-shaped eyes like Amris, her brown skin, and that smile that he'd remembered about her after so long. When he ordered her XXX-rated movies his mind and body became seduced and made up. She had one of the illest bodies he'd ever seen. The way he had witnessed her being fucked like a slut by different men was mind-blowing. And she had to have magical pussy, too, with the speed she could make them lose their nut. And her mouth. She had them lovely Jennifer Hudson's joints – lookin' like she could suck the paint off a New York fire hydrant in the middle of Times Square.

Kaz had spent the entire night watching females suck her fat ass and juicy cunt. And then, what had made Kaz shower, get dressed, and speed across the city to ring her apartment buzzer was one particular masturbation video via *Onlyfans.com*. She had a rabbit dildo which she used on herself but out of nowhere – like forty-five minutes into the hot, sweaty, act – she'd dropped the dildo. Then she frigged her small erect clitoris for what seemed like a thousand times…

Then the ultimate happened.

She cried and whimpered for a minute straight. A full *one-minute* as her pussy cream *geysered* like the steamy blast of a hot spring in the morning sun. Eddie Murphy would've been proven wrong: some females indeed do have sunshine and sparks shooting out of their vaginas, (Eddie Murphy's "*Raw*").

When Kaz had been let up into Amris Brazil Heighlon's apartment, he'd looked her in the eyes and said, "Of all the women I've met, nobody except you told the truth even when you know a nigga or see a nigga you like and think he'll ditch your phone number, call you a ho, or diss you some other way."

She had sat with him in her living room. "That's why I just say it. I tell it all – even though I don't do that no mo!"

"What do you do?" he'd asked her.

"CVS security guard, and cook coke, bag crack, bag boy for hustlaz," she'd admitted with a shrug. "I mean whatta happen when he ten, thirteen, and sixteen? I gotta be doin' somethin' else I told myself. I need Maseo to respect me for what I *do* not done."

He'd kissed her. Really, really, kissed her and said, "I been doin' *NOTHING BUT* thinkin' boutchu since we re-met. And I need you, Amris. I-"

She'd smiled all giddily because she was feeling him. "Need?"

"I haveta be honest, too," he'd said, touching her soft face, small ears, and long silky black hair.

Her heart sank. "Are you gay? Married? Got a small dick? I can learn to love a small dick since -"

He'd hushed her. She was so funny. "Nah, I got one of them marvelous eight inchers all clean-shaven."

"Boy sheeiiiddd!" she'd stated. "Make yo fine ass have my baby."

"Imma hitter," he'd admitted. "And me and my team been hired as drug enforcers and assassins for a New York drug Kingpin. We 'bout to go live in New York. Ain't nuttin' in L.A."

She'd stared at him. "I'm not afraid…Been around Killaz and D-boyz my whole life. But if you askin' me to go, I'm goin' as one unit or just leave us here and I'll see you when you visit. Maseo need a real man around. So do I. Is thatch?"

He'd nodded and that's when they first made love and fucked. Human for a period and a wild pair of beasts from the bottom of the sea. A male and female megalodon with limbs. Hours later…

"Just one more thing," she'd requested in that sweet voice of hers. "Before we do anything or go anywhere, I need you to watch my movies so…then I'll know you won't judge me."

"I watched 'em all night yesterday," he said and laughed. "I loved everything. Youse a fuckin' hustla… bitch deserve respect and them niggas who you tried it wit, should be on they knees kissin' your feet. As for lil Maseo, he need a father and a Daddy. You gon' be my wife and Imma adopt him soon as we get solid. Word on my flag."

She loved Kaz since 2nd grade. He was her hero then, accepting her, and he's her hero now, not judging her.

They drove the van into an abandoned shoe factory, soaked it inside out with twenty gallons of gasoline, including two twenty-gallon bleach bombs with timers attached. Kaz exited the van and got inside the Riviera with his fiancée. Cumba and Ammo sat in the rear. Cumba waited until they were about seven blocks up before he used two burner cellphones to call into the cellphones attached on the bleach-bombs. Within twenty seconds they looked back and saw an enormous black plume of smoke rising into the air.

"Where to, Daddy?" she asked her man.

"Let's head to da crib," Kaz stated with a sigh.

Nobody mentioned what had happened. That's not how they rolled anyhow.

"Love you, baby," he said, kissing her.

"Mm, you better," she stated back. "I love you more than all the love in da Empire State."

CHAPTER TWENTY-ONE

"Your son's killer is dead."
Chicago, Illinois

Although Sage may still had some very profound reasons not to sign off on the final (so-called) hit list, to hear that the Rollin 60's Assassins had punched Bugout's ticket was extremely good news. Rocky Taylor could Rest In Peace now. Coldhearted called Tanya.

"Your son's killer is dead, Ms. T," C.H. told her. She gasped and began to cry. "We got justice for him the way Rock woulda wanted it."

"This family is your family, Sage," she told him as she controlled her emotions as best she could. "I love you- okay?"

"Love you back." C.H. texted Chubb next, Rock's baby

brother. **Go be wit ya mom right now. She heard what happened to Bugout.** C.H. texted him using the TextSecure encryption app. Chubb, Sonja, Sunny, and Choir Boy were all tucked away at the ritzy house in Larchmont working on the cellphone and other digital devices as ordered. That plan had started out slow but the fruit the Coldhearted organization was harvesting from "*drug clientele poaching*", they couldn't make it up nor ask for more.

"Ayooo!" C.H. banged on the door to the Sprinter where Tate and Deuce were both snoozing. "They got da nigga Bugout!"

Tate and Deuce stretched, "Dead?" they chorused.

Sage nodded. "Buzzard meal my nigga. *Food*. Morgue Cemetery."

"Zombie, ghost, Tupac, B.I.G., Bill Cosby ... oh wait, he still alive, he jus' look dead! Ha! Ha! Ha!" Tate burst out laughing.

"In da case *Joe Biden*!" Deuce said. "Skelator from *He-Man* lookin' -"

"Oh my god! That nigga look like ready to snap a limb!" Sage exclaimed. "Skinny fucker from Delaware he was the Senator who wrote, the fuckin' 1996 *Crime Bill* – fuckin' leadin' to prisons burstin' at the seams wit Blacks and Latinos. And who votes him in as President? DUMB ASS BLACK LIVES MATTER ass mufuckaz. Like bendin' over-*naked* this time – spreadin' open da globes and sayin' to da goddamned cracka *'STICK YA BOOT RIGHT HERE, MASSUH BIDEN, SIR.'* And what old Biden do?"

"Shoved that shiny old black shoe dead up the Black, Latino, Non-white assholes," Deuce finished. "He ain't just put it on da left cheek or right cheek but up da ASSHOLE of every Steve Harvey ass mufucka who fought each day to get that crack an even *bigger noose* for niggas necks."

Tate was nodding. "That's right. When it come to the Black man Joe Biden is Doctor Death. AmeriKKKan President Reagan gave the okay for us to be intentionally poisoned with 98% pure Bolivian cocaine Marine Lieutenant Colonel Oliver North was told by Reagan under no circumstances are the Nicaraguan Contras to fall to their knees during the Contra-Sandinista war. So Oliver North conspired with Bolivian mega-drug lord Roberto Suarez Gomez, his cousin General Meza (Bolivia) and the CIA to overthrow duly-elected Bolivian President Lidia Guellier and make Garcia Meza *dictator*. In public Reagan called it a *"Cocaine Dictatorship,"* because Bolivia's #1 Gross Domestic product (or GDP) is the coca plant. As Dictator, in 1980 to 1981, his beloved cousin Suarez Gomez is manufacturing in excess of *100 tons* of 98% raw and uncut cocaine per month and these staggering amounts of narcotics were entering the United States daily with the help of President Ronald Reagan's *do-boy* Oliver North and the CIA."

"No shit," C.H. stated as he texted Liza.

"Yeah," Tate said strongly. "They overloaded the Long Beach/L.A. Ports. You heard of Freeway Rick Ross."

"*I'm a hustla, Imma, Imma Imma hustla,*" Deuce started reciting rap lyrics. "Rick Ross. That black nigga?"

"Imposter. Nope. Not the real one," Tate stopped him. "*RICKY DONNELL ROSS* was a CIA scapegoat who was approached by CIA by dark operative Norwin Meneses to move the coke... to the poor. To Blacks. We were the intentional target of the poison. That wasn't the plan. The ghettos of Los Angeles, San Bernardino, Riversdale, El Centro, San Diego. California was first. Then Phoenix, Mesa, Tempe, Arizona. *CRACK*. That's why Gary Webb wrote the book *Dark Alliance* with the foreword by iconic black U.S. Senator Maxine Waters. And Lou Garden Price, Sr's book *SOSAFROMSCARFACE* highlights the dark truths about modern day slave masters like Biden, the Democratic Party, and even *niggers* like Michael Jordan who are profiters in private prisons. Yet we out here financing his black ass by wearin' his funky ass sneaks and other apparel."

"You said Democrats? My mom always vote Democrat," Deuce mentioned. "Obama's Democrat."

"Man...only thing good about Obama is Michelle's ass and them pretty cock-suckin' lips Malia and Sasha got," Tate scowled. "That nigga didn't remove all them slave owners off da U.S. Currency...He used drone strikes to kill more brown people...And like all the other Democrats they create policies that make them richer, the country poorer, and they're repeating the same old lies just to stay relevant. Following Democrats will eventually strip us all of our souls."

"But why? For real. Why you say dat?" C.H. asked him. Tate grabbed his attention with that last comment.

"My family, we came up in the church," Tate told him. "We believe in a right to life. Democrats, a right to choose. Meanin' abortions. Once a child is conceived that child has a natural right to live. To be born. I believe that. Democrats would do away wit my rights to guns...okay, the God I know says homosexuality is an abomination. Democrats – many who are powerful closet homosexuals in Government – create laws that contradict God's Word. In fact they are making many perversions of the Holy Bible such as *The Queer's Version*. And gay congregations."

Liza finally called Coldhearted. "You do what I say, sweetie?" he asked her.

"Kaz, Cumba, Ammo, Amris – Papi, I don't know all your men's names but them three and they ladies are here like you told me and we on lockdown 'til you get back," Liza told him. "Where's my cousins at?"

"We told them to make a day of it shoppin' and err'thang while we slept," he explained via RedPhone app. "You on RedPhone right?"

"Duh, I'm a gangster's wife for life," she snapped. "What I need to ask I can't ask but I miss you."

He knew what she wanted to ask. Exactly when would the

E.T.A be for their return from Chicago. They normally came to the Windy City and pulled into "Fiji Gold" on 47th and Indiana which was one of those rare strip clubs that had superb food. And not just any food but delicious Mediterranean cuisine. This time, they dropped in just to make contact but there was going to be a full day's delay, Don Armadillo's courier told them.

So they'd left Fiji Gold and took a ride through The Loop and ended up at Premium Storage on Grand Boulevard. They ordered a 20' x 30' unit and parked the Bronco inside. Before leaving C.H. had removed all four tires and placed two GPS trackers in clandestine areas of the SUV. Last, he'd placed a tiny spy camera on the edge of the opposite rooftop and brought it up onto his cellphone. He'd had to unsheathed one of his machetes to adjust the camera. It had all been exhausting but necessary in order to safely stash $1.7 million in cash."

"Yeah, I know whatchu wanna ask. I wanna answer. Times like these, I'm glad money allows cats like that around. Y'all know how to lock yourself in downstairs – not even fire could get to y'all under there," he said, tapping Tate to grab his phone. Tate and Deuce were playing Xbox.

Tate shot Noni and Deca the directions to give their Uber driver. "Da girls comin' back."

"Don't hang up – Facetime me, matter fact," C.H. stated as he drove into the storage unit parking lot. "Tate, the Uber comin' here or da telly?"

"Here- stop fuckin' cheatin', Dee! I saw you hit reset, nigga! Every time I buss ya ass on da first round, you hit reset! Pay up nigga, dats sixty, no, now *eighty*!" Tate stuck his hand out.

Deuce paid up. "Fuck you, Unc."

"Daniela here, too," Liza mentioned, hanging up the *RedPhone* line and switching over to an iPhone for Facetime. "Shit like this make me say you was right. 'Bout not sellin'."

"You mean the house?" She nodded. "Told you. How you do at auction?" he almost forgot to question her about that.

"Oh! God, man, really good," she stated. "The Rolls hit for $40k…the Winnebago $28k," she paused to look over some paperwork.

She spoke again moments later. "Babe, 'member da Italian repos done in same 14th and 15th Century periods? I thought I'd get $19k each for the Masaccio, Donatello da Vinci, Raphael's *Galatea, Madonna*…I got even more: $100k for all of them."

"*Jesus Christ*! You serious?"

"As cancer. And the cars are ready," she reported. "Just saw the email and the text."

"Babe, Imma say this once, ya feel me?" he stated really carefully. "Don't let me back out of it either. Okay?"

"Uhn-huhn. What is it?" she commanded now.

"We sellin' da house at a very steep price. Three million five hundred thousand – completely furnished," he decided which mildly surprised her. "And we leave for the Dominican Republic next Wednesday."

She was very happy to hear it.

"Hold on, babe…" He had to answer another burner. They were ready to take the truck and the cash. "Gotta go handle it, *mi amor*."

"Love you."

CHAPTER TWENTY-TWO

"I hug a snake, kiss an enemy."
P-Man's Rage

C.H. called Taizhan and she picked up the phone on the second ring. "I heard what happened and I need to talk with P-Man to try not goin' to war!"

She was hesitant. "My fuckin' god. Sage, are you usin' RedPhone or anything?" Taizhan inquired.

"RedPhone," he told her. "917-386-4388. But tell him I'm in Chicago. Have been for the last couple days – wit my fuckin' capo and lieutenant so it couldn't been us goddamnit."

Within minutes C.H. was on Facebook Live standing outside of the iconic Sears Tower. "See dis shit? See my capo, head of security?"

Tate looked into the camera.

"And my lieutenant Double Deuce," Coldhearted stated.

"So what, nigga? Youse in fuckin' Chi-Town, My Town, while you had ya folks murk mine!" P-Man barked at him.

"P-Man. We had a fuckin' understandin' so we could get dis KREAM. Imma risk the peace for a daylight fuckin' hit on your men?! LOOK in my eyes, son. It was no one on my team. I owe two million in consignment and bills out da ass to da bank…" C.H. added on. Then, with an incredulous look on his face he raised his palms. "And look… with one text, you could have us shot, diced up, and scattered at the bottom of Lake Michigan. So, this where I call you from if we had anything to do wit it?"

"Yeah…" up to that point, C.H., Tate, and Deuce had only been able to see the Almighty Black P. Stone Gangster's head and deep-set dark brown beady eyes. He was a 6-foot 1 inch brown-skinned brolick ass motherfucker. Someone was holding the phone for him. "You ain't think this raggedy old crib was mine did you?" he stated as he walked through what looked like a crackhouse.

"Nah- I mean I ain't thank nuttin', son," C.H. told him.

"They told me youse a beast wit the Internet, the dark web, especially that VULKANYK store y'all had, right?"

C.H. didn't answer that. "We encrypted so you understand."

"I do," P-Man told him. "You know we encrypted, right?"

Sage nodded. "Yeah, P."

"But you realize we up inside one of yo traphouses. You *guessed* it! Didn'tchu?" His voice was calm, assertive.

"Yeah. C'mon, to da car," he told Tate and Deuce. "To da city. We mashin' out."

"Hold ya horses, Blood!" P-Man demanded, walking to the kitchen. There was a small child in a highchair holding a spoon with oatmeal falling from it. He was eating plus making a mess.

On the floor in the kitchen, facedown, were four black adults. P-Man had his mask on now, his brown hoody pulled upwards over his head.

"I believe you," P-Man said as he turned over one of the bloodied, motionless people on the linoleum. He looked back at the camera not having to show any more.

C.H. was driving the ultimate in luxury SUV's. The GMC Hummer EV Pickup Edition 1. Interstellar, white over jet black, light gray alligator leather interior, air ride adaptive suspension, clean Carfax, trailering package, rear theatre configuration and shooting star headliner. The high-end coast-to-coast cars that Don-Armadillo's sons got their hands on were something out of *Fast & Furious* franchise. The GMC Hummer was price at $279,000 and C.H. was definitely trying to make a play for a million-dollar fleet. All papers and titles *clean.*

"You with me, Coldhearted?" P-Man called out to him.

"Yeah, who you got there witchu in that house?" C.H. wanted to know. He was getting real angry about that shit.

He looked at Deuce and asked, "Who was in dat fuckin' video?"

"Don't worry 'bout it, kiddo," P-Man waved him off. "You scared I snatched ya family up? Nah, nigga, I ain't getchu like that yet. Don't think I can't though. This shit happened when Bugout nem got killed. These some of yo Bronx homiez."

He paused.

"Then I know y'all poaching our clientele," the well-built hardened killer expressed. "People tell me y'all are cold-calling my fiendz, passin' out free crack hits and dope cuz y'all got a superior product. My ear is all over da city, son. Tell 'em Wham, yo Stacy -"

Two other goons who were in the room mumbled something. Coldhearted stopped at the hotel to get the Sprinter and the girls, Noni, and Deva.

"It's Junior nem!" Deuce recalled because they had a fucking army of niggas. "Big Junior."

"We P. Stone, you *Sixty,* so what?" the big blood boss shrugged. "I hug a snake, kiss an enemy, cuz only green means shit to me. But y'all mufuckaz not playin' fair. You riggin' da game up. I start out respecting you out here instead of playin' Russian roulette witchu…cuz I like Russia. I hear your story and I'm like let da young nigga do what he do. Now I see I gotta use *steamy tactics,* too."

"Y'all go on up outta there," C.H. finally said when the baby kept crying. "You made ya point."

"I hope so," the Almighty Black P. Stone leader stated.

"Now see? *Leaving.* C'mon y'all. Untie da lady. She prolly grandma. Mommy one of da ones still occupied…Let's see."

As he walked to the first bedroom a naked dark-skinned man was forcing a heavyset, pretty, brown skinned teen to perform an oral sex act upon him. The man had on a face mask.

"This sick fuckin' freak!" Coldhearted cursed as he stared at Deuce and Tate. "I was at Junior's, you sure that's one of his peoples? That girl look 13 or 14."

Deuce nodded and used his cellphone to call Junior.

When there was no answer they just packed it in and drove on out to New York. They had no idea just how sick and twisted P-Man and them other Almighty Black P. Stones turned out to be.

Absolutely shocking the hell one human can take another human being through.

CHAPTER TWENTY-THREE

"Stood Face to Face with Junior"
Mt. Vernon, New York

Instead of heading directly to Mt. Vernon first, Sage, Tate, Deuce, Noni, and Deva drove on up to the PRAY dealerships where they turned over the Sprinter. Tate opted to drive the obsidian clearcoat black Maybach while Deuce followed in the metallic blue Bentley Continental-GT Speed.

An hour later they were following the luxurious white Hummer- EV pickup truck as it negotiated its way up through the driveway and into the garage for each of the three opulent vehicles. Almost as soon as the garage doors closed they began to remove the kilos of heroin and cocaine from the Hummer.

Once the narcotics, illegal drug proceeds – and illegal weapons – were all stashed inside of the house's clandestine underground security boxes (not even the best Police K-9 could find them), C.H. always breathed better. Only he and Liza knew how to access these particular stash units which were located beneath the underground panic room/workshop. C.H. never allowed Tate, Deuce, or anyone else to see the *"trick wall."*

"Boss, come upstairs," Tate heard C.H. whispering or talking in foreboding, sinister tones in Spanish with Liza, Daniela, and someone on Snapchat. "You got company outside."

Coldhearted walked with Tate out into the garage where the Escalade was parked and they had the side door open. C.H. stepped out onto the patio and stood face-to-face with Junior. Liza appeared with her husband because she was feeling *bothered* and just flat out missed him. Coldhearted stepped aside and let Junior in.

"It's – my fam in the car and -" Junior started, pointing a thumb over his shoulder. "I-I don't…"

"Ayo Junior!" C.H. stated firmly. "Don't come up here like you broken or a bitch."

"I ain't neither, cuz. Just tryna respect yo shit and Liza's!" Junior snapped angrily.

C.H. nodded. "More like it."

They walked together out to where Junior had his silver 2011 Tahoe parked and idling. Liza, Tate, Deuce, Kaz, Cumba,

Ammo, and Daniela were standing around. Everyone knew that P-Man and at least a dozen of his goon's had followed Junior from Garter's strip club and caught Junior slippin'. That's how he'd got got.

"The Mercedes G550 Squared," Ammo said to the huge man with a pistol-whip gash above his right eye. "I don't see it."

"Err'body out," Junior ordered. He looked at Ammo. "Me and wifey was comin' outta Garter's when we was jumped, hit over da head, and zip tied. Threw us in the back of da G-wagon. They search me and my address is on my crib in the B-X. They tie up my sister Delores; they see our apartment is full of our girl's wit a slumber party."

"P-Man and nem followed yo blue G-550 Squared Wagon all day way from Garter's to yo crib on Carpenter Avenue?" C.H. questioned Junior. "In the Bronx?"

Junior nodded. "Yep."

Junior's sister, Delores, was his complete opposite. Although she was slender, for some reason, she walked with a hunch in her back – as if she carried Junior's huge ass around on her shoulders all day.

"So they jacked the G-550, right?" Liza wondered aloud.

Junior nodded again. "That's right."

There were five eerily quiet young brown skinned girls who stayed glued to their seats inside of the older model Chevrolet. Two of the girls – ages 9-year-old were named Ingram and the 10-year-old was named after Junior and

Delores' mother who was no longer around. Her name was Betilda – Betti for short.

Junior's daughters were all bigger than they should be at their age. Not *"heavyset"* and certainly not *"overweight."* Such terms at their new charter school were not allowed. Bigger *than she should be* was perfectly acceptable.

Junior's youngest baby was eleven. Her name was Cassara. His baby in the middle was Jubilee. "Juby" for shot. She was thirteen years old. And last was his fifteen-year-old, Michelle.

"Y'all comin' outta da truck?" Junior coaxed his oldest child. "Michelle, why dontchu take da girls inside where it's safe?"

Michelle climbed out of the Tahoe and followed Liza and the other women indoors. The men stayed in the attached garage structure at first to hear from Junior. And when all of the details emerged it had just about everyone getting behind Junior for blood…

Liza, Delores, Lilly, and Daniela gathered up themselves and Junior's daughters for dinner, snacks, and Netflix inside of the living room. All the men headed into C.H.'s home office-study.

"First off, for da record, Junior had been behind on some payment, and I cut his ear off not that long ago," C.H. stated with a shrug. "He paid up one hundred percent."

Kaz shook his head, laughing. "It ain't funny but C.H. a funny nigga."

"Nah," C.H. started. "Point bein' that Junior's Rollin 60 and he real flashy which is prolly why dem 550 niggas was huntin' him and his fam down. Nobody condonin' shit. Three top Almighty Black P. Stones nem snatch Junior, Delores… Junior's wife. Them little girls."

Sage excused himself for a few minutes and returned with two suitcases. He removed a M-67 grenade from his jacket pocket. "This kinda revenge will bring out the FBI, ATF, and ultimately prison," Sage commented.

He replaced the grenade and opened up one of the suitcases. And then the other.

"The grenade was Door Number 1. These suitcases are Door Number Two and Door Number Three," Sage told them as he opened up one of them and then the other.

Junior stood up shaking his head. "I can't fuck wit Number Two or Three. I'm barely a clean shot up close, son. That shit there's some guerilla Army Ranger sniper shit from a fuckin' *Jason Borne* movie or somethin'."

"I couldn't fuck wit a can opener 'til I practiced witta can opener, son," Tate pointed out to him. "Now, Number Two… that's made to order. It's why they have a sniper school in the U.S. Army. This shit is the M-107 Semi-Automatic Long Range Sniper Rifle. It's a .50 caliber system capable of delivering precise rapid fire on targets 2000 meters out. Extremely valuable in military operations in urban terrain where greater firepower and standoff ranges increase the effectiveness of counter sniper tactics."

"This one looks less intimidating," Junior observed. "Number Three here."

"I don't agree." Tate held it up. "This one is total opposite of Number Two. The M-110 sniper system is 7.62 mm's. This fires 7.62 double-m ammo to a range of 800 meters not 2000 – huge difference. But it's like an AK-47 on steroids... 800 meters out. It's a *maneater*."

"Can we be trained?" Junior asked. "I mean in a short time?"

Tate looked Junior in the eye. "I was in the Army long enough to learn how to teach y'all how to handle these type weapons. So, yeah. Fuck yeah, mufucka."

"Aight," Sage state with a serious nod. "C'mon, get yo family comfortable. We got a lot to unravel. But we gotchu, son. Tate get online to Air BNB and find a remote upstate New York ranch where y'all can do some shooting at without being disturbed by the State boys. Use the SHZ, Inc. debit account."

"Somethin' cheap?" Tate asked him.

"Son, we sittin' on *millions* in boy and girl... it's a *Maybach* and *Bentley* outside," Sage reminded him. "Get the right spot and don't cause attention."

An hour later Tate had located an upstate New York mansion in Sidney along the Susquehanna River. The price tag was decent $38,00 for a week. Tate booked it for two weeks and rented two helicopters. They were Model 22 Robinson helicopters. Both were black and white in color and were at the Sidney, New York, ranch-style home when Junior, his family, and Tate arrived.

The plan was simple. Tate would immediately set up a long-distance training course, which was what he did. The land was set up as a ranch, but the previous owner had died and left it behind to his four children: three women, one man. The siblings did not want to maintain the livestock, so they had to be sold off.

What the children had decided on was to lease out the 27-room ranch house and 108-acre spread and do away with all the animals. They had brought in a landscape architect with a first class resumé and reputation and he created a fabulous piece of land.

Tate ordered a truckload of coconuts and another which was loaded with cool spring water. They had wooden 6" by 8" posts with 4' x 6' foot aluminum signs with various numbers and either the word FEET, YARDS, MILE MARKER 1, or MILE MARKER 1 ½ on them. On the top of them were four seven-inch nails with spiked tips which were affixed there to secure in place the coconuts.

"Baby, you hired all them?" Tate asked Deva when he, Junior, and his nephew Spooky arrived to the rear of the mansion after double checking the shooting range set up. There were at least ten coconuts at each marker. When they made it back to the main house there was a group of about 55 Latinos who had used the "$5 vans" from out of Binghamton,

Syracuse, Hudson County (New York) to answer *"labor wanted"* ads on Facebook Marketplace and Craigslist.

Deva looked at her man when she stepped out of the front of the house in her white goosedown Burberry coat, black women's Coogi sweater, and Apple Bottoms jeans. She had on black ladies Timberland high ankle boots with black leather gloves. "Babes…" she said back to her soon to be husband. "What Imma do, send 'em back and we end up needin' them all? Right guys?" she asked an older woman who was standing with a younger female.

"That's right, ma'am," a Black man answered as he eyed Deva's beautiful plump buttocks as she approached the group of drivers of the vans that had brought the workers from all over upstate. Their advertisements had specifically stated that they would pay only for those labored workers hired who were among the first fifty applicants accepted. She paid each of the van drivers and added an extra $25 tip to wait.

Everyone she pointed at to dismiss, she gave them $25 for coming. The man who had just answered her minutes before saying, "That's right, ma'am," had to be at least 40 maybe even 50 but he wasn't even Latino like the others. He was 'bout 6 feet 6 or so, bald-headed, reminded her of Kobe Bryant. But he had dimples. "I almost dismissed you, Old Man. Don't let my fiancé see you checkin' my ass out like that. He'll kill you up here," she said in a low voice. "You're not Latino. Why would an AmeriKKKan be on Latino labor van lines up north this far?" she questioned him. "And what's your name?"

"Antwán but I did like how you call me Old Man. Can I speak to you on the sidebar please?" he asked, wanting to break away from the group.

She walked about five feet away and he followed her, glancing at that beautiful backside of hers again. He wanted to touch it.

"I can't lie to y'all," he said honestly. "I got a gun charge from outta da city. I skipped court."

"Why be honest wit us? We could just text the cops… and be done witchu," she said, shrugging. "You know what… fuhgeddaboudit. Get ya tall sexy ass back in line. Yo gon' get me in trouble." He made her pussy wet instantly.

"Old Man" stepped back in line. He felt the attraction too.

The dismissed people numbered nine which left Deva with 46 workers. "Papi, you wanna let them know the mechanics or what?" she asked Tate.

"Choose a Foreman or Forewoman," Tate told her. "And make the supervisor and let them choose an assistant. Supervisors make $250 more than their assistant and assistant make only $100 more than everyone else. Regular pay is $370 each week. We're not quipped to take everyone inside the main house but there is a three-bedroom cottage and a brand-new unattached luxury garage at the end of the white stone road – next to the old barn. It looks sort of like a house but it's not. The rest of you can stay out there until the tour buses and

Windstream trailers arrive. Y'all can bunk ten in each of those buses. Imma tell you right now…"

Tate saw young – *very young* Mexican, Guatemalan, Honduran, Colombian – women in the group. He counted about *twenty*. The other seven women were older and not obvious targets of the men. "If I hear of any stealin', Imma street nigga. No cops will be called, just us cuttin' off your hands. And we *despise* rapists and child molesters. Any man that take advantage of any of these women, or kids, your hands – and your dick -will be cut off. Matter fact, Imma let her do it so if she want to cut out other parts, we gon' let her, right, Deva?"

"That's right, Papi," she stated. "Damn right!"

Once the help had settled in, Tate hit up Deuce and let him know he was chilling. "Look, Neff, I got Junior up here and those two Robinson civilian helicopters. I have some basic knowledge about flyin' but da boss is payin' for private lessons while we up here. So I got an old friend of mine who gonna teach all of us. Ayo, is Kaz around?"

"Damn, he was just here wit Amris," Deuce informed him. "I'm here. It's rainin' like fuck and I gotta go to drop." He meant cash for the boss man. "You and me already made fifteen grand for the K2 and pills he let us have."

"Awesome, Lil Daddy," Tate told him as he entered his and Deva's room. The bed was GIGANTIC. He took a photo of it and texted it to Deuce and Sage. "This shit is an actual brand called *ULTRA-KING-SIZED* Inc. Crazy huh? Fourteen feet across, eleven feet long. Wow. I'll holla. I'm 'bout to shower, son."

He texted Deva and told her to come shower with him. She texted him back: **Be there in ten. Talkin' with one of the Guatemalan girls.**

The sun had set already on the posh green land of the Sidney mansion. Deva was inside of the women's bathroom which was located on the eastern end of the tennis courts inside of the same building as the men's bathroom and the showers. As she was coming out she ran into "Old Man" who had taken it upon himself to shower before anyone else became aware of the nicely laid out office area back there.

"What are you up to, Old Man?" Deva smiled as he told her to follow him real quick.

"I figured I'd check it out." He walked into the building and the office actually had a long black sofa with pillows on it as if the previous owners had been aware of the comfortable sofa. "I hope you don't mind, sweet, beautiful thing. It'll be just me in here. There's a computer, Internet, WI-FI. I should be payin' *you*."

He had a towel wrapped around him and a NYU sweatshirt on. She smiled. "Maybe you should," she flirted.

He stared at her, liking her perfume, everything about her.

"I told you to stop lookin' at me like that," she stated.

"I want to. I will. But you so fuckin' bad and thick, I just… *mm!*" He licked his big juicy lips like LL Cool J. And it made her cunt have a contraction. She could feel it actually dripping.

This old head nigga was *sexy*. As a young girl, like millions of others just like her, Deva loved older men. Didn't matter if they had money or not. The "Daddy thing" was in. He could be 60 and sexy, too. Deva could remember her own father Heriberto Honoret… and he never showed her any love or affection and the same went for Noni who was only a year younger than Deva. Deva really liked Deuce but her heart melted when older, wiser men look at her. Older playas made Deva's pussy wetter, too.

And that's where the weakness began: the warm, loving, way older men looked at her. That longing look of adoration *as if Deva was Old Man's daughter or something*. That's how it was for most of them. Deva had that sweet creamy color of *Telemundo* actress Genesis Rodriquez or *Game of Thrones'* Wife of Rob Stark, Oona Chaplin, perhaps a bit lighter. But hands down, she had the ass of Jessica Parker Kennedy from the *Black Sails* series or Regina Hall from *Girls Trip*. Once older men got past the body and looked into Deva's face, a look that gave her great comfort, safety, care, and protection like a million people's belief combined… That look just penetrated the beautiful Puerto Rican cupcake's Latin soul…and affected her hairless little pussy like a motherfucker. She was such a sucker for them old daddies.

Give him a Viagra – or even the *Cialis* would do – and Deva was his. Like right now, Old Man didn't know that she had become the huntress, and he was the hunted. The pieces would drop soon though.

"Hey, Old Man, you gonna get dressed before you get all ashy?" she asked him. "And it is a lil nippy, ain't it?"

He removed his sweatshirt and opened up his black leather carry-on bag. He also reached inside of it and took out a bottle of Baby Oil. He applied some to his upper torso, arms, face, and lower back. She walked up on him and made his towel drop. He had a semi-hard light brown cock.

"*HOMBRE-HOMBRE!!*" she whispered. "*Dios Mio!* That's a big one! Huh? Does it get… I mean could we…?"

"Make it bigger? Yes. Yeah goddamnit. Hell yeah. Pull your jeans down, mami," he pleaded with her. "I been dreamin' of that prize-winning ass and … even your titties. They bring out the rest of you… there you go. Put your fingers in that clean-smooth-shaven thang!" She fingered her pussy. It was very bald. And very wet.

She got totally nude for him. "No touchin'. I don't cheat. My god, I wanna suck your dick! And your balls really smell masculine. Look at me real close."

He looked down at her little thirteen-year-old girl's feet. They were slender, small, very soft, and pretty. Her left foot had a lovely tattoo of a *Mini Milky Way Galaxy* and the other *enormous* cock with the names *Deva & Bobby Tate*.

She grabbed both of her juicy and soft asscheeks and opened them as if she were opening up the curtains in the master bedroom at 10:00 AM to let in the morning sunlight.

He looked closely at her feet, studying the tattoos on each.

He had to ask her, "So this tattoo of your man bussin' your asshole in...wow look at it now!"

She looked back at him. "You like it? Is it pretty?"

He nodded. "I love how tender, pink, and innocent it looks. Can I smell it and kiss it?" he asked, dropping to his knees to stare.

"Umm," she said, feeling her anus quivering as she turned back around to study how raging hard, long, and thick it was. Measuring it, she deduced it to be at least two and a half inches wide. Maybe three. "No. No, I'm not a cheater. Just smell it. No kissing."

"Oh my god, Deva, I can smell your flavor!" he said, standing up close to her. He hooked his pinky finger into hers. He was taller than her, his face looking down into hers. Her breath hitting his nose. She had the nicest scent. "Baby, you thinkin' what I'm thinkin'? You wanna kiss and fuck, huh? I wanna lick your anus."

"I wanna kiss you, too, you tall, beautiful man," she whispered because his closeness cut off her speech. He smelled like the Mercedes cologne for me. "I know you see and smell all the coochie juices smeared on the insides of my thighs, dontchu?"

He nodded yes to her. "Baby, you have the best breath ever. Lemme just kiss you."

"Can't," she mentioned as she backed up. "My pussy too wet. If I touch you... Imma weaken and let you push that gigantic dick all up inside me. And what if you cum in me?

I'm not on the pill and all I want is my man's baby. But, listen."

He bent over to see if he could sniff her wet steamy heat again. She made his heartbeat fast. "Just open them phat ass juicy thighs, Mami Boriquena. Watch what your special feminine arousal scent does to my big balls and dick. Don't blink, Mami."

"What-?" she mumbled but did as he instructed. She literally observed the veins on the exterior of his monster cock expand in size. They pulsated and throbbed as if air were inside of them and his enormous racket balls moved to the right and left, and then piled up and in tightly.

"See? The smell of that Latina heat, coming from your wet gash, make me nearly splash all my cum out all over this place," he said so seductively that she wanted to slurp and suck on him like a newborn on mommy's titties. She almost ate his warm cum nut on the spot.

She heard herself cry-moaning. "B-because of how it smells to you?? O-Ohkay…"

Silent lust passed between them.

"Jeezus. Lemme tell you a secret, Old Man," she said as a very shy and sexy smile spread across her lovely face. She had one that could never be forgotten like the distinctive voice that came with it. BEAUTY. COURAGE. EDGE. PAIN. LOYALTY. One name came to mind for some reason: "*CARMEN ZUMBADO*" from *CHICAGO PD* – on NBC network television.

Well, it was without a doubt that Carmen Zumbado and Deva Honoret-Garcia both had distinctively lovely face, voices, skin color, natural hair color, and perhaps even more. That was the only reason that the great actress had come to mind for the most part. To draw a comparison between the two women.

For now, Deva was blushing with the secret she wished to reveal to her new "*lust crush.*"

"Secret? I think I like the sound of this particular secret," Old Man replied with a warm chuckle.

"Well..." she figured if she was going to say it then the best way to let it out was not hesitate. "Some people like to see their husband, or boyfriend, or *fiancé*, have sex with another female while they watch. As a woman, I'm open-minded but I'm also only in my early twenties and lost my virginity when I was almost eighteen. This relationship now is my most serious."

"You mean Tate. I can tell from one meeting he's a Los Angeles gangster," Old Man noted. "He looks very serious."

She nodded. "We have *amazing* sex. Truly amazing sex. But he has a fantasy, I have a fantasy. But my fantasy, I'd run before I ever did it. And that is to fuck my stepfather."

Old Man laughed. "Why?"

She laughed and shrugged. "I had the hugest crush on him. My mom was a bitch and he was hot. He's why I like black men. I was nine when he married Mom. He loved to play with us. He never realized it, but he got me off all those times I'd wrestle with him and sit on his powerful muscular legs."

"You were a freak," Old Man said.

"I admit it, yes." She paused. "They sent us to a boarding school in Canada but it became too expensive. I was fourteen, my mom had split with him. That was the issue. I came back home with Noni in her room. Me in mine. I'd play this game knowing he'd come to wake me very early in the morning. It was still dark out. When I'd hear him in Noni's room, I'd pose in my tightest gray satin panties. I'd use a Visine bottle to make a wet puddle in the crotch."

"He'd think your pussy was hot each morning," Old Man said turned on by the visual. "He ever take the bait?"

"He'd come in very quietly and I'd feel his eyes all over my little ninety-five-pound body," she explained. "I wore night shades. So, I'd wear pajama T-shirt, lay on my back, legs spread. I realized then that he was enjoying the scent of my pussy. I'd literally be *leaking* cunt juice in front of him and he wouldn't touch! He'd sit there! And then, one day, out of nowhere, I got so intense of him, his face there. I could *smell* the musty hot heat of my virgin pussy and my sweat and I just started masturbation! Finger banging! One with fingers inside of my anus and the other the back of his head. And I *begged* him! He ate me and I *exploded like a volcano!* When I was done the mattress felt like a rain hit it."

"So you fucked him!?" Old Man surmised.

She shook her head. "No…fourteen-year-old virgin had

squirted again and again! And to this date, I still fantasize of fucking my pervert stepfather. He taught me everything oral and I mean *everything*. He had the prettiest six-inch prick ever."

"What about the *secret*?" Old Man asked her. "You forgot."

She nodded. "The secret. OG Bobby Tate and I were watching *PornHub.com* now…and still talkin' about fantasies. I told the one that make me wettest, my nipples the pointiest. So: *'Hey Tate…what's your fantasy?'* He never loved a woman like he does with me. He says nothin' in the world would give him a harder hard-on than to see me at the *nastiest* and *sluttiest* I can be, I absolutely love to fuck and be treated like I fucked like a *whore* – but by Tate. I adore that man. However… what he is proposing is the ultimate act of liberty inside of love."

Old Man reached for her hands. He took her left hand and wrapped it completely around the warm, hairless, and heavy scrotum below that she already had deemed to be a formidable cock. Additionally, he folded her right hand round his gigantic still-hard penis.

"Whenever I'm needed, however I'm needed, I gotchu," Old Man told her. "Hook that threesome up. You already lemme smell all them roses you got and let me see that lil rosebud asshole. You ever take a cock this big in there?"

"Tate thick as fuck," she all but swore. "Maybe not that long but I know my asshole can stretch."

"Okay. Go!" he stated.

CHAPTER TWENTY-FOUR

Playing Bottom Bitch For The Day
Garter's Strip Club

Daniela was becoming known for the expensive cost of membership to her Latina Chocolaté parties she threw at her Eastchester mansion. What happened there was a word-of-mouth event. For example, the *Latina Chocolaté* party was what Daniela called it but that's not what it was an exorbitant hookup membership. Tonight was what was called, "*A Black & White*" affair or event.

A Black and White affair was when black couples, black singles, or even black people in groups, would enter the party to mingle with members of white couples, white singles, or white groups. (However they chose to do it). The endgame was always about sex. And the way it was all set up was through what was and still known as *VULKANYCKACY-D.onion.*

Don Armadillo, like a handful of other Mexican and South AmeriKKKan drug lords, had become billionaires with so much cash that rats were eating it and making nests out of it. Others, like El Chapo, the Medellín drug cartel members, etcetera, tried to invest cash inside of the U.S. stock markets and U.S. Department of Treasury agents – the IRS – shut them. For instance, José Gonzalo Rodriguez – Gacha of the Medellín Cartel had $67 million of his money seized by the U.S. Treasury Agents.

Mexican drug lords [like Armadillo] were now using their kids like Daniela, to legitimize their fortunes. Others-such as El Gulfo, Juarez, and Sinaloa Drug Cartels have generational "Game Money (e.g., *El Señor de los Cielos'*/The Lord of the Skies – Amado Carillo-Fuentes) – had grandchildren/great-grandchildren who had located $30 billion dollars of safely buried gold/silver/and platinum they'd "inherited" and had paid estate taxes on which was left for them.

Flavia Naomi Santiago alias Daniela Esmé Vallillo (AKA "La Comillo") was the smartest and most effective child of Don Flavio Santiago alias Don Armadillo. His three sons, not as much. They were better at killing rivals and protecting the Santiago family. Don Armadillo let his lawyers in Mexico use the $500,000,000 in precious metals and stones that *his* great-grandfather had placed in a will [for Don Armadillo] be sold to an Indian Mining Company based out of New York. That sale was over $684 million dollars. After the IRS payments, the cash was about $400 million.

Daniela knew that her family was one of Mexico's richest and they had a lot of enemies on her father's side. She had many private investments she'd made with banks, companies, and various individuals. She was far from dumb. Her graduation from USC was proof of that. Additionally, when she'd come to New York, she only stuck around but a hot minute at Sage's house. She adored sex more than a volunteer whore especially when the girls looked like Liza and the boys as nasty and as sexy as Sage. He was a bad as boys came and he loved to kill more than a cat. Death didn't put fear into Daniela. If Liza was dead, Daniela would shoot straight over to Sage and show him how wet that shit made her.

In fact, she thought she attended the Gold & Green Affair at one of Latiná Chocolaté parties. The "Gold" standing for anyone worth one billion dollars or more. The "Green" stood for anyone worth one million dollars or more. This mansion was brand new. It contained forty lavish bedrooms Jacuzzi's or SCARFACE hot tubs were inside of each. A "Scarface hot tub" was set into the floor just like the movie. Her new mansion was in Danbury, Connecticut and was once owned by Curtis "50 Cent" Jackson and it was nothing short of *amazing*. If Robin Leach was still alive 50 Cent's former Danbury super-mansion - now owners: "*LMLC, Corp.*" better known as

La Mexicana Fiesta Latina Chocolaté Corporación - would be in the lead-off credits of the show's weekly premiere.

What Daniela was doing was actually genius. Risky. Daring. And, prior to doing it, she got all of her ducks lined up in a razor-sharp row. That meant *muscle* was behind her. #1 Don Armadillo. #2 Sage Michael Thomas, the Mastermind.

"And what made you think of it?" Daniela had asked him a little while back. They were eating ice cream after an extremely torrid and raunchy fuck in the back of her Rolls-Royce Phantom.

"Out of every person I fuck wit in da clique, Garter's bartenders, Tanya Taylor, Luca Sirocco – not even Liza," Sage had mentioned as he'd intentionally let strawberry ice cream drip onto her left thigh. He had licked it all off of her. That was the day – or night – two white female undercover police officers had rolled up on the $450,000 white vehicle which was parked alongside a fence at Iona College in New Rochelle. "Cops. Don't move. Fuck 'em." Sage had said.

"Police, window please." One of the white female police officers had asked.

"How we know?" Daniela had replied.

The officer had put her identification up to the right passenger window in the rear. There was a light tint all around the white Phantom. "Y'all ain't gon' start shootin' at us when that window come down are ya?" Sage had asked, laughing.

"Why would you say that, sir? And, if that were the case,

would a window save you?" the veteran cop with the identification had reasoned.

"This one would," Sage had said with a smile.

"This is only a check. We saw the – sir...?" the two female officers had only to see Sage's barefoot and leg...to know that he was naked.

"Officers, y'all just gimme a sec," Sage said as he'd stepped proudly outside of the car, both hands raised, boner at half mast, naked as a newborn. "If you'll allow – I'll find my clothes, show you ID."

"No, you're okay. Sage Thomas. We know you." The other female officer was actually a brunette lieutenant. "We thought something sinister was going on. I know you heard about the college girl rapes."

"The guy had a Rolls Royce Phantom – yeah," Sage had stood there flexing his muscles, making his pectoral (chest) muscles bounce up and down like Terry Crews on Ameri-KKKa's Got Talent. "Rapist in a Phantom. Heard of that one."

"You know what we're talking about, Mr. Thomas!" the brunette white woman exclaimed as she was rewarded with what Coldhearted had been showing off to her and her partner. The brunette was actually a great-look woman with light brown eyes. Those eyes did something to him. No. No. Not to him, *for* him. Her eyes did something for him. "*Blackstone,*" he had said aloud.

She'd stared at him. "Yeah," she nodded his way, watching

him watch her. And the look became ever more intense. His dick was a granite diving board.

"Claudia Blackstone," he'd said her full name as he got dressed. Daniela had punched him in the back and *made* him get dressed. "I see that Lieutenant's badge."

"Yes, sir." She nodded, passed him a business card, and it was over.

"You knew her by name," Daniela had said. "How?"

"She run the Westchester County Municipal Drug Task Force, da WCMD," was all he had said about it except, "She moved her family outta White Plains. We gotta find out where she weak at. Okay?"

Daniela had nodded as she drove them to her Eastchester mansion. "You never finished talkin' earlier. It's very important that I know. My father will ask. My brothers. The -"

"YOU," Sage stopped her when they had entered her ranch-style villa. She had the best and most lavish estate in the entire Eastchester.

"Me?" She paused as her Mexican butler and maid waited on her. She hugged him. "What's that mean?"

"*Piensalo* (think about it)," he had reminded her. "You were the only one to come to me and say that them bitches at Garter's was fuckin' me outta my fuckin' bread. You had told me that *I needed something*. You recall?"

"A *bottom bitch*," Daniela had said in that cute little giggle of hers. "What'd you do?"

He had closed the door to the bathroom and pulled the

beautiful Mexicana-Irishwoman up against him after they'd stripped themselves nude for a scented bubble bath. "Wait! Don't get in yet little freckle nose!"

She'd struggled with him to get away. "No, Big Daddy. Lemme go!"

She was strong as hell. And slippery, too, due to the steam that had filled up the bathroom. He had wrestled her to the floor which was all covered with a herringbone plum color which blended well with the Night-Tones of the walls, ceilings, and showers. She got him onto his back and then…there they were in a 69 position.

Daniela and Liza were alike in this way. They loved it when he treated them rough. Daniela loved to be tied down and spanked until the skin was red.

"Hey, damn you taste mad salty-sweet," he told her after having his fill of smelling her little cunt *before* all of the Chanel of Burberry aftershower body spray stole away that natural sweet scent of her pretty little body. Daniela and Liza can leave the house for eight hours – drive here, there, sit to have a pedicure…When they return home they just have to wash away all the imagined "sweat/funk" they'd accumulated form the motherfucking MMA 30-round matches they just had. To Sage, there was no greater joy than to smell his woman, not the perfume and cosmetics.

"Baby!" he called out to her. "You gon' miss it."

"My Empire State Daddy." She had hopped up onto her

bed where he'd been sitting with a cellphone video ready to show her. "What's that? *Que eso?*"

"Me playing bottom bitch for the day," he'd explained to her. "Like you said. My age doesn't prevent ownership but it puts restraints on management."

"Why's everyone bein' corralled down into the gambling rooms?" Daniela had inquired. There had to be at least 75 to 85 women taken down there. Half were sitting, the other half standing around looking nervous.

"Okay, okay, okay! Let's start!" Coldhearted boomed as he walked in clapping his hands. *"Dominic step forward. Hold it down! Shut da fuck up! Or you fired – get da fuck out! Straight up,"* he scolded everyone.

On the video, there were over 100 men in there. Sage called out 20 of them.

"*Sand Man, Nigel, Owen, E-Money, Dave C., Tony B., and Blackburn,*" Sage finished calling them out. "*The email is Garter s6660@gmail.com or Instagram: Garters6060. Upload the videos now. Deuce, start first video now. Nobody leaving either.*"

All the women had already left their cellphones upstairs in the locker room. As the videos were shown clearly on a 71-inch Toshiba HDTV Smartscreen TV, it soon became clear that Sage had used 20 different men to record 33 women being given "Pink Room" ($200 Sex Specials) and "Blue Room" ($100 Lapdances/Handjobs) where 20% went to Sage and 10% to security.

Naiba was among the thieves caught stealing the entire $100 or $200 amount.

Sierra was another.

There were many of them. Nearly three dozen.

"*Aight, check it out,*" Sage could be heard saying on film. "*You thievin' bitches who stole from me...y'all gotta pay. Who was coverin' at the Pink Door and the Blue Door? Yo, Tate, where's Luca?*"

Luca was called down. As soon as he came in, Sage was in his face. "*Watch the fuckin' video! On the time stamp of each date, go back and check to see who was at the fuckin' Pink Door and Blue Door!*"

While Luca figured out the dates/times on the video, Sage had Deuce go retrieve the logs. There had been two Rollin 60s security who had been in cahoots with those thieving hoes. *Ben-G* and *Cheech*. Sage spotted them both. The 33 females who'd stolen the money were put inside of a smaller room and carefully searched. Then made to wait.

Three men had arrived at the back of the club in an unmarked white van with stolen plates. They each had on black and white demon masks. As soon as they entered the room Sage was on Cheech's ass like a painful pimple. He just started banging in on the nigga's head and face! Each time his knuckles landed it sounded like a bone or a tooth broke!

"*Move on them dirty bitches!*" Sage barked at his Rollin' 60s men as he dragged Cheech across the floor. "*Youse dead to me!*"

Now the 33 women in the room were truly frightened. A pushcart with two large boxes on top of it was pushed into the room. The thieves, two at a time, were shoved into chairs and held down while all of their hair on their heads, eyebrows, and eyelashes were shaved/cut off. Once that was done, each of the angry and crying women was forced to write down their social media passwords, emails passwords, bank information – Sage wanted it all.

"These hoe with cars- all those titles is getting signed over to the organization tonight, I don't care if we here all night," he ordered his men.

Cumba, Kaz, and Ammo transported Cheech and Ben-G to the slaughterhouse, sedated them, and locked them in the deep freezer. As day was turning to night and night to day, these 33 thieves didn't even have a goldfish, dog, cat, bank card, zero. There was one thing left to do.

"I called this Albanian Brooklyn Besa Boy. Load them bitches up in the van, sedate 'em, and take 'em to 1442 Bergen Street," Sage said to Kaz. *"Any questions?"*

"Nah." Kaz and his team was ready to roll.

"Ain't them Besa niggas Albanian Mafia?" Deuce wondered as Luca came down. *"Sex traffickers, too huhn?"*

"Trust me, them bitches stealin' days is done." Sage told Deuce. *"Luca...Kaz and them need an extra man."*

Luca hesitated. *"Okay, boss."*

"You don't want him to come back?" Kaz questioned Sage about Luca.

Sage told him to kill him. "*I don't need nobody who gon' let people sneak thief me.*" And then the video stopped.

DANIELLA WAS STUNNED.

"You lookin' at me like I did too much," he mentioned to her.

"No," she said in return. "Maybe I'm lookin' like you didn't do enough."

He played with her long red hair as they laid cuddled close with her head now against his chest.

"That mix of Mexican blood with Irish Republican Army is *catastrophic*!" he told her. "You comin' to the Dominican Republic wit us?"

"Yes," she said slowly. "Do you think Liza will show her teeth if she feels I've fallen in love with you?" Daniela asked.

"Will she...wait. What? Have you?"

"I think you know," she stated. "It's not obvious?"

"I do. And same here."

"I know," she said, rubbing his abs. "What. Marry us both?"

"I'd need you to love her, Lilly, and Izzy the same," he expounded while stroking her head. "Let it happen organically."

He moved on top of her, stared into her eyes, and kissed her small, sweet face from ear to mouth on the left and then from her soft little right ear, across her cheek to her cute bubblegum pink lips. And he was possessing her lips, breath, tongue like this woman was something top caliber. No doubt about that. Her father a billionaire.

"I've been kissed before," she whispered.

"I'm sure," he said.

"My god," she sighed as she was cradled into the spoon with him. "No man can kiss a woman like that and not be in love with her or vice versa."

"I agree," he told her. "We gon' talk about it all in the D.R. And by the way, any man who has been around you – especially when you wear those very thin terrycloth shorts with no panties on – and hasn't tried to kiss you.. he probably owns rainbow socks, T-shirts, and bedsheets."

She giggled. "You are so stupid." She said. "I know."

She wiggled and felt his penis swell up. "I love it when it's against my pussy lips like that…sleep papi."

CHAPTER TWENTY-FIVE

Blue Chapman was something
Blue's Story

Liza had been to both Ponce, Puerto Rico, and "the D.R." (The Dominican Republic) seven times in her life. Especially when she was between 4 and 12 years old – the last time had been around the time she'd first laid eyes on the boy she would one day end up eloping with: Sage Michael Thomas alias "C.H." or Coldhearted.

They decided to use *The Cabo Frances Macoris* Travel and Luxury Real Estate agency who had offices in Los Angeles, Miami Beach, Chicago, New York City, and of all places Ponce, Puerto Rico. On the evening they were crossing all T's and dotting all I's a brand-new *Bell 429* helicopter hovered over the Thomas house until Liza turned on the bright lights at the rear end of the property's wide grassy backyard and newly constructed blacktop basketball and tennis court.

Out front, an auto-transporter truck came to pick up Liza's Bentley and Sage's Maybach. "Don't go nowhere," Sage told the two men with the truck. They were armed drivers hired to take the luxury vehicles to PRAY AUTO for further upgrades and safe storage while they were in the D.R.

Kaz, Cumba, and Ammo had just arrived. "Park and give them the keys to the Escalade," Sage told them as he looked behind them at the black 1961 Riviera. "Who dat, Amris?" Sage asked because of the glare of the bright streetlight reflecting off of the Riviera's windshield.

"Who else would it be?" Amris yelled back.

"I don't know!" Sage stated with a flirty smile. "From what Kaz and nem tellin' me, you done brought in ya whole old runnin' clique from out West!"

As Sage ran to the backyard he looked up in the sky and wondered what the fuck Liza had goin' on with the helicopters. "Dog, what up wit da ghettobirds?" Ammo pointed up at one hovering out back.

"Ain't no ghettobirds, cuz. If it was… we'd see da pigs down here too." Kaz lit up a Newport and handed the Escalade keys to Sage's auto-transportation people.

Inside of the Riviera, Amris hit the horn to get Kaz's attention. "Ayo, man!" she snapped on him. Kaz came to the window where Amris' sexy ass was sitting behind the wheel. "Daddy, it's already four of us in here. When you said y'all was droppin' off the Escalade, we only got the RIVVIE and it's four of us in here," she complained.

Cumba and Ammo were in earshot. Ammo laughed and handshake hugged Kaz saying, "Ammo, it's a Riviera. Big leather seats front and back. Plenty of room wit them honeys on our laps."

Amris had opened the door to her and Kaz's new house to her cousin Charlotte Sparkles, a 20-year-old R&B singer and dancer killing it on YouTube, and she already had an album out and at least 17 single releases on iHeartRadio, Spotify, iTunes, and most of the other music distributors online. She'd just gotten fired from her job at a grocery store in Long Beach and was about to do some stripping in a Compton night club when she connected with her big cousin on Facebook. As soon as Double J heard her sing he'd taken her into SHZ and she was signed that night.

The other two women had worked with Amris on lesbian XXX-Production when they were all still part of Pinky's Porn Film distribution company. Vaynale, who everyone just call "Vee", and Blue Chapman – a light skinned "mulatto" chick with natural hair that was so blond that her thick eyebrow were even blonder. She had blue eyes but not the ordinary light kind. Hers were very dark, just like her outlook on life and what was inside of her heart. And she was only 25.

Vaynale "Vee" Churchyard came to stay with Kaz and Amris with work ethic and hope as her momentum and what got her up in the morning to go to Savage Hoodz Records, to write, see the voice coach and to sing. She almost had that PUTRI ARIANI voice in her single entitled "Loneliness." *Almost.* No one in the music world was better than PUTRI. Not Adele, not Kelly Clarkson, not "Ri-Ri," not Taylor. Not even the Queen of All Queens, legendary Bey herself. They were all as good...and have had their chance to hit homerun after homerun, Grand Slam after Grand Slam. But PUTRI ARIANI, a 17-year-old blind Indonesian piano prodigy? She had not had her chance to shine. And if the same people who'd got behind Adele got behind PUTRI she'd *kill* it. But since she was of a "certain" culture, or religious belief "OLD FAITHFUL" would be OLD RACIST BIGOT...And the same old black fools *and* Latino fools would continue to drop money on the same small group of talent in the rigged-up music industry. Sort of how SAG and the WGA controls actors and writers of color; sack them and kill their careers by overlooking them in Academy Awards/Oscar talks and Tony Awards. Or because a woman was a woman (especially if she's a black woman or black woman film director), to pay her less or pay her nothing at all.

PUTRI should be the next big voice. Like a Whitney. But knowing power, race, and bigotry in AmeriKKKa, or course, Adele would win the promotion contest. She's a white woman. Taylor would also win. *White record corporations would demand* that she did.

In the meantime the 26-year-old Vee Churchyard must continue to hope and grind harder than an organ. And, as to the 25-year-old Blue, no one should ever judge a book by its cover because looks were deceiving. When Kaz was watching his fiancée – Well, at the time the XXX-rated movies were made of course, Amris was not even in his life – in the lesbian movies, the mulatto babe may have been second to Amris but Blue Chapman was something ALL men wanted…

Blue's father had been a Norwegian Fisherman who'd spent two-thirds of his life fishing on a ship named, The Stavanger VAASA. All throughout the Barents Sea, up and down the Scandinavian Peninsula, The Baltic Sea, and – when prices were up for giant sea crab, lobsters, and Marlin – his ship would be chopping through the risky waters of the Chukchi, Beaufort, and Bering Seas. Capi Chappy was what his crew of 79 called him, according to her mother around the time she'd turned 12. Her mother had been a waitress at the famous Playboy's Club in Hollywood when a large group of fishermen had come into the chic establishment back in 1993.

The only thing Blue's then 17-year-old mother (Tiffany) could recall was Capi Chappy's corduroy blue jeans, a nice white turtleneck, and the "*$50 tip*" he'd given to her. The comeback of the Playboy Clubs in California at the time had been a big deal and management was strict and the girls' obligation to wear a complete uniform which was a one-piece bathing suit, he rabbit ears and the fluffy white cotton ball tail. The night the two had met, Tiffany had somehow lost her tail and was sent home. But she had no ride, no money for cab fare, in fact no money at all.

The Norwegian fisherman had been observing everything. "He's a dick. No, a pussy. I should show him not to treat you like that."

That was another reason she'd been so pissed off that fateful evening. She'd seen the blue-eyed blond-haired dreamboat and she'd felt her young 17-year-old heart get swept out to sea. Capi Chappy was not tall, but he was herculean. Tiffany had lied to get the job at Playboy Club because one day she'd wanted to be a movie star. She was a huge *"Baywatch"* fan for instance. And she had quite the body for it. Her titties were D-cups but the small "D" not the bigger "D."

A big "D" would be 38 or 42-D. She was more like a 32-D cup which was the quintessential perfect for a female her size. In any case the night they'd met she'd accepted his offer to take her home safe which he did. However, since the evening had been young and he was leaving out to sea in the next day, they'd gone walking.

They'd driven out to Venice Beach and spent the night on the boardwalk. Before daybreak they were cutting through the back of the Venice Beach Police Departments Horse-Back Training Division. It had started to rain so – since there was no one around – they'd undid the latch and went all the way in.

"Wanna see somethin' funny?" he'd asked her.

She'd smiled. Her beautiful brown face had lit up with mischief. "What. Ride a horse?"

"Uh uh. The horse gonna ride this time. Did I tell you how

pretty you looked when you changed?" he'd asked her as he'd let one of the male horses out. There were two mares in the next two stalls over.

"No, thank you. It's all I had other than the Playboy Club uniform." She'd ran her little hands over the red and white polka dot summer dress. She had deliberately left off her bra because she'd known men looked at her tits. Plus, when she'd changed at home, she had left her black panties on the floor in her room. Her virgin pussy didn't grow much fur, but it sure felt good when the Santa Ana winds blew up her short dress. "Was she doing, Capi?" she asked about the stud's behavior. The horse was drooling and making noises.

Capi pointed at the two-tone tan and pink extremely hard horsecock. "It's two mares in there. One of 'em or both are in estrus. We can tell cuz of the sounds he makes and his penis is like an etiolated vegetable. Like a cucumber is normally all green. Peel it… it's a complete pigment change. Open that gate, honey," he'd instructed her.

His long arms were around her waist and she'd melted back onto him, feeling his own thumping, hard, lengthening manhood. Her buttocks trembled but inside, she'd been very excited. She heard him sniffing her neck the way the boys at school had always liked to do. "Capi," which stood for Captain, and "Chappy" for Chapman, had never been with a black girl but once he'd laid eyes on Tiffany, he was completely locked in. That dress she'd changed into had her dark pointy nipples pointing out…and although Tiffany hadn't known it, Capi had hugged her from behind to check for panty lines. That fabulous round, perfect ass. Those titties. Women weren't shaped this perfectly in the entire Norway. It was a land of white – (chalky white) – bitches with asses shaped like the head on Gumby. SpongeBob SquarePants.

"What's estrus?" she'd asked Capi as she'd opened up the horse stall. Capi's hands were underneath the flowing – outward – at – the – hem dress. He turned her around as the male horse walked up to the mare and sniffed. Long strands of saliva and snot were running from the stud horse's nose and mouth.

"You're so beautiful." He'd kissed her soft, wet lips and she'd kissed him back. His hands were bold, he'd palmed her bottom with the left hand and her creaming pussy with the right. She'd started moaning and groaning and seeking his tongue with her clean white teeth. "Estrus is…*what is this?*" He's showed her the "*wet*" on his fingers and she'd blushed red. Her brown skin was lighter than brown. More like Jada Pinkett-Smith, Gugu Mbatha-Raw, or Nathalie Emmanuel so the red blush was apparent. He had loved the Playboy Club Tiffany less because her 32-Ds had been right there like the bait he could not touch. "Say it for me…" he'd teased as, once more, with the left ring finger he'd circled her anus from behind and, with the right…he'd played with her pea-sized clitoris…he pinched it until she gasped and nearly sounded like the stud horse until he'd pulled both hands away from her clenching love holes.

"*MY HORNY AMERIKKKAN PUSSY HONEY,*" he'd wanted her to repeat. "Please say it. Say it slow and lick your lips."

She laughed. "You sound so sexy with your accent when you say it."

"Okay show me what the horse does so we can leave. Then I want you to keep touchin' me, okay? Cuz if the cops see us, we're in trouble and my mom will kill me," she'd mentioned.

"Your mom? Why? You work the Playboy Club. You're twenty-one at least," he'd said. "*Right*?"

She nodded. "Yeah. Twenty-one. I just meant it would trip my mom out because Catholic girls don't do this."

The stud horse walked pointedly into the next stall where a much smaller all white mare met him face to face at first and tried to mount her. She'd raced up at him and he did the same. Then he'd bit the shit out of her neck and mounted her again. She was in submission at that juncture. Tiffany had watched as that huge stud horse's cock located the small opening of the mare's vagina due to her will and submission caving totally in. How could the mare take a log inside her?

Capi Chappy had his pants down and she felt his thick hot dick slide across her delicate wet feminine parts. Watching the mare get fucked by such a mammoth penis was making the teenage Tiffany lose all of her senses. Although she had never been fucked she was only waiting for the best opportunity to present itself. Watching the small mare get fucked made Tiffany lose control.

As her eyes were glued to the mare being hammered by the stud horse, Capi had somehow gotten her on her hands and knees and pushed his cock up against her wet love lips. He pulled her dress over her head and started to push into her. She'd whimpered something about being a virgin and not to get her pregnant but by this time, he was already halfway inside of her. And before they knew it he was inside of her, balls deeps, and he was taking her in and out, fucking her hard. Her sweet black cunt opened up, pouring out her honey.

Then he'd cum inside her pussy. They'd gotten the hell out of there. Capi had taken her to a hotel and they'd kept having sex. In all, he'd busted off seven times inside of her. But he never got to see her. Tiffany had only been a great lay to the fisherman. He had turned his back on Tiffany. And his baby she'd conceived.

Blue's dark side had reared its head long before she was even born. Her name not only described her eyes but also the mood her father had left her mother in. Tiffany had turned to other men, depression, pills, booze – she never was able to rebound from the heartbreak. Her darkness was inherited by her daughter…

No one called Blue a mulatto to her face because anyone with three brain cells would know that the term was derogatory. No wonder Jermaine Dupree didn't sign the nitwit idiot who went on to win his reality show *The Rap Game*. Blue Chapman and females like her all over the country were wishing that they could whup that rapper's ass for calling herself a derogatory term like Mulatto and thinking it cool. Now any white motherfucker she did business with was shaking her hand and smiling while he or she had a free pass to call her *"Nigger"* to her face because that's all "Mulatto" was and ever was.

During slavery periods in the 15th and 16th Century, the female slaves with lighter skin were *"trusted"* more than their darker female counterparts. These lighter slaves were *"prettier"* and also considered to be selected for special duties inside of their master's mansion such as maids, cooks, nannies, and "sex objects/toys." The master never called *a mulatto* his mistress, she was just a whore or a nigger wench.

The mulatto fucked and sucked all the master's friends, family members, and business associates' dicks. They fetched a higher price because they were bathed and dressed better than the "field niggers." Ask a Ku Klux Klansman or a Neo-Nazi skinhead what or who was a mulatto and they'd say: *My superior white semen inside of your cup of black coffee,* (meaning anus, mouth, or vagina).

Houses were developed and some were even guarded like prisons where the biggest and strongest slaves were brought to bed mulatto women. Inside of each room the woman was chained. It was a baby factory. When the child was born, in many of these "baby factories," if the child was born female, it would immediately be slaughtered and fed to the hogs. It was the male black child who was worth feeding and raising because (A) He could either be sold for a high price; (B) Traded for guns, horses, and other livestock; or (C) Made to work…This was only a small piece of ugly truths about mulatto. Nothin' proud in that word as a name.

However, the whole reason why Kaz had agreed on letting Amris' cousin, Charlotte Sparkles, stay was because Blue Chapman had been looking for a fresh start and Kaz had been one of like a half million of her fans that masturbated while watching her XXX-rated movies. And she did not disappoint! On her second night living with them he was woken up from catching Blue and Amris making soft, sweet love. The woman that he loved and admired, Amris, the lovely former adult film star, being made love to by the *other* adult film star that he idolized. He had watched them for a while and, instead of trying to join in, he'd kissed Amris.

"Y'all enjoy ya privacy," he'd said, kissed Amris, and exited.

She loved him for that and it had made Blue feel really good. Kaz had made her feel comfortable, which was what she'd needed.

Snapped back to the present, Kaz heard Coldhearted whistle. "Neighborhood!" Kaz said loud enough to get Sage's attention.

"Tell the auto-transport to go-head and go. Y'all get outta here," Sage instructed Kaz, Cumba, and Ammo. "Go to PRAY

Auto Dealers in a coupla days. Tate and Junior 'bout to come back soon so..."

"Boss, we got it. Liza and your babies are back there," Cumba said. Both helicopters had landed in their back yard. "Son got two helicopters out back!"

Kaz drove the Riviera out of there while Cumba and Ammo travelled with the transporters in the extended cab trailer. Their destination was to the PRAY Auto Dealership in Connecticut. The house was placed on a tight security lockdown. Sage contacted the security company to let them know that he'd be out of the United States, probably two weeks.

Tanya Taylor arrived with Diamond Girl and Bertha. "The club is a mess!" Tanya chided Sage who'd refused to tell her anything. "Have you thought of selling it?"

"It's a cash cow. Why would we do that?" he asked Tanya but looked at Liza. "On beer and wine alone, we make $200k per year."

They were standing inside of the family room when Lupé, Elizabeth, and then Daniela arrived. Tanya hugged all of them. Liza was holding Izzy one minute but when Elizabeth came, Isabel didn't know anybody anymore. She was happy to see her grandma.

"Giiirrrrlll, you have to tell me about *Latina Chocolaté*!" Tanya gushed to Daniela.

The coppery-haired daughter of billionaire drug lord Don Armadillo grinned. "People keep asking me about my new *sex club*."

Lupé put her hands over Isabel's baby ears.

"Well?" Tanya had a look on her face like she was about to start munching on the popcorn.

"It's more than that," Daniela stated. "I'll explain when we get on the jet or once we're in the D.R."

Sage opened up a suitcase and showed Tanya a printed out list of *MUST DO* items. "The suitcase is one. There's a green army bag next to the door filled with singles. Fifty-eight thousand worth and all the coins are rolled up. In all, there's a million dollars. Be safe wit it."

Within minutes the helicopters were ready to take Sage, Liza, Daniela, Lilly, Isabel, Lupé, and Elizabeth over the city and down to JFK International Airport. Suddenly, a phone call came through that made him yell to the pilot, "*WAIT!* Lemme off!"

"WHAT?!" Liza was signaling him from the other shiny burgundy BELL 429 chopper.

He sent her a text which she read seconds later and looked up at him. **SOMETHING EXTREMELY SERIOUS I GOTTA DO. MEET YOU AT Jet. Send chopper to football field behind Evander High. Tell him re-fuel first then send me E.T.A.**

CHAPTER TWENTY-SIX

"Out here round born headhunter."
The Slaughterhouse
Mt. Vernon, NY

"You're fuckin' wit my wife's nerves cuz you got me hoppin' off the helicopter," Sage started to say as he walked towards the front entrance of the *G-Bop-A-Lot (EC) Hip-Hop T-shirt Shop*. Where everyone he had just sent along to the PRAY Automotive dealer in Connecticut was at the T-shirt front shop "owned and ran" by the Rollin' 60's Assassins. "Where's my cars?"

"They went on up to PRAY. No need in bringin' them over here wit da merchandise we got in da basement," Kaz conveyed with cynicism.

"I'm hip. What's so important that I had to jump literally out the fuckin' helicopter?" Sage demanded.

"Hi, Sage," Amris said from behind the glass display counter where she was helping three customers with questions and several items they each had bought.

The store had several rectangular glass display cases. Although they were built and advertised as a T-shirt shop they sold way much more. Things like watches, 14k jewelry, walkie talkies, school supplies, expensive apparel for all the major professional teams, "high-end hip-hop" fashion, candy, chips, and a few other items. Kaz, Cumba, and Ammo were all about flipping cash which was why the store looked like it was doing very well. When Vaynale Churchyard, Blue Chapman, and Charlotte Sparkles came along so did extra help. Well, since Sparkle's career had been taking off, she hadn't been helping out. But that had been no problem because there just so happened to be girls that lived nearby who could use the work.

Kaz, Cumba, and Ammo went out through the rear and let their boss down into the basement. As soon as they began descending the stairs Sage removed his twin heavy reinforced nickel and titanium Browning. .380 semi-automatics.

"Ain't no imminent threat like dat, cuz," Cumba mumbled as Sage saw who was tied down to the steel table.

The assassins had performed every upgrade a so-called slaughterhouse or death house would need.

"Whatdafuck son do?" Sage pulled out his cellphone. He wrote to Liza: **At fuckin' bailbondsmans. Holla soon.**

It was Tanya's son, Chubb. "Aight, you said get Sage. Here he go," Ammo said.

"Read this." Kaz handed Sage a printout.

"Those cellphones? The forever phones? You don't think I knew, Sage?" Chubb asked him.

"Then why'd you not use another phone? Another system? You committing suicide, son!?" Sage was enraged.

Wherever Sage found it possible, he had set up a system like that of a police or FBI *Pen Register* to tap burner phones like TracPhones or cellphones that he had "bootlegged" or reactivated through a particular Internet Service Provider/Cellular Phone Service Provider. These days one merely only needed TOR, the onion router, bitcoin/cryptocurrency, and the darknet.

"Y'all gonna *listen* to me or kill me?" Chubb winced as he struggled to see due to the cut above his eye and swelling.

"Get him up. Give da nigga some water," Sage said. "Chubb, you was my fuckin' nigga. I'm readin' the texts from *your* phone. This your shit, dog. (914) 686-4738."

"Son, listen to me!" Chubb cried as Cumba unloosened his arms but not his legs. Then Cumba punched the shit out of him. "*Fuck*! Man fuck you, nigga!" Chubb cried.

"Chill, cuz!" Sage snapped. "I'm tryna hear da nigga!"

"Man, he *admitted* it!" Ammo interjected.

"I don't give a fuck! Obviously, the fuckin' shits important enough you fuckin' called me!!" Sage was out of his seat.

"Miss me wit dat loud boss shit in yo voice, too!" Cumba boomed at him. "You keep doin' that shit."

"Man chill, cuz," Kaz tried to calm his manz. "He da boss, nigga."

"Man, Imma *man* at the end of the day, homie! *Nobody* humpin' me! West Coast Neighborhood Crime Mob! You sittin' here entertaining the words of a snitch who had been textin' back and forth wit a fuckin' *cop* for months!" Cumba emphasized every word. "Fuck."

Sage nodded and sat back down in his chair.

"Son, I know it looks fucked up," Sage said as he took a deep breath. From one instant to the next, it all looked normal until Sage had them two .380 Browning twins in his hands again. "Man, y'all coulda handled this shit. Get his feet loose, get em' in the big walk in."

Cumba used a shackle key to unlock Chubb's legs and he started to put up a vicious struggle. Ammo and Kaz rushed in to help.

Sage affixed his silencers to the gun and even before they could reach the big walk-in deep freezer, he blasted the shit out of Cumba! All that big mouth bullshit. One pointed at Kaz and the other at Ammo. *PHFFTT!! PHFFFTT!!!* Kaz had on a Kevlar vest but Sage knew to check on niggas like these. But before he could, even with two cracked ribs, Kaz had been able to answer!

PHFFFT! Came the flash from the black .40 caliber which contained a short professionally manufactured suppressor. The shot ricocheted off of the freezer door and struck Sage in his cheekbone. Stunned by the impact of the round, he sent two more well-placed rounds at Kaz's head, point-blank.

"Any more, nigga?!" Sage screamed, feeling the warm blood pour from his face.

"Ammo movin'!" Chubb pointed at the assassin.

Ammo was slowly crawling towards the stairs. Sage smiled and took aim at his head. "Where you think you goin'?" Sage asked as blood dripped from his face. *PHFFFT!!*

"Sage, you was shot," Chubb indicated at his face.

Sage shook his head. "Fuck that shit, nigga. Ayo, Chubb, please tell me I ain't take out these good ass gangster niggas… on yo behalf when *you* was in the wrong."

"I been workin' wit that woman cop on some quid pro quo shit," Chubb said as they sat on the ground facing each other. "When Rock was murked, this cop named George Macon and Claudia Blackstone -"

"Stop. Blackstone? What she look like?"

"White. Mid-thirties, brown hair, light brown eyes. Nice Natalie Martinez figure. The actress."

"What-you got somethin' more, nigga?" Sage cut his eyes at Chubb. "You like her… You fucked her?"

Chubb kept shaking his head.

Sage wanted to fuck him up. "What then?!"

"She was actin' like she like me," Chubb admitted. But then he went ahead and laid it all out. "I, at first, thought she was Bomb Squad working with Sergeant Macon and FBI cats that came around. My moms, aunts, uncles, everyone were crying about MVPD not doin' shit. Then, one day, the Blackstone chick pulls up aside me and says: *'Follow me.'* Takes me to Bronx Lebanon Hospital, to *The Morgue.* Shows me bodies stacked on top of bodies. No body bags, becuz the city budget cuts. So, employees are bringing regular trash bags from home. A man wrapped up wit fuckin' Hefty black bags. Another three-hundred pounder man – word ta mutha – turned over why I was standin' there! In a white, small ass, yellow bread bag type bag under him – the nurse says, *'That's pure laziness. Somebody left they lunch next to a corpse.'* She 'bout to throw it out when the pathologist says, *'No, don't throw that thing away. The baby got hold of fentanyl. That's **a baby**. They try to hide the crime by putting the baby in the oven…And that three-hundred-pound man is a woman. The baby's mother. She OD'd and died while the baby fried'.*"

"Blackstone took you there?" Sage questioned the crazy story. "For what? That shit was the 52-fakeout."

"She wanted me to see all that carnage to make Rock's death seem like it was your heroin and coke's fault," Chubb revealed. "And she let me know that she'd been appointed Westchester County Municipal Drug Task Force lieutenant and that they were after you."

"Rock's death was a fuckin' *minute* ago!" Sage snapped angrily. "You was s'posed to come to me and let me know!"

"I didn't give them shit on you," he said. "I don't see you in cuffs or no one close to you. I've been pickin' P-Man's crew apart wit a laptop. Now, if P-Man was here torturing me and wanting to kill me for what I've done and still doing... what could I do? You was right. Savage Hoodz was never no gangstas."

Sage's phone rang for the 100th time. "Hello?"

"C'mon, Papi, what the fuck?" Liza complained.

"Y'all go ahead, I'll follow tomorrow," he promised.

"Why?"

"What'd I say? Everything kosher. Somethin' happened so I have to move some serious bread around. I'll be there." He hung up.

"So, what now?" Chubb asked. "Them niggas chicks is still upstairs. Want me to get them to come down here?"

"Nah, homie, you don't need to do dat. I will." Sage assured him. "You? You just rest on up."

PHFFFTT!!

Execution.

PHFFFTT!!

Day.

Sage stood up onto his feet. Sighing, he said, "I got a lot of cleanin' up to do! And... West Coast Crime Mob! Bitch niggas. That's y'all problem. Smokin' that bullshit, swallowin' any pill they make, ya listenin' to an undercover homosexual sayin' hard murder lyrics he never even lived…and came out here round a born headhunter poppin' off and gotcha fuckin' whole faceplate blasted in. West Coast Crime Mob. Fuck outta here, nigga! Ain't where ya from, it's where ya at!"

UP NEXT: COLDHEARTED 3

Did you enjoy the read?
Let us know how much by leaving us a review on Amazon and Goodreads.

OTHER BOOKS BY

URBAN AINT DEAD

Tales 4rm Da Dale

The Hottest Summer Ever

Hittin' Licks For The Holidays: Atlanta

Wet Dreams On Lockdown: The Nurse

How To Publish A Book From Prison

By **Elijah R. Freeman**

Despite The Odds

By **Juhnell Morgan**

Good Girls Gone Rogue

Good Girls Gone Rouge 2

By **Manny Black**

Hittaz

Hittaz 2

Hittaz 3

Hittaz 4

Coldhearted

By **Lou Garden Price, Sr.**

Charge It To The Game

Charge It To The Game 2

A Summer To Remember With My Hitta

Snatched Up By A Hitta

Santa Sent Me A Real One For Christmas

Wet Dreams on Lockdown: The Unit Manager

Thug Me The Right Way 2

Thug Me The Right Way 3

By **Nai**

A Setup For Revenge

Wet Dreams On Lockdown: The Librarian

By **Ashley Williams**

Ridin' For You

Ridin' For You, Too

Trickin' on a Heaux for Christmas: A BBW Love Story

Homie Hoppin' For The Holidays

Wet Dreams on Lockdown: The Female C.O

Letters Of His Love

By **Telia Teanna**

The State's Witness

The State's Witness 2

The State's Witness 3

This Time Won't You Save Me

By **Kyiris Ashley**

Stuck In The Trenches

Stuck In The Trenches 2

By **Huff Tha Great**

The Swipe

By **Toōla**

Melted the Heart of a Menace

Wet Dreams On Lockdown: Lieutenant Grace

By P. Wise

Merry Trapmas: Ice & Frost

By **Mia Sky**

Thug Me The Right Way

By **DiamondATL & Nai**

Atlantastan

By **Chris Green**

IN The Streetz

By **Tron Hill**

Wet Dreams on Lockdown: The Male C.O

By **Tamyra Griffin**

Wet Dreams On Lockdown: The Counselor

By **Paris Iman**

Wet Dreams On Lockdown: The Warden

By **Shawnice**

Wet Dreams On Lockdown: The Captain

By **TN Jones**

COMING SOON FROM
<u>URBAN AINT DEAD</u>

The Hottest Summer Ever 2
THE G-CODE
Tales 4rm Da Dale 2
How To Invest In The Stock Market From Prison
By **Elijah R. Freeman**

Hittaz 5
By **Lou Garden Price, Sr.**

The Swipe 2
By **Toola**

Good Girls Gone Rogue 3
By **Manny Black**

Despite The Odds 2
Hittin' Licks For The Holidays: Chicago
By **Juhnell Morgan**

Charge It To The Game 3
By **Nai**

A Setup For Revenge 2

COMING SOON FROM

By **Ashley Williams**

This Time Won't You Save Me 2
By **Kyiris Ashley**

Ridin' Forever
By **Telia Teanna**

Pretti & The Beast
By **P. Wise**

Atlantastan 2
By **Chris Green**

IN The Streetz 2
By **Tron Hill**

BOOKS BY

URBAN AINT DEAD's C.E.O

Elijah R. Freeman

Triggadale

Triggadale 2

Triggadale 3

Tales 4rm Da Dale

The Hottest Summer Ever

Murda Was The Case

Murda Was The Case 2

Murda Was The Case 3

Hittin' Licks For The Holidays: Atlanta

Wet Dreams On Lockdown: The Nurse

How To Publish A Book From Prison

STAY CONNECTED

Follow
Elijah R. Freeman
On Social Media
FB: Elijah R. Freeman
IG: @the_future_of_urban_fiction

www.ingramcontent.com/pod-product-compliance
Lightning Source LLC
LaVergne TN
LVHW021235080526
838199LV00088B/4355